This I Believe –
For This I Fight

A Cold War Novel
by
Ted Hovey

ISBN: 978-0-9908097-4-6 (print)
        978-0-9908097-5-3 (ebook)

This I Believe – For This I Fight is a work of fiction. Names, characters, places, and events are the products of the author's imagination or are used fictitiously. Any resemblance to actual persons, living or dead, is entirely coincidental.

Blue Prairie Publishing
Roseville, MN

This book is dedicated to all who served during the Cold War to support and defend the Constitution of the United States of America — especially those who lost their lives.

ACKNOWLEDGMENTS

Few writers can say that they did it all by themselves. I'm not one of them. Without the able assistance of Jessie Hennen, Patti Frazee, and Gene Noirot, the publication of this book would have been much more difficult.

First of all, thanks to Jessie Hennen for her expert editing work. Her knowledge of writing and her artistic skill were of the utmost help in making this a better book.

I am also grateful to Patti Frazee, who is a highly competent master of the technical side of publishing. She has now helped me with three books with amazing professional skill.

Gene Noirot, a fellow veteran of the Cold War Era, did an excellent job of colorizing an old black and white photograph for the cover. Thank you, Gene.

Of course, any errors or other flaws in the book are entirely my responsibility.

Mine honor is my life. Both grow in one.
Take honor from me, and my life is done.

William Shakespeare
Richard II. 1.1.182-183

1

HANG FIRE

Grafenwöhr Training Area in Bavaria
Monday, 22 August 1960

There should have been a roar like the door to hell being opened.

Instead — there was nothing.

Nothing happened.

The fifty-two ton Patton tank should have been rocking from the gun's recoil. Nick should have been feeling a thrill rush from seeing that old truck target, a remnant of the war, disintegrating into streaks of flame and flying metal.

But there was nothing.

The only sound was the tank's engine idling.

"Try it again, Nick," tank commander Stark said over the intercom.

"ON THE WAY," Nick yelled into his intercom mouthpiece.

Nick pulled his electronic trigger again, and yet again — Nothing.

There were fifty-four rounds of ninety-millimeter main gun ammunition in the turret — as well as thousands of rounds of machine gun ammunition. There were hand grenades and small arms ammunition. The fuel tank still held almost one hundred gallons of gasoline. If the round in the main gun exploded in the breech while the crew was in the tank — well, Nick knew they would all die instantly.

The voice of Sergeant Stark came over the intercom again.

"Okay now, boys, it looks like we got us a hang fire. Driver, shut down your engine. Now, youngsters — everybody keep calm. Let's do what we've been trained to do in a situation like this. We're going to evacuate the tank, then get at least fifty meters away, and wait until the gun cools down and the round can be safely removed from the breech. Slowly now, men — quietly and carefully — no sudden movements — and don't bump into anything on your way out."

Sergeant Hollis Stark had seen combat as a tanker during World War II. He had experienced destruction and seen death. Nick respected him not only for his knowledge and experience, but for the way he remained calm in the face of danger.

Nick heard Vince Delvecchio shut the engine off, open his driver's hatch, and scramble out of the tank.

Sergeant Stark climbed out through the commander's cupola.

Nick unplugged his intercom cord from the radio switch pack that was strapped to his chest. He turned to get out of the gunner's seat, intent on moving his legs without hitting his knees on any metal objects.

Then he saw Danny.

Private Danny Maguire, loader on the tank crew, was frozen in place. He was standing on the turret floor with several empty ninety-millimeter brass shell casings and dozens of spent machine gun shells around his feet. His back was flat up against the turret wall.

"Danny — move. We've got to get out of here, now."

Danny's arms were outstretched, the left one reached to the rangefinder that went across the turret ceiling over the main gun. His right hand gripped the metal grid that protected the radios from shell casings as they ejected from the main gun's breech.

In the reddish half-light, Danny's white knuckles were almost invisible against the painted white interior of the turret. His eyes were huge — and they were not blinking.

"Come on, Danny, let's get out of here," Nick said as he settled back into his gunner's seat.

Danny didn't say anything or make any movement. His eyes were fixed on the blue-black metal breechblock. Danny's eyes seemed to widen further when Nick spoke   but he didn't move.

Nick turned the radios off to make their hum go away. He started to gag — it was the blend of gunpowder smoke, engine exhaust, gasoline fumes, and something else — like Danny had ...

"Oh no, Danny — no," Nick said under his breath.

Nick squeezed his nose with his thumb and index finger.

"Danny, let's go, let's move it — this is serious — this thing could blow at any second. Don't be a chickenshit — not now of all times. Do you want me to leave you here?"

Nick looked up through the open hatch above him. A late-summer wind blew through the trees, out there in the darkness where safety was. Time seemed to fly and to stand still — both at the same time. Any second could be his last.

Nick reached up and turned on the turret light — blinking in its brightness.

Sergeant Stark's head appeared in the loader's hatch above Danny.

"What's up with you two? Get your butts out of this tank right now. Nick, help him get out of there."

Nick reached carefully over the breechblock and grabbed a handful of Danny's field jacket.

Danny stiffened with a surprising strength.

The smell of him grew stronger — the weakness in his bowels.

Nick let go.

"Danny, come on, we can't stay here any longer, there's no time to lose," Nick pleaded. "Get yourself up through that hatch — now."

Danny still didn't move.

Outside — Section Sergeant Crawford was shouting at Stark, as if he was to blame for the hang fire.

Nick heard Crawford climb onto the tank.

The new section sergeant's red face peered in through the hatch.

"What's the matter with you two assholes? Get out here — right now."

"Sergeant, we've got a problem here," Nick said.

"Look, Holloway, you get the hell out of there — now. That's an order. I'll deal with Maguire."

"Sarge, let me talk to him first. Please, sergeant."

Nick had seen it before. Officers and noncoms who thought that all they had to do was give soldiers an order, and then things would happen — happen in the way they wanted, as if they were God himself.

Crawford was already climbing in through the loader's hatch. He was a large man, and he put his foot on top of the breechblock as he came down into the turret.

Nick watched as the gun bobbed up and down.

He thought that his heart had stopped. Would the gun explode? His mouth went dry and his knees felt like jelly.

Crawford turned and pointed a finger at Nick, then up at the tank commander's hatch opening.

"You. Out. Now."

Nick didn't move.

Now Crawford was in Danny's face.

"Private Maguire, you little shit — are you a man, or are

you a fucking yellow belly? Get your miserable bag of pus up out of this tank — *mach schnell.*"

Danny stayed. It was, Nick thought, as if his mind was in a trance, and his body glued to the turret wall.

Crawford grabbed Danny's jacket with both hands and yanked, trying to break him loose. Danny was rigid   he didn't give.

"Come on, asshole — do you want to die?"

Crawford let go of Danny. He looked at him with disgust, and then he looked at Nick.

"Didn't I tell you to get out of the tank?"

"Sergeant Crawford — I think it's important that I stay with Danny. I know how to talk to him. I'm sure I can get him to go out."

Crawford tried one more time to pull Danny away from the turret wall. Again, he failed.

"I'm reporting the two of you. In fact, I'm going to recommend court-martials for both of you."

With that, Crawford climbed up and out of the turret.

* * * *

Shouts and murmurs outside.

The silence inside the steel coffin was broken only by the pings and cracks of cooling metal.

Nick took his helmet off and carefully laid it on the turret floor. He shivered at the touch of cold sweat on his back.

"Danny — I know you're scared. I'm scared myself. This is bad. But it's going on five minutes now, and the shell hasn't blown. That's a good sign — the gun is starting to cool, it probably won't cook off now. But we shouldn't push our luck. We should go — now."

Danny finally spoke.

"I, I don't want to die, Nick."

"Neither do I, Danny. We're young, and we've got too

much to live for. You like to draw, and you're good at it. You could go to an art school."

Danny's body moved, and his eyes were blinking. Nick could see tears growing under his eyes. Danny looked old to Nick, even though he was only nineteen.

Nick held his hand out.

"Come on, Danny — take my hand — we'll go out together. It'll be okay, you'll see."

Danny let go of the rangefinder and took Nick's hand. Danny's skin was cold.

Then Danny let go his right hand. He leaned away from the turret wall.

Nick helped Danny get his right foot up on the turret ring ledge, and then Nick pushed him up. Danny put his elbows on the turret hatch opening, pulled himself up, and crawled out.

Nick gagged at the nearness of Danny's bottom.

Once Danny was on top of the turret, Nick got out and helped him off the tank.

Nick drew in several deep breaths of the fresh night air.

It had started to drizzle.

Outside, safely away from the tank, Nick and Danny stood by the lieutenant's jeep. Sergeant Crawford screamed at them so hard that there were blue and white lines in his temples.

"I've just talked to the lieutenant and he agrees with me. Private Maguire, you'll be court-martialed for your cowardice. And you — Private Holloway — yes, you heard me right, you're being busted down to private as of right now. You'll be court-martialed for disobeying a direct order, and for whatever else I need to come up with. I hope you both end up in Leavenworth, but I know I can get each of you at least six months in the division stockade in Dachau — and then, dishonorable discharges."

Crawford walked away.

Nick was numb with confusion and rage.

Possibly, he thought, there were two kinds of soldiers — those who thrive in a peacetime army — the go-by-the-book guys, who look good, can kiss ass, and can march straight. Then there were those who thrive in violent combat on the battlefield. He suspected that Sergeant Crawford was in the second group, and now was just a frustrated and mean noncom waiting out the inactivity of the Cold War.

And then there were the men who shouldn't be in the Army at all.

Nick looked at Danny.

Danny grinned self-consciously, then he reached over and half-punched Nick in the shoulder.

2

DIVINE INTERVENTION

Monday, 22 August

The jeep pulled up to the company command post tent. Second Lieutenant Richard Jensen and Sergeant Crawford went inside.

"Wait outside," Lieutenant Jensen said to Nick and Danny.

Almost immediately, loud voices came from inside the tent.

"What's going on, Nick?"

Nick couldn't be angry with Danny. What good would it do to alarm him?

"I don't know, Danny."

Nick had known a kid in high school — Eugene Wallis — who was like Danny in several ways. Not very smart. Anxious, most of the time. A target for bullies. One day, when Eugene's clothes smelled like he had been in a barn, Nick and others put him under a shower with his clothes on. Nick cringed when he thought of his own role in bullying Eugene. When Gene turned sixteen, his parents let him quit school, to help out on the farm, they said. Nick vowed to himself that when he got home, he would visit Eugene — maybe take him to the drugstore and buy him a chocolate sundae. And say he's sorry.

A few minutes later the tent flap opened again, and 1st Sgt. Kermit Dixon stepped out.

"Why don't you men wait in here, out of the rain."

They followed.

The tent was a standard World War II-vintage dark green squad tent, with a canvas partition that separated the first sergeant's front area from the company commander's field office in the rear of the tent.

Sergeant Dixon sat at a small table on the left. A set of radios sat on a platform on the right in front of an operator. There were several portable chairs along each side of the tent entrance.

"You boys want any coffee?" Dixon asked.

"Sure."

Nick strained to hear the voices behind the partition.

He guessed that Captain Charles Elliott, his executive officer First Lieutenant Patrick Dolan, Second Lieutenant Jensen, and Sergeant Crawford were discussing the court-martials that Crawford wanted for he and Danny.

Turning to Nick, Sergeant Dixon said:

"I'm not sure how long it will take, Holloway, a real argument is going on in there. It depends on how much patience the captain has."

Five minutes later, Jensen and Crawford left the tent. As he walked by Nick, Lieutenant Jensen's face looked like that of a scared puppy — his walk looked like that of a dog with his tail between his legs. Sergeant Crawford, on the other hand, looked like a pit bull, with red eyes, and spit foam on his lips.

Back in Ohio, Nick had never known anyone like Sergeant Crawford.

Nick graduated from high school in 1957, but in defiance of his parents, he did not go to college. He knew he could do college work, but he couldn't settle on what he wanted to study — what he wanted to be. He was interested in many things.

He worked in his father's lumber yard after high school, and finally decided to enlist in the Army. All healthy young men faced the draft and a six-year military obligation. Nick decided he would go into the Army and get it over with. Maybe then he would discover what he wanted to do with his life. He enlisted in early January 1958.

Danny was called into Captain Elliott's office. Nick tried to make out what was being said on the other side of the partition — but he couldn't. The voices were soft — no yelling — and Nick took that as a good sign. Nick knew Danny lacked the emotional skills to successfully cope with people of authority. He was easily intimidated — Nick had seen Danny several times unable to speak when a superior used a rough tone of voice with him. Why was he drafted into the Army at all? Nick wondered.

Nick ran his hand through his short, sandy brown hair.

The door flap from the captain's office opened, and Danny ran out. He was sobbing as he ran past Nick, and toward the outer tent flap.

Nick stood up.

"Danny — Danny, what's wrong?"

Danny rushed past him — out of the tent.

"You're up, Holloway. The captain wants to see you next," the first sergeant said.

Nick went in and stood at attention before Captain Elliott's desk.

"Specialist Nicholas Holloway reporting as ordered, sir," Nick said as he saluted his commander.

From behind Elliott, Lieutenant Dolan stared impassively.

Nick forgot about Danny for the moment. Now his own future was at stake. He dreaded the idea that he might be court-martialed. He could never explain that to his dad and his uncles, who had served bravely in World War II. They wouldn't understand. In their minds, Nick knew, only cowards and criminals got themselves court-martialed.

His knees felt weak and his head ached. Nick struggled to maintain his poise and to project a sense of dignity.

"At ease, Holloway. This is one big mess you've laid at my feet. What were you thinking of — ignoring a direct order from your section sergeant?"

"Sir, it is true that I did not exit the tank as ordered by Sergeant Crawford. At the time, I was only thinking of Private Maguire and how best to help him get out of the tank safely, sir."

The captain sighed. He continued, his voice tired.

"What makes you think you know more about how to handle a hang fire situation than Sergeant Crawford? Do you know that he was a decorated tanker during the Korean War? Saved my life, actually. But that's beside the point, isn't it? This is the Army, and you do what you're told — you follow your superior's orders — no ifs, buts, or maybes."

Nick didn't respond.

"Sergeant Crawford wants you court-martialed for insubordination, and Private Maguire for cowardice. Lieutenant Jensen, your officer, agrees with him."

Nick remained quiet. His face showed no expression. He looked straight ahead.

"I tend to agree with them. But Lieutenant Dolan here has convinced me that such punishment would be an extreme overreaction to this incident. You should thank him for the fact that you guys aren't going to the Army prison at Leavenworth."

Nick shifted his glance and caught the impassive eyes of Lieutenant Dolan.

"Lieutenant Dolan reminded me that you are one of the best tankers we have, not only in Headquarters Company, but in the entire battalion. He also pointed out that caring for your men is one of the most important responsibilities of a combat leader. I agree with that. Also, with the Soviet's Eighth Guards Army facing us across the border, we've got to be ready for them. If the Ivans come at us, I'm going to need you, Holloway. Finally, since you're on the track to attend the Noncommissioned Officers (NCO) Academy, I've decided to let you off the hook this time — and, you won't be demoted. But don't let it happen again. One more incident like this, and I'll be inclined to throw the book at you. Sergeant Crawford is not happy with my decision, so you'd better work extra hard at getting back on his good side. For my part, I am putting a hold on your application for the NCO academy, until I'm sure you've got what it takes to be a sergeant yourself."

Nick fought off his wanting to smile as elation filled him inside.

"Thank you, sir."

"You're dismissed."

Nick saluted Captain Elliott, and then pointedly saluted Lieutenant Dolan as well.

Nick found Danny in his tent at Tank Section's bivouac area. Danny's face was buried inside his sleeping bag.

"Danny, what's wrong?"

Danny's face appeared and he looked at Nick. Danny's eyes were red. He sniffled.

"They've put me on KP duty, Nick — permanent KP."

Danny started sobbing again.

"Permanent KP? Every day? Are you sure, Danny? Is that what they said?"

"Ye-yes, that's what they called it. They said I should sleep now and report to the mess sergeant at 0400. Nick, I can't sleep. What am I going to do? Tell me what to do, Nick."

Nick put his arm around Danny's shoulders.

"Try to get some rest, Danny."

Danny blinked at him and rolled over.

Nick laid on his air mattress and sleeping bag and

replayed the events of the night. The good thing — maybe the only thing that mattered — was that the hang fire shell had not exploded in the gun's breech chamber. They were still alive.

Thank God for that. But Danny's situation was another story. Nick had never heard of another soldier being punished with permanent kitchen police (KP) assignment. He wasn't even sure that it was legal under the Uniform Code of Military Justice (UCMJ). KP was a once-in-a-while duty for lower-ranked enlisted men. It was grueling work. It was demeaning work. Up early, then to work all day and into the evening. It was hard work — especially when it had to be done outdoors, in the field.

* * * *

Thursday, 25 August

One evening several days later, the men of Tank Section were gathered near one of the tanks, still talking about Danny and the hang fire.

"You never know, do you? I mean, one defective shell, and, wham, bam, thank you, ma'am, it could all be over for a tank crew. Damn, just like that," Ned Lafontaine said as he snapped his fingers.

Specialist Fifth Class Fred Carson, one of the tank commanders, was the first to see him and to shout *Attention*. The men jumped up and stood at attention as Capt. Bruce Reynolds, the chaplain for the battalion, walked up.

"At ease, men — as you were," the chaplain said with a mild voice and a gentle face.

"Have a seat, Father," said Joe Flores, driver on Sergeant Crawford's tank, as he put a .50 caliber ammunition box down for the chaplain to sit on.

"Thank you very much, I will sit down — but I'm afraid

14

I'm not a priest. I'm not Catholic, so you can just call me Chaplain Reynolds."

"Yes, sir," said the men in unison.

Nick Holloway was confused. He had never seen an officer, other than Lieutenant Anderson, come around to just talk with enlisted soldiers before — and Lieutenant Anderson had been their section leader before Jensen, so you expected him to do that.

Nick had seen Chaplain Reynolds only once before, at a mandatory morale talk at the Henry Kaserne Theater. Nick had been raised in the church, and believed in God, but he didn't go to the chapel services because he didn't feel comfortable among the officers and NCOs.

"So — where are you men from?" Chaplain Reynolds asked.

The men answered him in turn. They were from big cities such as Baltimore, Providence, Wilmington, Chicago, and Los Angeles, and from small towns and farms in states such as Oregon, Kentucky, Ohio, Wisconsin, and Vermont.

"And how is the training going for you?"

"Fine."

"Good."

"Great."

"Couldn't be better, sir."

"No complaints, chaplain, sir."

"Do any of you men have any questions you want to ask me?"

No one spoke.

"Come on now, I'm not going to bite your head off, or turn you in, or anything like that. But if you have any questions, or need any help, or know somebody who needs help — anything — tell me about it."

This was not how the men were accustomed to being talked to by their superiors. And the chaplain was a captain, after all.

Nick hesitated, thought about Danny, and then spoke up.

"Chaplain, sir, there is one thing you might be able to help with. There's a private in our section — his name is Maguire — Danny — Daniel Maguire. He's been put on permanent KP duty by Captain Elliott. Maguire's been on KP for several days now, and he's exhausted. It isn't right what he's going through."

The other men were quiet.

Nick had been on field KP when he first arrived in Germany — when he was still a private. It was a long day of setting up and cleaning up of the large wash and rinse cans, and the garbage cans. And then there was the demeaning task of serving officers who carried on as though he wasn't there. But Nick's experience had been for one day only — but now, for Danny, there was no end in sight.

"What did he do to get such punishment?" Captain Reynolds asked.

"We had a hang fire in our tank, sir — that's when a shell doesn't go off, but might explode inside the gun and then, if that happened, the whole tank would blow up. Danny was terrified. So, when Sergeant Crawford ordered him out of the tank, Danny couldn't move — he was actually too scared to move."

"Private Maguire, eh?" the chaplain said as he wrote in his notebook.

"I'll have a word with Captain Elliott. Now I must take my leave — there are miles to go and people to see yet tonight. Do you men mind if I offer you all a word from scripture, and then a prayer?"

No one objected. He was an officer, after all.

The chaplain opened his Bible.

"This is the Twenty-third Psalm — maybe you men remember this. I find hope and comfort in these words. Here it is, a psalm of David: The Lord is my shepherd; I shall not want. He makes me to lie down in green pastures; He leads me beside the still waters. He restores my soul. He guides me in straight paths for His Name's sake. Yea, though I walk through the valley of the shadow of death, I will fear no evil for thou art with me. Thy rod and thy staff, they comfort me. Thou preparest a table before me in the presence of mine enemies. Thou anointest my head with oil, my cup runneth over. Surely, goodness and mercy shall follow me all the days of my life, and I shall dwell in the House of the Lord forever."

The men were quiet.

Chaplain Reynolds closed his book, bowed his head, closed his eyes, and folded his hands.

"Dear God, look with kindness and compassion on these men who are your children and your servants. We pray now in the way your Son taught us: Our Father in heaven, Thy name be hallowed; Thy Kingdom come; Thy will be done, on earth as it is in Heaven. Give us today our daily bread. Forgive us the wrong we have done, as we have forgiven those who have wronged us. And do not bring us to the test, but save us from the evil one. For thine is the kingdom, and the power and the glory, forever and ever. Amen."

Some of the men also said amen, and then it was quiet.

The only sound was the faint buzz of the radio from inside the tank's turret.

* * * *

Friday, 26 August

The following evening Nick and other men in Headquarters Company's bivouac area gathered closer to the command post tent.

Inside the tent, out of sight, Captain Elliott and Chaplain Reynolds were having a shouting match.

"I'm in charge here, and what I say goes," Captain Elliott said.

"You don't have the right to use excessive punishment for trivial offenses."

"Trivial you say — trivial? Nothing is trivial out here. We're training to hold the line against godless communism. You, of all people, should understand that. We've got to be ready to fight. We can't have marginal soldiers who shit in their pants before they're even in combat — not clumsy little incompetent peckerheads like Maguire. Jesus fucking Christ, chaplain — he deserves to be put on permanent KP. He's lucky I didn't have him court-martialed for cowardice."

Nick heard what sounded like his company commander pounding his fist down hard on a map table.

"Don't you use the Lord's name in vain with me, captain. You may think you're the god of this company, but let me remind you that you are an officer of the United States Army — serving the United States of America and its Constitution. Private Maguire has rights."

"Who are you — you, you — you, a measly chaplain — to come in here and tell me how to run my company?"

"I'll tell you who I am — I am the person who has the ear of your battalion commander. Remember that. Think about that tonight — tonight, captain — as you also rethink your treatment of Private Maguire."

The tarpaulin flap was whipped open, and the chaplain walked quickly away toward his own tent, about fifty meters away.

The men who witnessed this encounter stood in stunned silence.

Nick wanted to start clapping.

The next morning, word went around that Danny Maguire was no longer on KP duty.

3

TRAGEDY

Friday, 2 September

The Third Medium Tank Battalion of the 34th Armor spent the next few days in combined tactical training with an infantry unit. No gunnery was involved, so Danny was not required to do his duties as loader of the main gun. He was, for the most part, just going along for the ride. Nevertheless, Nick watched Danny. He had known Danny for about five months, and if anything, Danny had become sadder and quieter than before. Nick worried about Danny. Danny seemed ready to snap under the strain.

Nick worked extra hard to do his job so well that Sergeant Crawford would have no reason to single him out for harassment. He found, to his surprise, that he was developing a certain respect for Crawford — at least for his knowledge and experience with the tank.

* * * *

Nick had deflated his rubber air mattress and was rolling his sleeping bag when he heard the explosion. He stopped, letting the bag unroll, and looked at Vince. Together they stared in the direction of the noise.

"That was close," Vince said.

They finished packing their gear in duffel bags and carried them to their tank. Then they waited for the order to move the tanks to the railhead to be loaded onto flatcars for the journey back to Munich. It was their last day at Grafenwöhr. They had been there for a month, by evening they would be back in their own barracks in Munich's Henry Kaserne.

Nick saw Sergeant Crawford running towards the command post, which was now just a limp tent laid out on the ground, ready to be folded up.

"Nick, what's going on?" Danny Maguire asked.

Nick's patience with Danny grew thin at times. It seemed that Danny thought Nick knew everything and could do anything.

"I don't know, Danny."

It was a dappled gray morning, and it was raining off and on — the men called this kind of rain *Bavarian sunshine* — one minute the sun was shining, and the next it was raining.

The men were standing by their tanks when Crawford returned.

"Men, here's the skinny on that loud boom you heard. An eight-inch howitzer shell blew up in the tent city at Camp Chaffee, not far from here. No word on casualties yet. That's all I know."

"When will we move our tanks to the train, sergeant?" one of the men asked.

Crawford grinned in that way that made Nick cringe.

"Don't know yet. Why? Can't wait to get back to your girlfriend?"

The man looked ashamed.

Crawford returned to a serious tone.

"I'm going back to the lieutenant and the captain. I'll let you guys know when I learn more myself."

The men stood waiting under the dripping trees in their rubber-coated ponchos. Nick shivered as the rain came off of his helmet and down his neck. He put the hood over his helmet.

"Hey, Nick — what do you think is going on?" Paul Becker asked. Paul was the gunner on tank four.

"Beats me, Paul. I'm guessing the German railroad has us on their schedule, so we should get the order to move out at any minute."

They waited almost a half hour, and then Sergeant Crawford returned.

"Okay, maggots — we'll be moving out in a few minutes." Crawford had that grin on his face again.

"First, I've got to provide two boys to serve on a cleanup detail at Camp Chaffee. There were casualties there. I want two volunteers. Hmm — let me see."

Crawford made play out of his selection. He walked around and looked over each of the men.

"Ah — you, pussy Maguire — yass, you'll do — now, who else?"

Crawford was looking at Billy Dryden — a private who was the loader on tank four.

"I'll go," Nick said.

Sergeant Crawford looked at Nick. His grin went away as he stared at Nick.

"Okay, Holloway — you're on. Report to the CP, someone will drive you guys over."

Nick knew that Vince and Sergeant Stark could move the tank to the railhead and get it loaded and tied down on the flatcar by themselves. He knew also that Danny needed him.

* * * *

At Camp Chaffee, Nick learned that fifteen soldiers of the 12th Cavalry were killed, and twenty-seven were wounded, when a large howitzer shell fired by the 18th Field Artillery overshot the impact area and landed in a tent.

The camp looked like a scene from a horror movie. A pit where the tent once stood. Lumps of dirt and sod in a circle around the hole. Bits of paper flying around from the helicopters' wind. What really shook Nick were the bodies lying on stretchers, and parts of bodies lying helter-skelter. And the color red.

Officers and NCOs were shouting, ambulances came and went, and two helicopters with red crosses on their sides were parked nearby. Screams from some of the wounded men rose above the shouts.

A sergeant came up to Nick and Danny as they stood looking at the frenzied activity in front of them. It wasn't until the sergeant had yelled at him for a second time that Nick responded.

"Specialist Holloway and Private Maguire reporting for a cleanup detail, sergeant." Nick said.

Danny stood there, transfixed by the scene.

"Follow me."

They walked to where a group of men were gathered beside a truck. Two men in the back of the truck were handing out shovels, rakes, and gunnysacks.

The other men in the cleanup group were, like Nick and Danny, from other nearby units, some from line companies in Nick's battalion.

"Okay, men — here's what we're going to do," said the sergeant in charge of the cleanup. "We're going out to the edge of the debris field and start there — then we'll work our way in. That way we shouldn't interfere with any of the medical people that are still here or the guys trying to piece together what happened here."

The men formed a line at some distance away from the center of activity. They moved slowly forward and picked up whatever was obviously fallout from the explosion.

Nick looked over at Danny. He was standing there with an olive drab piece of canvas. The canvas had a dark blotch on it that could have been blood. Danny looked as though he was in a trance.

Nick picked up an empty boot and put it into his sack.

Nick kept his eyes on Danny. Danny wasn't doing well at all. He moved slowly. He walked past a piece of wood from a cot frame.

"Danny — pay attention — you missed that stick of wood there."

Nick pointed behind Danny.

Danny turned around.

"Huh? Nick? What?"

Nick stopped. He and Danny were falling behind the line of men.

"Oh, now I see it. Thanks, Nick."

The pieces of debris were more numerous as they moved forward. Nick picked up a helmet, a cartridge belt, a shaving brush, and a shredded rubber air mattress. And then he saw a bloody thumb.

It was about two inches long, severed at the second knuckle. It was red, except for the pink flesh where it came off.

Nick didn't pick it up.

"Sergeant, can you come over here?" Nick said.

"What you got, soldier?"

Nick pointed at the thumb.

"Okay. I'll have one of the medical people come to get it. They'll know how to handle this."

The sergeant marked the place with a peg.

Bile rose in Nick's throat as he bent over to do his job. He had to stand erect and breathe deeply before he could continue to put pieces into his bag. He wondered whether someone would have found his own thumb if that hang fire shell had exploded in the tank.

Danny sat down on the ground. He was crying and retching.

Nick dropped his sack and went over to Danny. He put his arm around Danny and assured him that it was okay to cry — and to get sick. Nick said he felt like doing the same.

Nick talked to the sergeant in charge and convinced him that Danny would be more useful with a rake to smooth the ground they had already covered. The sergeant looked at Danny, and agreed.

So Danny stood there, raking the same patch of ground over and over as the sky grew dim.

* * * *

It was dark when Nick and Danny arrived in Munich in one of the company's trucks. Sergeant Stark and Vince had already cleaned the tank at the wash rack, parked it, and covered it with a tarpaulin.

Nick stood under the shower for fifteen minutes. He scrubbed himself with soap and a stiff hand brush until he felt raw.

He tried to sleep. He thought about Danny — why didn't the Army send Danny home? Was it because they couldn't admit they had made a mistake by taking him in the first place? Could it be that simple?

4

VINCE DELVECCHIO

Munich
Saturday, 3 September

Nick couldn't sleep. He thought about Danny, and he thought about Sergeant Crawford. He kept asking himself the question — why? That word kept floating in his mind. Then many *whys* — embedded in bright red thumbs and other body parts, floating randomly behind his drowsy eyes. Maybe he slept some, but Nick didn't think so. In his dreams, he saw himself running down an endless hallway, with Danny riding on his back, and Crawford close behind, chasing them.

At 0200, Nick got up, went down the hallway to the latrine, and took another shower. He stood under the shower stream for a long time. When he sensed he had been there ten minutes, he shut the water off, grabbed his towel, and dried himself. As he looked at himself in the mirror, he looked old. Was that what the Army did to a man? He was only twenty-one. Nick had recently learned that Specialist Fifth Class Reuben Ortiz was only twenty-six years old — Nick had assumed that Ortiz was closer to forty.

Back in his bunk, Nick could hear every breath of his

roommate, Vince. He heard the footsteps of the sergeant in charge of quarters (CQ) in the hallway as he made his rounds, and every jeep, car, and truck that drove near the barracks that night.

At 0530, the CQ was in the hallway, blowing his whistle to wake the men. Nick was the first man up in Tank Section. He went directly to the latrine and shaved. He was dressed and sitting on the edge of his bunk when reveille was sounded.

Vince looked at Nick and just shook his head.

"Nick, you don't look so good."

"No shit, Dick Tracy, who clued you in?"

Nick regretted saying that to his best friend. When Vince returned to the room, Nick tried to undo the damage.

"Hey, buddy, I'm sorry I snapped at you like that. I shouldn't have said that."

"No problem. But Nick, how can I help you get past whatever is eating you? It has to be about Danny and Crawford."

"I don't know, I don't know. It just isn't right the way Crawford treats Danny. And all the thoughtless guys who are mean to Danny."

* * * *

The Saturday morning inspection was routine. After noon chow, Vince suggested that Nick and he go to the Enlisted Men's (EM) Club and have a beer or two.

"I promise you, Nick, that I will listen to you. Listening is not one of my strong suits, but I'll try — I'll try real hard."

Vince Delvecchio was Nick's best friend. Nick had heard his life story in detail.

He'd said once that his first day in the Army had been the worst day for him. That was the day when a barber at Fort Dix turned Vince's ducktail hairdo into a regulation military buzz cut. After he got over that, Vince enjoyed much

of the Army's training and routines. He was a good soldier —
steady-minded, slow to anger, quick to forgive.

Vince's family owned and ran a successful Italian
restaurant in Providence, Rhode Island. His father wanted
Vince to work in the business — in fact he wanted to turn it
over to Vince someday.

But Vince thought otherwise. He had other talents —
he was a good student, an athlete, and he had a good tenor
voice that could have been great with training and practice.
He was popular with Nick and his other Tank Section mates.
They loved his cadence calling ability. Not only was his voice
nearly perfect, but, he had an uncanny skill of calling the
count just a fraction off the regular tempo. He learned this
in basic training from a black sergeant. The fact that Vince, a
white soldier, could do the same made it special for him.

Vince didn't share his parents' passion for cooking and
the restaurant business. So, in his first outright act of rebellion
against his parents, he had gone to an Army recruiter and
started the enlistment process. Nick's parents had been proud
when he enlisted, but Vince's mother and father reacted with
anger and tears. Still, they wrote Vince faithfully each week.

Nick first met Vince when he was assigned as driver on
the same tank crew with Nick. The two hit it off immediately.
There was mutual respect because they were both smart and
competent, and they took their roles as soldiers seriously.
They stood together when in fights. On their free time, they
enjoyed exploring Munich together.

And then *it* happened.

It occurred one winter night at Grafenwöhr in December
1959. Vince was told to take a jeep and go out to pick up two
guards who were standing on forest roads several miles away
from the impact area where tanks had been firing into. The
guards were supposed to prevent any vehicles or individuals
from getting too close to the dangerous impact area.

One of the guards was Nick Holloway.

After picking up Nick and Billy Dryden, the other guard, Vince was on the way back to Tank Section's bivouac area. The day had been warm — here and there on the road were sheets of ice where snow that melted during the day had frozen during the cold night. Talking and laughing while driving, Vince hadn't realized how fast he was going — he overcompensated his turn when the jeep slid on the ice.

The jeep flipped over. Nick and Billy were thrown clear, but the jeep landed on top of Vince.

Nick hadn't hesitated. He directed Billy to use the jeep's radio to call for help — for an ambulance and a medic. Through Vince's screams, Nick assured him that he would be okay — that the medics would soon be there.

Nick tried to lift the jeep off of his friend. It was too heavy — the jeep wouldn't budge.

Nick ran into the woods and returned with a tree branch about four inches thick. He dragged the branch to the jeep. A pool of blood was forming under Vince's hip.

"They're sending an ambulance right out, Nick," Billy said.

"Here — help me with this branch. We've got to get the jeep off him so that we can see where all that blood is coming from."

Using the branch as a lever, the two men were able to lift the jeep up on its wheels. Vince was free.

Nick saw that the blood was coming from Vince's right leg. The amount of blood made Nick think an artery might have been severed. He took his web belt off and buckled it tight around Vince's thigh as a tourniquet.

Now Nick thought the only other thing he and Billy could do for Vince was to cover him and keep him warm, and to keep him awake.

The ambulance reached them shortly thereafter. Nick had been afraid that the ambulance driver might get lost in this dark part of the Bavarian forest.

Vince spent three weeks in the U.S. Army hospital in Munich. He had suffered a broken pelvic, a leg broken in two places, and a broken ankle. Luckily, he recovered fully with no limp and no other lasting injuries.

Nick came to the hospital to visit Vince often, usually every other day and on both Saturday and Sunday.

Vince believed he owed his life to Nick. Nick demurred and said the medic would have been there in time anyway — but Vince wouldn't hear of it.

"You saved my life, Nick. I'll never forget it."

There was nobody Nick trusted more than Vince.

At the EM club, with Löwenbrau beer on tap, the two soldiers sat at a table on the far side of the room, as far away as possible from others in the club.

"Vince, you should have seen that place. The mess, the shouts — hell — the screams of the wounded guys. It was chaos. It shook me up. I can't imagine what that was like for Danny. Blood-stained stuff. I even found a guy's thumb. Damn — I can't get that thumb out of my head."

"Drink up," Vince said. "I'll get us a couple more beers."

When Vince returned to the table, Nick was playing one of the slot machines that stood along the wall. Vince caught Nick's eye and held his mug of beer in the air. Nick went back to the table.

"I thought the slots would help me get Danny and Camp Chaffee off my mind."

"Nick, buddy — you've got to forget all that shit. It's not good for you to keep going over it, and over it, again and again."

"I don't want to forget — I don't think I can forget it. I want to understand, not forget."

"Why do you care so much, Nick?"

Nick didn't answer him.

Nick thought about Vince's question. He had grown up in a small town in the Midwest. In Sunday school, he was taught to love others as much as he loved himself. In the Boy Scouts, he learned *on my honor, I will do my best, to do my duty, to God and my country.* The Scouts also taught him to be kind and helpful to everyone, especially the weak and the vulnerable. His parents talked about the kind of person he should be — they not only talked about that, they were models of practicing what they preached.

And then there was Eugene Wallis. Could Nick atone for his bad treatment of Eugene by being kind to Danny?

After a while, the two men ordered a pizza. Nick believed the Henry Kaserne EM Club had the best pizza in Munich. Actually, it was one of the only places to get an American-style pizza.

"Well, then — have you thought about talking to someone else who might be able to help you work through this?"

"What? You think I need help? Professional help? Do you think I'm nuts, Vince? Is that it? You think I'm crazy?"

"No, Nick — I don't think you're crazy. It was just a thought. I don't think I'm doing you much good. You sound worse now than you did this morning. Your feelings are eating you up."

"So, now you think you're a fucking expert on my feelings?"

Vince held his hands up, palms facing Nick.

"No — no. I'm no expert. I just thought someone who knows about these things — you know, maybe you could talk to them?"

"Yeah — like who? I'm not going on sick call and say I need to see a doctor for psychos."

"Oh, I don't know. Maybe Lieutenant Dolan, or top sergeant Dixon, or even that chaplain guy — what was his name? Oh, yeah — Reynolds, Captain Reynolds."

Nick and Vince ate their pizza in silence. Nick continued to drink beer.

When Nick almost fell off his chair, Vince stood to help him.

"Come on, Nick. It's time to go."

With Nick's arm over Vince's shoulders, the two men started to walk towards their barracks. For Nick, the sky was spinning. When they reached the middle of Patton field, Nick fell down to his knees and vomited. Vince held him so that Nick wouldn't fall forward into his own puke.

5

EARL CRAWFORD

Tuesday, 6 September

Sergeant Earl Dellmar Crawford was thirty-one years old. He was a large man, standing six feet two inches tall, and weighing about two hundred ten. He had put on weight in recent years, but it only served to further intimidate the soldiers under him, just by his size. He also used words to instill fear in his soldiers.

"Men — I'm Sergeant First Class Crawford. I'm from the old Army — the brown shoe Army. I was commissioned as an officer on the battlefield in Korea — but the powers that be took that away from me. I'm still pissed off about that — but so be it. I've killed the enemy — lots of 'em. That's what we warriors do. That's what you're here for — to kill commies. I know how to start a tank engine when it's ten below zero, and I can tell the difference between a gutless coward and a real man. Make no mistake about that. I've seen it all in this here Army — so don't think you can goldbrick and get by without working. If you do, I'll hang you upside down by your balls — I will — I will do it — I'll do it faster than you can blink your eyes. So, if you want to get along with me, you better do what I say — quickly and well. And no backtalk — I don't tolerate no backsassing. You hear me? When I say jump — all I want to hear from you is 'how high?' That's all — you're dismissed."

One of Earl's ways of maintaining his authority over his men was to pick out the most vulnerable soldier in his unit and then to get rid of him. And the most vulnerable soldier in Tank Section was, of course, Danny Maguire.

Maguire, Earl thought, was just a little piss-ant; a yellow-bellied imitation of a man. He was sure that the jack-off private was going to get them all killed someday.

Maguire couldn't keep his gear in order. He couldn't read a topographical map, or operate the radios. He was a menace with a weapon in his hands. He'd never be a driver or a gunner, and he wouldn't even be an adequate loader if it weren't for the color code scheme for the ammo that Nick Holloway devised and drilled into Maguire's pea-sized brain, over and over.

It was impossible, Earl was sure, that anybody in Tank Section actually liked Maguire. Certainly, Holloway and Delvecchio looked after him, but it was clear that they resented the little fart and saw taking care of him as a sort of Christian duty, which was, in Crawford's opinion, utter bullshit.

Holloway had said once that Maguire shouldn't be in the Army. If not for the fact that the puke could actually start marching on his left foot, he probably would have been washed out during basic training. He should have been sent home anyway. Geez, what were they thinking? Then the Armor School at Fort Knox, how had they passed him on? What a perfect storm - what a series of mistakes — by his draft board, then they passed him on in basic, and finally, some idiot at Fort Knox thought he could be a tanker in spite of the fact that Maguire found it impossible to learn.

Now it was Earl's job to get rid of him. To tell the truth, he was looking forward to it.

6

Bar Fight

During the following week, Nick put himself into his work with an enthusiasm that he hoped would help him deal with his feelings. Maybe Vince was right — maybe he should try to forget.

Saturday night found the boys of Tank Section at one of their favorite bars on Goethe Strasse, near the Hauptbahnhof, the main train station in central Munich. At the Texas Bar, the young men quickly started the process of getting drunk.

And so, Nick Holloway was trying to restrain Jimmy Wapoga.

The words *smoke signals* had set Jimmy off. He'd thrown the thick glass beer mug at Ben, tipped the table over with all its beer mugs and ashtrays, and now — with arms outstretched — Jimmy was trying to go for Ben Bartlett's throat.

"No, Jimmy — no," Nick Holloway yelled, not exactly sober himself, as he grabbed both of Jimmy's arms from behind his back.

Jimmy couldn't move forward, so he sat back down in his chair.

Ben stood there, puffing defiantly with his fists up.

Finally, he bent over and helped right the table and pick up the mugs and ashtrays that weren't broken. A barmaid came with a broom and dustpan and cleaned up the broken glass. She mopped up the spilled beer, staring at them with doleful eyes.

A bouncer came, stood and looked for a moment, and then seeing that the fuss appeared to be over, he returned to his stool by the front door.

"You sum-bitch, Holloway — whyn't ya let 'em fight," Ned Lafontaine said.

"It's okay, Ned. We're all friends now — ain't we, Chief?" Ben said.

Jimmy Wapoga glared at Ben.

Still — they'd invited Danny, and they'd invited Jimmy, too, the other man who bore the brunt of Tank Section's teasing.

Jimmy was an angry young man. All Nick knew was that Jimmy was an American Indian from Nebraska. Nick had never so much as asked him if he had grown up on a reservation — it didn't seem important. But other men in Tank Section made fun of Jimmy — letting out war whoops and dancing around him, and asking him how many white men he had scalped.

And now, still panting, Jimmy looked not at Ben, but directly at Danny Maguire.

"Sergeant Crawford is right about you, worm face. You are useless — you are the lowest scum of the lowly — you are lower than whale shit. The only thing you're good at is drawing pictures in that little notebook. What good is that for us? We're all gonna die anyway. Fuck your pictures."

Danny sat there with his mouth open.

"C'mon — knock it off — that's enough of that talk, Jimmy," Nick said.

Ben Bartlett and his pals had big grins on their faces.

Danny was about to cry.

"Maguire, you scruffty little leprechaun," Jimmy continued. Why don't you do us all a big favor and go AWOL? The MPs will catch you because you're so dumb, and then they'll put you in the Dachau stockade — and then I won't have to see your ugly paleface mug around here anymore."

Nick and Vince stood up at the same time and went for Jimmy across the table. Nick had one knee on the table as he reached for Jimmy.

Then someone landed a fist to the side of Nick's head. He shook his head to refocus, and then he went after Ned Lafontaine, who was nearest and clearest.

Nick knew the reality of fights such as these. He knew the best way to win a fight was to stay out of it. Too many men, he thought, believed the way to fight was like it was done in the movies. But real fighters lost teeth, had broken jaws, and suffered concussions. Nick saw a fight while in basic training where a soldier's cheekbones were shattered from a hard fist. After surgery, the man looked strange because that cheek didn't move when the man tried to smile.

It was a melee. Ten GIs, including some strangers from other tables. Two boys were rolling on the floor, locked in mutual bear hugs — unable to break free from each other.

At one point, in an odd moment of silence, Nick heard Hank Williams singing the *Honky Tonk Blues* — still playing on the jukebox.

With grunts and curses, glass breaking, men yelling and girls screaming, the men fought — hitting, kicking, biting, clawing and scratching. If a chair or table broke, the youngsters grabbed any pieces that could be used as clubs. The fight would not end until all of them became unconscious, or hurt, or too exhausted to continue, or until the military police stepped in to stop it. Bouncers were too few to stop a melee such as this, so they didn't try. Also, the Army had an agreement with the Munich police — in the end, U.S. Army Military Police (MPs) would police the soldiers.

Nick hammered his fist into someone's nose, saw blood covering his hand, and then he heard a woman's voice calling his name.

"Nick. Nick. Over here."

It was Trudy, one of the barmaids that Nick had flirted with before.

"They call MPs, Nick — MPs coming," Trudy said as she stood by the bar motioning for him to come to her.

"Thanks, Trudy," Nick yelled at the woman.

"Let's go, Vince — Danny — MPs."

Their clothes, already saturated with cigarette smoke, now were like sponges, soaking up spilt beer and blood on the floor.

Nick pushed aside Joe Flores, who was kicking Danny. Danny was on the floor, his knees held to his chest by his arms. His face was bloody. Nick helped Danny get up on his feet.

"This way, Danny."

Nick, Danny, and Vince followed Trudy to the back of the bar. She led them through a passageway, past storerooms and toilets, to a door that opened onto an alley.

Trudy kissed Nick on the cheek as he went out the door.

"We should never have started that dumb game," Nick said.

It had all begun, he recalled dimly, with someone's suggestion that they go around the table and tell everyone else exactly what they thought of them. With all the alcohol they had consumed, there was no way it couldn't have ended badly.

"We needed that like we need a third nipple," Nick said.

"You've got that right," Vince replied.

"How you doing, Danny?" Nick asked.

"I'll be okay, Nick — except I've got an awful pain in my side."

Danny's face and shirt were covered with blood. He had a gash on his cheek that oozed red.

"Don't worry, Danny — we'll get you cleaned up when we get to the dispensary at the kaserne. The medics will check your ribs. Hopefully, they're only bruised."

They walked through alleyways until they saw a taxi on a cross-street. The taxi took them back to Henry Kaserne. Nick didn't want the Munich police, or anyone else, for that matter, to see them before they got Danny to the kaserne.

"Never again," Nick muttered to Vince as they helped Danny into the taxi.

"Roger that, Nick."

7

LOVE AT FIRST SIGHT

Saturday, 10 September

Medics at the Henry Kaserne dispensary cleaned Danny's face and stitched up the deep cut on his cheek. His ribs were only bruised, not broken. Nick and Vince had Mercurochrome applied to the cuts on their faces and hands. Vince had black eyes and fat lips. Nick had a small cut and a bruise on his right cheek, and needed a few stitches in his left eyebrow.

In the barracks, Nick took Danny to his room and helped him onto his bunk.

"If any of the other guys give you a hard time when they get back, just ask Billy to come get me," Nick said.

Back in his own room, Nick saw Vince — with a smile on his face.

"What are you so happy about?" Nick said.

"I put our names on the pass list for tomorrow. We're going out on the strasse and get drunk."

"I don't get it — one minute we go drinking and get in a fight — and in the next, you've got us going out drinking again? To get drunk?"

"It's just an expression, Nick — a figure of speech. We

need some fun, some genuine fun. You've got to get away from Maguire for a while. If he can't take care of himself, then so be it. But you, my friend, you can't save Danny or anyone else in this man's Army. It's a hard world, and as much as you don't like to hear it, Danny will have to sink or swim in it. You need some fun for a change. I know I do."

* * * *

Sunday, 11 September

After lunch on Sunday, Nick and Vince changed into civilian clothes, picked up their pass cards at the orderly room, and headed for the front gate of Henry Kaserne. They walked the quarter mile on Kollwitz Strasse to the bus stop on Ingolstadter Strasse. The bus took them to Parzival Platz where they transferred to a streetcar that would take them to downtown Munich.

In two important ways, Munich was a great duty station for young soldiers — there were lots of beer halls, and many pretty young women.

The two young men went first to the *Zigeuner Keller* — the gypsy cellar — for a drink, and to decide where to go and what to do next. Their decision was to visit the famous *Deutsches Museum* and then to have dinner at *Café Figaro*, Nick's favorite restaurant in Munich. After dinner, they would visit the dance clubs in Schwabing and try to meet some girls.

They finished their drinks and went up the stairs to the street level. As they came out into the bright sunshine, they stopped and stared. There, not ten feet away, were two cute girls studying a city map. Nick guessed they were Americans by their laughter, and by the way they were dressed.

Nick didn't hesitate.

"Good afternoon. You lovely ladies look like you need some assistance, and we are here to assist you. How lucky is that? Now, how can we be of help to you?" Nick said.

The girls looked up with open mouths that quickly turned into smiles.

"Oh — hi. We were looking on this map to see where the Hofbrauhaus is," said the girl with the full lips and the light auburn hair.

A glow inside Nick rose. His smile was warm as a sun soaked soft blanket. The worst thoughts of Camp Chaffee, Danny, and Sergeant Crawford disappeared.

"No problem. It's not far from here. In fact, we were on our way there ourselves — weren't we, Vince?"

Nick looked at Vince and winked.

"Oh, yes — the Hofbrauhaus is one of our favorite places in Munich."

Nick held his arm out and the girl with the big smile put her arm through his.

Vince offered his arm to the girl with the dark blond hair.

"Hi — my name is Vince and I'm funny and charming, but totally harmless. By what name are you called?"

"Barbara."

"Barbara — that's a nice name."

Nick was silent. He couldn't take his eyes off the girl at his side. Green sweater. Gray skirt. Penny loafers. Like a vision from home.

"I'm Nick — Nick Holloway," he finally said.

"I'm Carol — Carol Benjamin. Do you mind my asking who you guys are? I don't mean your names. What are you doing here in Munich? I thought the only young American men here are students like us, or those soldiers we sometimes see riding around Munich in trucks. You don't look like students and you don't look like soldiers."

Carol's look lingered on Nick's cheek and his stitched eyebrow.

"Thank you, Carol Benjamin, thank you very much. You noticed — now I guess our cover has been blown."

Nick spoke softer — almost in a whisper.

"You see — we are from outer space — from Mars. We came down to your planet earth to carry out a very special mission."

Carol's smile was still there, but she furled her eyebrows, and leaned slightly away as she looked at Nick.

"Really — and what is your special mission?"

Nick changed his voice — trying to imitate Cary Grant.

"You see, my dear, we must find beautiful American girls and learn as much as we can about them. Such as where they are from and what they are doing in Munich, Germany, on a gorgeous Sunday afternoon in early September."

Carol laughed.

"Okay, I'll tell you what I'm doing here, if you'll tell me what you're doing here."

"Fair enough."

"Barb and I are students at JYM — the Junior Year in Munich program of Wayne State University. We're just starting."

"And where are you from, earthling?" Nick said in his affected voice.

"Michigan. Monticello, Michigan, to be exact. Both Barb and I are from Monticello, and we go to Wayne State University in Detroit. I love school. I want to be an English teacher, but I have a second major in German. JYM is a Wayne State program. Now it's your turn — you promised to tell me what you're doing here."

Nick went back to his normal voice.

"Believe it or not, but Vince and I are soldiers, stationed here in Munich. This is a great place to be stationed, but being in the Army can be an out of this world experience sometimes."

Memories of the past week flashed across Nick's mind. His smile disappeared.

"So — what do you and your friend …,"

"Vince — that's my buddy there — Vince Delvecchio."

Nick poked Vince in the shoulder.

"Vince — meet Carol Benjamin — Carol, Vince Delvecchio."

Carol and Vince acknowledged each other, and then Vince introduced Barbara to Nick.

"And you and your friend Vince — what do you do in the Army?" Carol said.

"We're tankers — you know — those fifty-ton dark green monsters you see, with the big gun sticking out of the turret — the turret with the white star. We operate those machines."

Carol didn't respond. She was looking straight ahead.

"Oh, come on. You've known soldiers before. You've known guys who've been in the service?"

"Yes, I have. In fact, my dad was in the Army in World War II."

"There, you see — your dad and I would get along just fine."

"Don't be so sure. Dad said I should be careful when I'm around soldiers. No — he actually said I should stay away from soldiers."

"Now, why would he say something like that? I'm just an all-American boy from Kimball, Ohio. Boy Scout, high school athlete, Sunday school, and my mom makes the best apple pie in the world."

"Boy Scouts? Sunday school? Now you're putting us on," Vince chuckled as he spoke.

Nick gave Vince a playful punch in the shoulder.

"Hey buddy — whose side are you on?" Nick said with a wide grin on his face.

"Okay, ladies — here's the Hofbrauhaus," Nick said as they approached the famous beer hall at Platzl 9.

The Hofbrauhaus loomed above them, venerable as could be. The girls gasped when they went through the swinging doors. Tables and tables of ancient Bavarians in knee-breeches and feathered fedoras, with waitresses spinning by in dirndls, each holding eight one-liter mugs of beer in their muscular arms.

"How do they do that?" Carol asked.

Nick shrugged his shoulders. He explained that the Hofbrau had been making beer for over three hundred and fifty years, and that there were six other major breweries in Munich.

They found an open table in a corner. When the waitress appeared, Nick ordered.

"Vier Mass Bier, und zwei Brezein, bitte."

Nick told how Hitler had launched the Nazi Party at the Hofbrauhaus in 1920, by presenting his twenty-five-point platform, including a provision that Jews were not considered real Germans.

"How do you know these things?" Carol asked.

"I had good teachers, and I read history — and Munich has seen a lot of history."

"Wow, that's great," Carol said.

"Oh, I don't know," Nick muttered self-consciously.

"No, really, I mean it. It shows that you're curious, that you want to understand."

They talked and laughed for over an hour.

"You guys look like you've been in a fight — have you?" Carol asked.

Nick lifted his beer stein in the air.

"Oh, we had too much of this ... and, you wouldn't believe it, but both of us walked smack dab into lamp posts."

"Really? Barbara said with sarcasm.

"I'll bet," Carol said.

"Not really," Vince said. "Mine was more of a kiosk, or a statue of some kind."

"I don't believe either one of you," Carol said.

Nick changed the subject.

"Say, Vince and I were planning to eat dinner at a great little place called the Café Figaro. They have some tasty

Hungarian dishes there — spicy, but not overly so — just lots of good food. Would you like to join us?"

Carol and Barb looked at each other.

Carol shook her head.

"Sorry, but we're expected back to have dinner with some of our friends," she said.

The girls and Nick and Vince exchanged telephone numbers, and then Carol said they could find their own way back. She and Barb thanked the young men for the good time they had.

And then they were gone.

* * * *

"I think I'm in love," Nick said. "I've got to see that girl again."

He grinned broadly.

"There you go again with that love thing. The real question is — would you take her home to meet your mother?"

"Oh, yes — no question about it. Mom and Carol would hit it off. It would be good."

The two soldiers went to the *Café Figaro* for supper. Flirting with Rozalia the waitress was fun. The Hungarian Reisfleisch was good, the Villany red wine was good, the coffee was good, the conversation with Vince was good — Nick was enjoying himself.

What were the feelings he was having? He had never felt that way before. They were pleasant feelings. They were a welcome relief to his recent struggles to keep Danny safe. Nick had just met a girl who was not only attractive — no, Nick thought she was beautiful. Not only was she beautiful — he saw that Carol was smart, smart in a people sense, and maybe also smart in a bookish sense. Nick marveled at how easy she was for him to talk with.

8

CAROL BENJAMIN

Sunday, 11 September

After dining with some of their classmates, Carol and Barbara walked to Carol's host family's apartment at Isabella Strasse 6. Barbara's family lived only a few doors away.

"Can you come in for a while, Barb? We need to talk."

"Yes, we do."

The Meier family was out. The girls sat on the sofa in the spacious apartment. The building was one of the lucky few in central Munich to escape being destroyed by allied bombers during World War II. In the short time that Carol had stayed there, she wondered about the history of the apartment. Had it belonged to a Jewish family before the war? Whoever it was, they must have had the means to furnish the apartment with expensive-looking furniture and furnishings. Her bedroom had plush velvety drapes and an oriental rug. And how did the Meiers come to get the apartment after the war? Maybe, when the time seemed right, she would ask Frieda and Arndt about these questions.

"Barb — be honest now — what did you think of Nick

and Vince? I know they're soldiers, but they're two good-looking guys — right?"

"Oh, yeah — not cute, not with those shiners and stuff — but still …," Barb said.

"I know what you mean. They were banged up, but they looked clean, and they … they looked good, right? I mean, Nick's blue eyes, oo-la-la."

Carol thought about what she had just said. Of course, she was attracted to him, what normal red-blooded girl wouldn't be attracted to a stud like Nick? On the other hand, was he a stable man? Was this devil-may-care manner of his just a front for some deeper feeling of inferiority? On the other hand, he had been polite and respectful to her and Barb. He wasn't stupid, at least he didn't act like he was.

"I looked at Vince's fat lips, and tried to imagine what it would be like kissing him," Barb said.

Both girls giggled at that.

"Seriously, Barb, you saw and heard the same that I did — would you like to go out with Vince again? I mean, do you see anything wrong with that?" Carol said.

"Wrong? Carol Benjamin — are you kidding me? I'd go out with that Italian stallion just like that — if he asks me."

Barb snapped her fingers in the air.

"Well, what I mean by wrong is … oh, you know what I mean. What would you say to your mom, or to the other JYMers — if they found out you were dating a soldier?"

Carol thought about her parents, especially her dad. He had been in the Army in World War II, and while he didn't talk about it much, he had said most soldiers behaved poorly when it came to women.

"Yeah, I see your point. But, Carol — how often in your life are two charming, utterly studly, good-looking guys, going to walk up to you and want to get to know you? So what if they're soldiers? At least they're American soldiers," Barb said.

"The question remains, Barb. What would your mom and dad think? What about our classmates? What about Herr Professor Kienetz?"

"My parents wouldn't like it one bit. They're very protective of me. As for the rest of them, I don't care what they'd think."

"I told Nick that my dad was in the Army during World War II, and that he had warned me about soldiers," Carol said.

"What is your dad worried about?"

"Oh, you know."

"No, I don't know. My dad was too old for the war. Come on, tell me."

"He said that all soldiers want to do is to get drunk and then to get into any girl's pants."

Both Carol and Barb went into fits of hysterical laughter. Carol fell off the sofa onto the floor, where she laid on her back and laughed so hard that her hands went from her face to holding her stomach, and then back to her face again.

"Carol, you are such a square — so old-fashioned."

Eventually, the girls calmed down, and Carol resumed her place on the sofa.

"Carol, no — I was wrong — you are so naughty."

"I know."

They laughed again.

"Now, Carol, it's your turn. Will you go out with Nick if he asks you?"

Carol's face turned red. She hesitated before responding.

"Yes. Yes, I would."

"Carol — you're blushing."

"No, I am not."

Carol rubbed her cheeks with her hands.

"There, you see, if I'm blushing it's from laughing so hard."

"Come on — I know blushing when I see it," Barb said.

"Well, okay, yes … the truth is, I liked him."

Barb poked at Carol, trying to tickle her.

"See, I was right. You've fallen for a soldier — a soldier from Ohio with a banged up face and a split eyebrow."

"Oh, come on, Barb. I haven't fallen for Nick — I just met the guy. How could I possibly fall for a guy who looks like a street fighter — a guy I just met today?"

"No problem — I get it, Carol. Now, the question you asked me is for you to answer. How are you going to explain this to your dad? What will you say to our class?"

"Please don't say anything to our classmates, Barb. Let's promise each other — you don't tell on me, and I won't tell on you."

"It's a deal. Of course, if the guys don't call us, then we won't have any problem at all."

"Good, and with dad and mom way back in Michigan — they don't have to know anything."

They sat in silence for several minutes.

Finally, Barb spoke.

"And if Nick doesn't call you — well then, you'll just have to call him."

They both erupted in laughter again.

"Barb, you are a bad influence on me."

"I know."

They laughed and laughed.

"Say, Carol. Let's have some of that cognac your host parents keep in the cupboard."

9

Tanks

Monday, 12 September

Most days when Tank Section was in Henry Kaserne were filled with maintenance work on the tanks. This Monday was no exception. The fifty-two-ton M48A1 Patton tank required constant maintenance in order to keep it in combat-ready condition.

There were ninety-nine tanks in the Third Battalion, 34th Armor Regiment. Four of the tanks were in the Tank Section of Headquarters Company. Nick Holloway was the gunner on tank 97, with the number 2 painted on the turret since it was the battalion executive officer's tank.

Nick took pride in knowing the tank as well as anyone in the battalion. From when he went through the armor crewman training program at Fort Knox, Kentucky, Nick took every opportunity to learn how to operate and maintain all of the electrical, mechanical, hydraulic, communications, and weapons systems on the tank.

In Nick's experience, the M48A1 was not a reliable tank — it was notorious for breaking down. Its twelve- cylinder Continental model AV-1790-5B 810 horsepower gasoline engine had four magnetos to coordinate the timing of the internal combustion cycle: intake, compression, ignition, and exhaust, or, as the soldiers called it: suck, squeeze, bang, and blow. With the tank bouncing over rough terrain, the magnetos were frequently out of sync and needed adjustment. Until adjusted, the engine was harder to start, and, once started, it ran roughly.

The tank also had a much smaller auxiliary engine called the *Little Joe*, which was used mainly to charge the batteries and to help start the main engine.

The transmission, an Allison CD-850 cross-drive automatic, had to be checked for fluid levels and leaks. The transmission controlled the steering of the tank by providing greater or lesser speed to one track over another. The driver made this happen through the use of rods and levers that were attached to the steering wheel in the driver's compartment.

The tank's tracks also required constant attention. The rubber-padded steel tracks were made in twenty-eight-inch-wide two-tread track block sections. These sections were linked together with wedge-shaped steel center guides and smaller end connectors. These metal pieces squeaked like mice when the tank moved. Many of these track parts shook loose, wore out, or cracked — needing to be tightened or replaced.

Road wheels, idler wheels — front and rear, return rollers, and the heavy rear track drive sprockets also needed to be inspected, and attended to or replaced if necessary. Broken tracks were common while tanks were used in field exercises — usually caused by poor driving techniques. Whatever the cause of a broken track, fixing it involved backbreaking work.

The M48A1 Patton tank was designed with a torsion bar suspension system that absorbed shocks while the tank moved over rough ground. The twelve steel torsion bars were each about eight feet in length and three inches in diameter. They were located inside the lower hull of the tank — not easily accessible. Only one end of each bar was visible from outside the tank. The torsion bars were anchored, alternately, inside the tank's hull, then they ran across the bottom of the hull to extend through to the outside, where they were fastened to an arm connected to each set of two side-by-side road wheels. As the road wheels went over an object such as a rock or a tree branch, the wheels and connecting arm would rise causing the torsion bar to twist. Once over the obstacle, the tension in the torsion bar would restore the wheel to equilibrium.

On a training exercise in May 1960, metal fatigue caused a torsion bar to break on Nick's tank. Because of the position of the bars inside the tank's hull, Nick and his crewmates worked around the clock with tank mechanics to replace the broken bar. First, the crew off-loaded all of the ammunition from the tank because the mechanics used acetylene torches to get at and cut out the broken torsion bar.

Tanks carried high explosive ammunition for use against buildings, bunkers, and soft-sided vehicles; armor-piercing ammunition with tungsten carbide steel cores, and rounds with shaped plastic explosives for use against other tanks; white phosphorous, or *Willy Peter*, as soldiers called it, to be used to start fires; and canister shot, filled with steel pellets, like shotgun shells, for use against enemy soldiers in the open.

In addition to ammunition for the tank's 90-millimeter main gun, the tank carried several thousand .30 caliber bullets linked together in belts for the coaxial machine gun mounted alongside the main gun. and .50 caliber belted rounds for the heavy machine gun mounted inside the tank commander's cupola. All of this ammunition had to be counted, inspected, and cleaned to ensure that it would work when necessary.

Repairs — both major and minor — oil changes, grease lubrication, battery maintenance, rust removal and prevention, painting, cleaning and calibration of optical devices, cleaning and inspection of ammunition, replenishing the first aid kits, and cleaning and oiling the set of tools stored on the tank — all of these needed to be done, and done right, if the tank and its crew were to be ready if and when the order came to go into combat.

The tank also carried radio and intercom equipment. Nick's tank had an AN/GRC-3 radio set. This set included an R-108 receiver, an RT-66 receiver/transmitter, a PP-112 power supply, an RT-70 receiver/transmitter, and an AM-65 power supply. The AN/VIC-1 intercom system allowed for the crew to communicate with each other. These systems were designed to be rugged because of vibration and the tank's bouncing motions, especially when in rough terrain. The radio sets and related equipment required testing and repairing as necessary. Crew training on radio operation was ongoing.

All of this work required competent and motivated soldiers as crewmen.

* * * *

Sergeant Crawford walked around the four tanks and their crews, asking questions and giving orders.

When he got to Nick's tank, Crawford said nothing to Nick or to Vince, who were cleaning and oiling hand tools. Danny Maguire was inside the turret. Sergeant Stark was away at the dental clinic at Will Kaserne.

"These front idler wheels need to be rotated — the inner wheel is worn down on the inside. When were you numbskulls thinking of getting around to doing this?"

Nick and Vince looked at Sergeant Crawford, and then at each other, and then back to Crawford.

"Sergeant, we did rotate the idler wheels, before you got here, just before we left for Graf," Nick said.

Nick stood to check for himself — Vince did the same on the other side of the tank.

"No, sergeant — the outer wheel still has plenty of lip left," Nick said.

"This one's fine too," Vince said.

"Are you two dumb fuckers telling me that I'm wrong?"

Nick and Vince looked at each other again.

Danny Maguire stuck his head up out of the loader's hatch.

Nick's mind went from continuing the argument and trying to convince Crawford he was wrong, or to agreeing with him and then just forgetting to do what the sergeant ordered. This was a tactic Nick used sometimes when given an obviously wrong and stupid directive.

"No, I'm not saying you're wrong. I'm just saying that since the tracks tend to pull to the outside, the outer wheel wears faster than the inner wheel. It's just a matter of physics, sergeant, that's all."

"Fuck you and your fucking physics, motherfucker — you've been reading too many books. I know what I'm talking about. If I say change the idler wheels around, that's exactly what I mean."

"Yes, sergeant. Right away. We'll get right on it," Nick said.

Crawford looked up and glared at Danny, and then he walked toward the barracks.

10

GREASE GUN

Just in case the sergeant was watching them, Nick, Vince, and Danny broke the track, pulled the idler wheels, and put them back on in exactly the same way as before — the correct way. If Crawford made an issue of it again, Nick would just play the self-deprecating dumb guy role.

"Oh gee, sarge, how dumb of us — of course you're right, sarge. We just forgot all about it. We'll do it now, right away," Nick would say.

Sergeant Crawford didn't bring it up again. Nick thought that Crawford was such a good tanker that he must have known the idler wheels were mounted okay. It must be that the sergeant needed to show them who was the boss — like the sheriff who twirls his revolver and points it at people, just to prove he has the power.

* * * *

Tuesday, 13 September

Sergeant Crawford stood on a raised platform in front of the soldiers. A flip chart easel stood behind him. On a table lay a gray submachine gun. Each soldier sat Indian-style on the floor, with a weapon lying on his poncho spread out on the floor in front of him.

Danny sat on his own poncho next to Nick. Actually, it was Nick who sat on his poncho next to Danny.

"Listen up men. The submachine gun, caliber .45, M3A1, is an air-cooled, blow-back operated, magazine fed, automatic shoulder weapon. It is light, compact, and rugged. The weapon is fed from a box-type magazine that holds thirty rounds. The submachine gun is most effective at ranges from one to twenty-five meters. It's ideal for wasting any bad guy who sticks his face in your tank hatch. With bullets that are almost a half-inch in diameter, a cyclic rate of fire of seven rounds per second, and a muzzle velocity of nine hundred feet per second, you can see why this lovely little killing machine is affectionately called a grease gun."

Nick's mind was elsewhere. *Carol. Carol Benjamin from Monticello, Michigan. Her seductive smile, full lips, and hair the color of ginger spice.*

"Now, men — pick up your weapons. Before disassembling the submachine gun, clear the weapon. Press in on the magazine catch and remove the magazine. Now, raise the cover, insert a finger into the cocking slot on the bolt, like this."

Crawford held his weapon up so that all of the tankers could see it, then he pulled the bolt to the rear, and inspected the chamber to make sure it was empty.

"Squeeze the trigger and allow the bolt to go forward. Then close the cover."

The sounds of bolts ramming home and covers clanging shut filled the room.

Carol with the light auburn hair. Carol with the cute smile, the light brown eyes, the upturned nose, the sensuous full lips, and the wonderful scent of her perfume. Nick imagined what it would be like to make love to her.

Slowly he realized that Sergeant Crawford was looking straight at Danny.

"Now men, to disassemble the weapon, watch me as I go through the steps — then you will try it:

1. First, you press in on the stock catch on the left side of the pistol grip and remove the stock by pulling it directly to the rear.

2. To remove the trigger guard, place one side of the shoulder rest of the stock on the housing assembly. Like this. Place the other side against the trigger guard and rotate the stock forward. Remove the trigger guard from the pistol grip. Rotate the trigger guard toward the front of the weapon and unhook the trigger guard from the housing assembly.

3. Remove the housing assembly from the receiver — like this.

4. Remove the magazine catch assembly by rotating it toward the right side of the receiver."

Carol — he should call her soon and ask her out again, and to save a day to go to the Oktoberfest, before she plans to do something else. Would she go without Barb? Doubtful. Vince should call her too. Carol's perfume smelled like cloves, like ginger snaps, like the color of her hair. Her voice was low and sweet — so feminine, so sexy.

Sergeant Crawford slammed his pointer hard onto the table.

"Specialist Holloway — wake up and pay attention."

"Yes, sergeant," Nick said.

Crawford went on with his lecture.

5. "To remove the barrel: with the bolt forward, depress the barrel ratchet and unscrew the barrel. Do not allow the barrel ratchet to touch the notches in the barrel collar when removing or replacing the barrel. The stock can be used as a wrench to loosen the barrel.

6. Open the cover and withdraw the bolt and guide-rod group from the receiver."

She'd been smart, too. She'd looked at him like she knew everything about him.

7. "Drift out the sear pin. The magazine catch, ejector, or the oiler stylus can be used as a drift.
8. Remove the trigger pin.
9. Withdraw the trigger and sear group from the receiver."

It was possible that he was in love. Love after one meeting. It was just like in a movie.

"There you have it, men. The submachine gun has been field disassembled. Now you try it. Here are the steps again."

Sergeant Crawford turned a blank page on the easel to reveal the nine steps written large.

Then he went through the steps to reassemble the weapon.

"Are there any questions? Private Maguire?"

Danny nodded his head.

"No? Okay — field strip your weapons and then reassemble them."

The dissonant clamor of clicking, clanging, and pinging rose in a crescendo, and then slid down to an occasional note after a few minutes. Sergeant Crawford walked around, watching and coaching the soldiers as they worked.

Nick finished taking the grease gun apart, thinking about Carol's smooth, small hands. Then he put the gun together again.

Of course, next to him, Danny was struggling with his weapon. Nick whispered instructions to Danny so that he could reassemble his gun. Danny was the last man to finish, but his submachine gun was finally complete, at least it looked like it was.

Sergeant Crawford came to Danny and picked up his weapon. The barrel fell off.

"What the fuck?" Crawford said as he dropped the gun in front of Danny, and then gave it a strong kick. The gun parts flew.

Oh no, Danny. Why? Maybe if Nick hadn't been daydreaming about Carol, he just might have made sure that Danny's barrel was tightened? Nick wondered whether he should stop trying to help Danny.

"We're going to drill on this over and over again until you can strip down the submachine gun and put it back together again, blindfolded. Your life on the battlefield, and the lives of the soldiers on your tank crew, might depend on it."

"Okay — let's do this again."

Nick didn't think about Danny — he was thinking about Carol, and the Oktoberfest — when was its first day?

Surely, he had to see her before 24 September. Yes, the 24th. Where could he ask Carol to go with him next? Maybe he should suggest to Carol that they visit the English Gardens?

Nick decided he would call Carol right after evening chow. He would have to talk with Vince first — they could talk during chowtime.

"What is the 24th Infantry Division?" yelled Crawford.

"It's you and I, sergeant."

"And what's your purpose in life?"

"To kill the enemy, sergeant," the men responded.

"That's right. The fucking commies are the enemy, and your job is to kill them before they kill you."

Nick looked at the men around him.

"What are you?" Crawford yelled.

"WARRIORS, sergeant."

"And what do warriors do?"

"KILL, sergeant."

"Dismissed."

Nick didn't feel like a killer. He would rather be a lover than a warrior.

11

Nick Calls Carol

That evening, Nick and Vince walked from their barracks, across Patton field, to the Service Club building near the front gate of the kaserne. The Service Club had several enclosed telephone booths where soldiers could make private calls.

Nick dialed Carol's number.

A woman answered.

"Hallo?"

Nick was taken aback for a few seconds.

"Ja, hello, hallo. Ich ... ah ... ja ... ish would like to sprechen with — mit — Carol — Carol Benjamin?"

"Just a moment, please," the woman said in English. "By the way, the phrase, if you'd like it for next time, is *Guten Abend, darf ich bitte mit Carol Benjamin sprechen?*"

"Hello, this is Carol."

"Hi, Carol — this is Nick, Nick Holloway. Remember me?"

"Of course, I remember you. How are you, Nick?"

"Great — just great. Say, I'm sorry for being so awkward with your host mother."

Carol laughed.

"That's all right, Nick. I know the feeling."

Then — silence.

"Nick?"

"Yes?"

"Okay, I just wondered if you were still there, or if we had lost our connection."

"I wouldn't want that to happen," Nick said.

"So, what have you been doing the last couple days?" Carol asked. "Have you gotten into any more fights, then?"

"Oh, no, no sirree, ma'am — keeping my nose clean, that's me — clean as a dentist's fingers."

Carol chuckled.

"So, what keeps you busy, then? What do you do when you're not fighting?"

"Oh, you know — soldier stuff."

"No, I don't know, but I'd like to know. Tell me what kind of stuff soldiers do."

Nick told her generally about the usual daily activities of tank maintenance and training classes. A little voice inside told him that Carol didn't care, not really care, about what he did — but that she was judging him on what he said and how he said it. So, he tried to keep it brief.

"Do you like doing soldier things, Nick?"

"Yes ... yes, I do. I'm good at it, at being a soldier. I know that. And, I like the feeling I get from doing a good job."

"Tell me how it feels, Nick."

"How it feels? I don't know .... I guess I was raised to do the best I can at everything I do. So, when I do that, it feels good. I think about how my dad would be pleased with me. Maybe it's how you yourself might feel when you get an A on a test. I don't know — I might be just prattling away here — you must be getting bored listening to me."

"Oh, no, Nick — I'm not getting bored. I like you ... I mean ... I mean, I like hearing you talk."

"You like me?"

"Well … um … you know what I mean, Nick. I just … I meant I like your voice."

Nick held the phone away from his ear, looked at it, smiled, and leaned back inside the phone booth.

"It's okay, Carol. I like you too."

There was silence for a few seconds.

"Nick — I'm sorry, but I don't understand why anyone would enlist. Getting drafted is one thing, but volunteering? I don't get it. Why did you do that?"

"Carol, you do know that every healthy male has a six-year obligation? By enlisting, I was able to decide when to go in, and I got a guarantee that I would be sent to Europe."

"Oh, I guess I didn't understand that. I still don't like it."

"Okay, now it's your turn. Tell me what you've been doing since Sunday," Nick said.

"Oh, I got incredibly lost at the university the other day. I wound up sitting through an entire biology lecture by accident, just because I was too embarrassed to leave."

"Did you understand it?"

"It was all in scientific German — I only got bits and pieces."

Carol went through her routine of classes and study.

Nick thought he would like that kind of life. He had always liked school. Maybe he should go to college instead of staying in the Army?

"Nick — you said you hadn't been in any more fist fights. You looked rough when I saw you on Sunday. How often do you do that — that fighting stuff?"

Nick laughed heartily.

"I only fight when I have to."

Nick laughed again. He hadn't really thought much about fighting. In some ways, it seemed he had to fight to prove that he was a man. And then, the Army encouraged violence. Actually, the Army had a double standard — on the one hand they trained you to be violent, and then, on the other hand, they punished you for acting out. If they caught you, that is.

"That's good — I'm glad of that. Now, I've been curious — you never answered my question about what you guys were fighting about. Will you tell me now?"

Nick went on alert. His mind was engaged in a fight of its own. One part of him wanted to keep some of the truth away from Carol. He was afraid she would judge him negatively if he told her all of the truth. She might think him unworthy of her friendship if she knew about his resorting to violence in an effort to protect Danny and ... and how important it was for him to fight for his own sense of manliness. Would she think he was just another thug? A guy who has to fight at the drop of a hat? Would she reject him for that reason? Should he risk telling her the truth? On the other hand, to lie to her now — to lie to her about anything at all — would gnaw away at him, at his sense of who he was, at what he thought a man should be and how he should act. Nick knew that if he lied to Carol now, she would sense it. Nick thought that if Carol was as smart as he thought she was, and she had the kind of character that he thought she had — that he hoped she had — she would understand. If she wasn't that smart, and didn't have that kind of character, then maybe it was just as well that he found out now.

The muscles in Nick's neck and shoulders were tight.

"There's this private on my tank crew, Private Danny Maguire ..."

Nick told Carol about Danny, about the hang fire; about Danny's punishment of permanent KP; about the cleanup business at Grafenwöhr; about the everyday harassment of Danny by the bullies, including Sergeant Crawford; and finally, about the fight at the Texas bar.

When he had finished, he waited for Carol's response.

He didn't have to wait long.

"Nick, I'm proud of you. To fight for someone like you did, for someone who is weaker and more vulnerable, is a noble thing to do. I'm sorry if you thought I felt otherwise."

Nick sighed, and relaxed again in the phone booth.

"Thanks, Carol."

"How is Danny now?"

"His ribs are still sore, and he'll have those stitches in his face for a while longer. He looks worse than Vince or I look."

Nick chuckled at his own words.

He saw Vince leave his telephone booth and look over at Nick.

"Carol, before we sign off, I want to ask you if you would like to go out with me this coming Saturday? Vince was going to ask Barb also, so we could double. We were thinking it would be fun to go to the English Gardens, if the weather is good."

"Oh, Nick — I'd love that, but ..."

"You can't go?"

"No, I can't. I've got other plans."

They said goodbye, and hung up their phones together.

Nick sat there for a minute or two before joining Vince.

Other plans? What other plans? Was that some girl talk way of telling him that she wasn't interested? Or not interested enough? Why couldn't she tell him what her other plans were? Did she have another boyfriend?

"Bummer about Saturday. Did you set something up with Carol for Sunday?" Vince said.

"Saturday? What do you mean?"

"The JYM field trip to the castle — didn't she tell you?"

"No, she just said she had other plans for Saturday."

"You didn't ask her about that?"

"No."

"I asked Barb to come to the kaserne on Sunday for my basketball tournament," Vince said.

Nick called Carol back.

"Carol, I just talked with Vince — about your trip on Saturday."

"Yes?"

"So, how about you and I meeting at the English Gardens on Sunday? Say, around 1400 — I mean 2:00 o'clock?"

"That sounds like fun, Nick. See you then."

"Auf wiedersehen."

12

MANFRED NEUMANN

Wednesday, 14 September

Sergeant Earl Crawford parked his car thirty meters away from the abandoned factory. He studied the building for several minutes before approaching on foot.

Rust and broken glass were the wrecked building's dominant features. Mud and puddles lay in front of Earl.

The hulk was in an old industrial section of Munich that had been mostly destroyed by allied bombing raids in World War II, and not yet redeemed by reconstruction. The Germans had done marvels with much of the city since the war ended in 1945, but, in 1960, there was still plenty of work to be done in order to restore the city to its pre-war condition.

Earl walked cautiously to a large open doorway. His eyes scanned the high open windows. He didn't trust German criminals. He laughed to himself — *and they better not trust me.*

He stopped short of the open doors, waited until his eyes adjusted, and then he peered inside. There were many places where a gunman could hide and ambush him.

"Good afternoon, Sergeant Crawford. Do you have what I want?"

The voice came from someplace close inside the dark interior of the building.

"Where are you? I won't talk unless I can see you, Manfred."

A man stepped out of the shadows and came closer to him.

"So, Manfred — are you alone?"

"You act as if this was some big deal. Relax, sergeant — we're only trading a few cigarettes for American dollars. Do you have them with you?"

"Yes — do you have the money?"

The German called Manfred laughed.

"You must have read too many detective books — you sound so tentative, so serious," Manfred said.

"I'm always serious. Let's get on with it," Earl said.

Manfred opened his briefcase and took out a paper bag. He opened the bag and showed Earl that it contained U.S. dollars of varying denominations.

Earl counted the money.

"There's only $350 here. We agreed on $8.00 a carton — fifty cartons — that's $400."

"My dear good sergeant. The supply of American cigarettes on the street has increased. You're not the only American taking advantage of the difference in prices. Also, I can't get enough when I sell them — my distributors drive hard bargains. It's only fair that you should share the market losses with me."

"Fair? You call going back on our agreement fair? We talked about this, and settled on $8.00. I'll take my cigarettes to one of your competitors — that's what I call fair. Or — I could break your nose and your fingers. Don't you think that's the fair way to treat a cheater?"

"Okay, okay, sergeant. There's no need to talk about violence — especially over a little cigarette transaction."

Manfred counted fifty dollars from his billfold and

handed it to Earl, who took the bag of money and went to his car.

Manfred followed.

Earl opened the trunk and lifted two open cardboard boxes out. As he turned to hand them to Manfred, a black Mercedes came from behind the building and pulled up beside them.

"Manfred — you said you were alone."

"No, I didn't, sergeant. You are mistaken. I said you took this transaction too seriously."

Earl's mistrust meant that he always planned ahead. If he had known that Neumann was bringing someone with him, Earl would have brought someone as well — just to even the odds.

Manfred put the two boxes in the trunk of the Mercedes, got into the car, and then he and his helper drove away.

Earl stared at the car. He kicked a piece of debris as hard as he could.

* * * *

It being Friday night, Earl Crawford went to the NCO club on Will Kaserne to drink and have dinner with his cronies from the 3/34 Armor. Crawford, Albert Richards, and Franklin Hairston had served together in the Korean War. Richards was the supply sergeant in Headquarters Company — and Hairston worked in the battalion's finance office.

These men still looked to Earl with respect for his leadership, even though he had lost his commission as an officer.

His demotion — because that's the way Earl Crawford saw it — was not the only resentment that he held against the Army. There was also that business about his father.

Lieutenant Colonel Winfield Scott Crawford had commanded a military school in New Mexico. Earl was a junior in the high school department when it happened.

His father was removed from his position in disgrace over a scandal involving misuse of funds. Forced to retire, Lieutenant Colonel Crawford urged his son to go into the Army and to do his best. He tried to convince Earl that what happened to him was not Earl's fault, nor was it the Army's fault. Earl was forced to face the truth that what had happened was his mother's fault. Her spendthrift ways had put the family in financial trouble, and Earl's father made a mistake — a costly mistake. Earl blamed the Army and his mother, but not his father.

Earl handed Hairston his share of the money he got from Manfred Neumann.

"Here you go, Frank — that cocksucker Neumann tried to cheat me again — but he finally paid up. I swear, one of these times he's going to go too far."

"Well, as the saying goes, all's well that ends well," Sergeant First Class Franklin Hairston said.

"All I can say is, he'd better watch out when he deals with you, Earl. He doesn't know he's trying to tickle the tail of a tiger. And, you know you can count on us to back you up — all the way, if you know what I mean," Sergeant First Class Al Richards said.

"There's no need to get rough, Al — not yet," Earl said.

They each, in turn, complained about how they didn't trust Germans.

"The cheap chiseler," Earl said. "One thing he did say that made sense to me though. The supply of cigarettes is getting larger for the Germans. American tobacco companies are licking their chops over the growing demand for smokes in Europe, and the Germans can't stand those dog turds the Turks sell them. So, what it all means is that there's going to be less money in it for small operator guys like us."

Hairston picked up his pack of Lucky Strikes and took a cigarette out. He lit it with his Zippo lighter. He turned the cigarette pack over and looked at it pensively.

"I can tell what you're thinking Earl, and it scares me," Hairston said.

"Okay — I'll bite — what am I thinking?"

"I'm hanging out on a limb already. Stealing cigarette ration books and falsifying official U.S. Army records is a serious offense. I could go to Leavenworth for that alone. But now, I'm guessing you want me to do something else, something more, in addition, don't you?"

Earl Crawford looked at Hairston with a practiced half-amused stare.

"You're right, Frank. I need more liquor ration stamps. I need full books of stamps. You'll have to get them out of that safe, and then fix the books."

Earl then looked at Al Richards.

"Al, you need to dip your oar in the water as well. I want you to gin up some more loss reports, and fair wear and tear claims, and get me some complete tool sets — new ones, this time, you know — the quality kind, the expensive ones. And paint, white paint — I can sell all the white paint you can get for me."

Earl was pleased. He got these men to go along with him. They were as money hungry as he was. He hadn't told them yet about his plan to sell empty brass shell casings to the Germans.

13

SOLDIERS

Thursday, 15 September

Earl Crawford had a love/hate relationship with the Army. He loved the feeling of recognition he got from being a good soldier, and he liked the predictable rituals of the Army. Maybe the most important thing about being a sergeant was the feeling of power he had over other men. He hated the fact that the Army took away the battlefield commission he earned in the Korean War — and for such stupid, bureaucratic reasons too. In his mind, he should still have been a commissioned officer.

At 0500 on this day, when Sergeant Earl Crawford was in charge of quarters (CQ), he walked through the barracks hallways, blew a shrill whistle, and yelled "rise and shine," "up and at 'em," "everybody out of those bunks," "drop those cocks and grab your socks," and "let me hear those feet hit the floor." He opened the door to each room, turned on the light, and made eye contact with at least one bleary-eyed soldier.

For men he didn't like, Earl blew his whistle inside the soldier's room — a painful ear experience for the men. He didn't think of that as mean — he called it *good training*.

Here and there, he heard a radio playing country music

— the *Hillbilly Reveille* show was the early morning offering of the Armed Forces Network (AFN) in Munich. Earl loved country music — his favorite song was *El Paso*, by Marty Robbins. Later in the day, AFN programming included the *Munich Morning Report, Luncheon in Munchen, Music in the Air, American Music Hall, Bouncing in Bavaria, Grand Ole Opry,* and *Hillbilly Gasthaus.* Earl listened to AFN as much as he could each day on his Regency TR-1 transistor radio.

Earl knew many soldiers who started their day with a cigarette, lit with the ubiquitous Zippo lighter. The soldiers had about fifteen minutes to dress and prepare to go outside for the company's reveille formation. The more energetic few popped right up from their bunks, grabbed their Dopp kits and towels, and headed down the hall to the latrine, to shower and shave before the call for formation.

Reveille formation was one Army ritual that Earl liked — it served both the purpose of getting everybody out of bed and starting the day together, and also to account for all of the soldiers assigned to the company. The roughly two hundred men of Headquarters Company lined up outside in the courtyard formed by their U-shaped barracks building. Soldiers lined up in ranks by sections, an arm's length apart, with section leaders in front. The company's first sergeant stood facing the company of men formed up. When he was ready, he gave the order to come to attention, followed by the command to report. Earl Crawford, as Tank Section sergeant, replied with *all present and accounted for.* The consequences of not being present or accounted for were intended to deter other soldiers from lingering in bed or otherwise dawdling in getting ready to go outside for formation. While this didn't happen often, the penalty could be something like two hours' extra duty each day for two weeks — called fourteen and two — and with no possibility of getting a pass to leave the kaserne during that time. Lingering and dawdling were not acceptable. Earl believed such punishment was an effective way to train men.

Earl got angry whenever a soldier in tank section was late for formation. Standard practice in the company was to punish all the men in a section for the failures of one man. Earl liked that — he didn't care if the men thought it unfair.

Far more serious was the offense of being absent without leave (AWOL). If a soldier left the kaserne without a pass, or while on a pass he didn't return at the end of his approved pass or leave term, he would be considered AWOL. Penalties for AWOL could be as light as a demotion in rank, or could be as severe as a court-martial resulting in a dishonorable discharge from the Army, or prison time, or both. Again, Earl thought it was important to set an example by handing out harsh punishment — it would stop others from going AWOL.

After reveille formation, Earl's soldiers had time to shower, shave, dress, make their bunks, and eat breakfast. The men of Headquarters Company ate in a mess hall in their barracks building. Food was abundant and well-prepared. The conventional wisdom was that when General Dwight Eisenhower became President of the United States, he insisted on the soldiers of the armed forces being taken care of properly. In his role as commander in chief, he made sure the troops had good food, reliable mail service, and other top-notch personnel services. Ike was a popular figure among the soldiers, but Earl Crawford wasn't one of them — he didn't like Ike. It was Eisenhower's people who took away his well-deserved battlefield commission. He also hated Harry Truman, because Truman fired General MacArthur during the Korean War. Actually, Earl Crawford hated all presidents and politicians. In public, however, Earl didn't criticize the president or talk much about politics. When asked about his opinion, he merely said that he was all for law and order.

Between breakfast and work formation, Sergeant Crawford inspected his men's rooms. He made sure that all bunks had been made in the prescribed Army way, with neat corners and tight blankets; that hardwood floors and other surfaces such as windowsills and foot and wall lockers were dusted; and that everything was clean and in good military appearance.

Meals, or chow, as the soldiers called it, were served in the company mess hall. The walls of Headquarters Company's mess hall were painted with murals. On one side was a large painting of General George Patton in a heroic pose with binoculars hanging from a strap around his neck. Patton was the legendary American tank general in World War II. Serious U.S. Army tankers revered him. The tanks of 3/34 Armor were named Patton tanks.

On the opposite wall was an equally large and romanticized painting of Germany's Field Marshall Erwin Rommel — hero of the North African campaigns of 1941 and 1942, and known as the *Desert Fox*.

From the stories he had heard, Earl respected both Patton and Rommel.

Around these mythic warrior generals were painted battle scenes, mounted cavalry on both horses and tanks — tanks, old and new — and inspirational expressions such as the question, *What is the 24th Infantry Division?* And the answer: *It's You and I, Sir."*

Evening chow was followed by several hours of free time for the soldiers. A movie theater, snack bar, ball fields, gymnasium, post exchange (PX) store, bowling alley, and an enlisted man's club (EM club), library, hobby shop, service club, and a photo lab, were all available on Henry Kaserne. In the barracks, there was a day room where men could play cards, write letters, listen to a radio, or just sit around and talk.

Earl thought these were all wastes of taxpayers' money. He believed soldiers would do better in combat if they weren't coddled with distractions while in the kaserne.

Not all days were typical — and Earl liked that.

14

Shakedown Inspection

Friday, 16 September

Shouts and whistles and bangs on doors. The dreaded shakedown inspection. Every few months, on a surprise basis, the Army showed how little they trusted their soldiers by conducting early morning inspections of the men's personal gear and other items that had no military purpose, but that meant something to individual soldiers.

Nick hated these invasions of his privacy. He didn't understand how the Army could trust him with a rifle, a pistol, a sub-machinegun, hand grenades, and a fifty-two ton tank, but they wouldn't let him keep a glass beer mug because it might be used as a weapon in a fist fight. Where was the logic in that?

This shakedown was at 0330. Instead of one sergeant going around to wake everybody up, the shakedown involved teams of NCOs and officers. The idea was to get all of the men out of bed and standing at attention in their underwear and bare feet in the hallways. If it was cold — well, that was just tough.

"Oh, no — not again," Billy Dryden whined.

"Shut your mouth and stand tall in the hall, soldier," Captain Elliott replied.

"This is good training, Dryden," Sergeant Crawford said, grinning.

While the soldiers were standing at attention in the hallway, NCOs and officers went into each room and rummaged through the men's footlockers and wall lockers. Also, each soldier had a small pack on top of his wall locker. This pack held three changes of socks and underwear, a bar of soap, an extra razor, an extra toothbrush, and a small tube of toothpaste. The purpose of the pack was for use in case of an alert — for practice or for real. The alert packs were also checked to make sure the required items were included. On an alert, soldiers were to dress, grab their alert pack, and go immediately to their tank. Practice alerts were conducted to time the soldiers — the goal was to disperse the tanks as quickly as possible.

Sergeant Crawford entered Nick and Vince's room with Captain Elliott, the company commander, and Lieutenant Jensen, Tank Section's leader.

After a few minutes, Nick was called into his room. He had been through the routine before. On his bunk were three familiar piles. One pile comprised items he was to keep in his billfold with him at all times. Documents such as his driver's license, which showed he was licensed to drive the Patton tank, the jeep, and the three-quarter ton truck; his weapons card for checking out his rifle, pistol, and submachine gun out of the company arms room; a card showing his chain of command, complete with names and telephone numbers — from Sergeant Crawford all the way to the President of the United States; a soldier's Code of Conduct card; and a facsimile Soviet military liaison license plate with a telephone number to call if he ever saw a vehicle with that plate on it.

The second pile included items such as his birth certificate and civilian driver's license from Ohio. Last time, the officers had looked the other way, but this time Captain Elliott told Nick that if he wanted to keep those, he would have to mail them home.

The documents in the third pile had already been torn in half — he was told they would be thrown away. These items included weapons receipts from Nick's former Army units, and names and telephone numbers of U.S. civilians and German citizens. During the previous shakedown, Nick had pictures of two German girls with their names and addresses and telephone numbers written on the back. He didn't believe it when he was told that Soviet and East German spies could use such information to prepare false identification papers, or to coerce the people into spying on U.S. armed forces. Nevertheless, they were destroyed as well.

This day found Captain Elliott tearing up the slip with Carol's telephone number on it. No problem, Nick had memorized the number.

"Holloway, you should know better than to keep this here," Captain Elliott said.

Nick vowed to himself that if and when he became an NCO he would be different — he would use common sense when asked to participate in a shakedown inspection. He would try to show more respect to the individual soldiers. After all, the soldiers were the heart of this battalion — the instruments of death and destruction that stood ready to die for their country and its Constitution.

The inspection ended for Nick and Vince. They were putting their things back where they belonged when loud voices came from a room across the hall — a four-man room — Danny Maguire's room.

"You are a sorry excuse for a human being — Maguire, you wouldn't make a good doorstop. You're as useless as tits on a boar. Your ass is grass now."

Captain Elliott was railing on and on, heaping abuse on Danny.

Nick took a step forward towards the door to Danny's room, but Vince grabbed his arm and shook his head — no.

Nick stopped.

He could not help Danny now. For one thing, he didn't even know what the issue with Danny was about.

In the hallway, Ben Bartlett, Joe Flores, and Ned Lafontaine, were all chuckling and whispering to each other.

The officers stepped into the hallway.

"Sir, I apologize. I'm terribly sorry that you had to see this. I promise you that it will never happen again," Lieutenant Jensen said to the company commander.

"Where do we get guys like that? We are a combat-ready tank unit — we've got to be ready to roll and fight when the balloon goes up. I want you to teach that young man a lesson he won't forget," Captain Elliott said.

"Oh, I will — you can count on that, sir," Lieutenant Jensen said.

The word went quickly around the men in Tank Section. When Sergeant Crawford opened Danny's alert pack, he had found that it contained dirty underwear. The open pack stunk. Captain Elliott and Lieutenant Jensen had reacted with disgust and anger.

Sergeant Crawford — followed by Jensen and Elliott, took Danny away.

Nick figured they were going to Captain Elliott's office on the first floor of the barracks. Nick was worried — how would they treat Danny?

Physical punishment was not condoned in the U.S. Army in 1960. Nick liked to think that President Eisenhower should get the credit for that as well as his other military reforms. Nick hoped that was the case. Nick had seen only two occasions when a sergeant kicked a soldier in the rear — but that was all. Therefore, Nick wasn't too worried that Danny would be harmed, physically that is. But Danny's spirit was close to being broken, and that bothered Nick — it bothered him a lot.

Nick got dressed and decided to wait near Captain Elliott's office. A jeep arrived and parked outside the entrance. Two MPs came into the barracks and were led into the captain's office by the first sergeant.

Five minutes later the door opened and Sergeant Crawford came out with Danny, who was still barefoot and in his underwear. They went up to Danny's room to get his clothes.

"Nick — it isn't true. I had clean clothes in my alert pack. Someone else must have switched them with my laundry. Nick — believe me — please — it isn't true."

"I believe you, Danny," Nick said.

15

DISNEY'S CASTLE

Carol and Barb sat in silence as the bus wound its way through the city of Munich.

The busload of JYM students was going to visit the castle of Neuschwanstein, near the city of Füssen, at the base of the alps in upper Bavaria. The castle was built in the nineteenth century by King Ludwig II of Bavaria. It served as an image many Americans recognized as that used by Walt Disney.

"You really like this Nick guy, don't you?" Barb asked.

"I don't know if I would say I r-e-a-l-l-y like him. I've only met him once — but ... ah ..."

"But ... ah ... what?"

"Well, so far so good. You know that fight the guys were in? Did Vince tell you what that was about?"

"No — he didn't. I asked him about it, but he put me off — again — with flippant non-explanations."

"Well, Nick said — he said it was to protect one of his buddies, a guy named Danny. Nick said this Danny keeps getting bullied, and Nick and Vince fought to protect him."

"Wow. I wish Vince would have told me that."

"Yes, I think that's commendable too. So, if that's a sign of what kind of man he is ... well ... I like that in a man."

"He's kind of a stud, too — isn't he? I mean, both of them are ... Oh, I better not say it?"

"Come on, Barb, you can't just leave it there, like that. Now — what were you about to say?"

"No, no — I won't say what I was thinking. Let's just say I wouldn't kick either one of them out of my bed for eating crackers."

Carol and Barb started laughing. They tried to stifle their laughter at first, but soon lost control.

Other students on the bus were staring at them.

Embarrassed — Carol put her hand on Barb's arm. Then with her palm flattened, Carol moved her hand down across her face. Her expression went from schoolgirl grin to mature woman — just like that.

They sat in silence.

Carol rested her head against the glass as she looked at the idyllic Bavarian countryside. Her thoughts were of Nick, the man she had met only a week before. She would see him again the next day. Who was he? Were her first impressions of him accurate?

She closed her eyes and leaned her head back on the cushioned seatback. To start with, Carol was attracted to Nick. She had to admit that. But she had known guys before who she was attracted to. Some of them were okay, but most were either into heavy drinking or made other bad choices, or were so shallow in their thinking that she couldn't have meaningful conversations with them. Carol knew who she was, and she respected men who knew who they were.

Carol was a realist. She didn't get sanguinely giddy when good fortune came her way, and she didn't get overly pessimistic when things went wrong. She was able to see the facts of a situation, and then to face them honestly as she figured out what to do.

So, what kind of man was Nick? A fighter, for sure. But if what he said was true, he was a man who fought for what he believed in. Carol liked that. She hoped that was a solid trait of Nick's character, and not just a one-off. On the other hand, he could be a man who fought just to prove something, like — in a perverse way — that he really was a man, a tough guy kind of man.

Carol believed that everyone had the capacity for doing both good and evil. Was Nick a man who could control his evil impulses? Again, she hoped that was the case. When they first met, she sensed that his somewhat cocky and glib manner was just a cover, so that he didn't have to talk openly and honestly with her.

His pickup line was clever, and it worked. The thing about being Martians was cute, and his imitation of Cary Grant wasn't bad. And, to be honest, there was something about Nick having been in a fight ... Carol shivered.

Her thoughts of Nick brought Carol to one important realization, she hardly knew him. She had to know much more about him before ...

"Oh, Carol. Helloooh. Hey, sunshine. Earth to Carol. We're almost there," Barb said.

The bus pulled into the parking area in the village of Hohenschwangau — the fairytale Disney castle loomed above them.

16

DANNY MAGUIRE

Friday, 16 September

Later that day, Nick learned that Lieutenant Dolan successfully convinced Captain Elliott that Danny might be telling the truth. Danny might have been set up by others. And if the captain went forward with court martial proceedings, it would be embarrassing if it turned out that Danny was framed. Nevertheless, Danny was given company punishment, a fourteen and two. Danny was ordered to sweep the streets, by hand, in the battalion area for two hours every evening for two weeks.

* * * *

Saturday, 17 September

After Saturday morning inspection and noon chow, Nick lay on his bunk reading a book — *Dear and Glorious Physician,* by Taylor Caldwell. He looked up to see Sergeant Crawford standing in the doorway. Crawford was on duty again as weekend charge of quarters (CQ). Vince had already left for the gym.

"Holloway — get your ass out here. Where is Delvecchio?"

Nick got up from his bunk and followed Sergeant Crawford into the hallway.

"He went to the gym."

Crawford then went into another of Tank Section's rooms, and came out with Danny Maguire.

"I've got a couple of jobs for you two morons today."

Of course he did.

"First, I want you guys to report to the mess sergeant. He tells me his garbage cans need to be hand scrubbed. He says the steam hose doesn't get them clean enough."

Crawford looked at Danny with eyes that Nick thought were meant to hurt, not simply to scare.

"And you — midget magpie Maguire — if I hear one word from anybody that you are screwing off — well, then — you will pay the consequences. So, give your soul to your Irish God right now, because I own the rest of you."

Nick and Danny got their field jackets, work gloves, and caps, and then headed down the hallway towards the mess hall.

Crawford gave Danny a hard kick in the butt as he walked by.

"Get a move on, you leprechaun asshole."

When would this end? It was incomprehensible to Nick that anyone could be so mean toward another human being — especially such a simple and harmless person as Danny Maguire. Why? Of course, Danny didn't belong in the Army — not in a combat role on a tank crew anyway. He could cause others to die if they were in combat. But that was the Army's fault — not Danny's. When would someone in the Army wake up — someone in a position with the authority and power to end Danny's nightmare and send him home? Or give him a job where he could be safe, and not a target for bullies. And what was Sergeant Crawford's purpose in treating Danny so poorly? Did the Crawfords of the world need people like Danny, just to make themselves feel worthy?

The mess sergeant gave Nick a bucket of warm water, some strong detergent soap, and two stiff bristle brushes. There were eight empty metal garbage cans standing upside down on the concrete garbage rack, outside the back door to the mess hall.

Nick couldn't believe his bad luck. He'd rather be anywhere else with Carol. His arm around her shoulders, the faint scent of her perfume in his head, seeing her hair in the sun. But Nick was an optimist — he had learned from Sergeant Cervenka how to take whatever the Army threw at him. Cervenka told Nick to keep his emotions out of it, because a soldier couldn't control much of what happened to him. Cervenka also told Nick to never forget that the Army didn't own his inner life. He could think whatever he liked, and as long as he didn't open his mouth and express what he was thinking, there wasn't a thing that the Army and its agents could do about it. And, as for his feelings, Nick had accepted Cervenka's advice there as well. *Nick, you own your own feelings, so don't blame Crawford for how you feel, and don't let any other mean and power-hungry person get you down.*

Look for something positive in everything you do. For example, he was here with Danny, and who was better to look after Danny than Nick himself?

Still — thank God that tomorrow he had plans with Carol. Sunday afternoon and evening. That at least was something to look forward to.

The job they had been given required Nick and Danny to get their heads inside the garbage cans in order to scrub clean the inside bottom and walls of the cans. Nick worked twice as fast as Danny, but that was partly due to the fact that Danny gagged and retched each time he went into a can. Nick inspected each can, when Danny said he was done with it.

When their heads weren't inside garbage cans, they talked.

"Danny, tell me, when you were growing up in Illinois ..."

"Decatur."

"Yes — Decatur, Illinois. What did you do for fun in Decatur?"

"I went to a lot of movies. I like movies."

"I do too, Danny. What's your favorite movie?"

"I liked the talking horse movies."

"Talking horse movies? I don't think I know ... oh, do you mean those Francis the talking mule movies?"

"Yeah – Francis — that's it. I liked it that Francis could talk."

"What did you think when the lieutenant in the movie was put in a psychiatric hospital for talking to a mule?" Nick asked.

"At least he wasn't a private," Danny answered.

Nick laughed.

When they finished cleaning the garbage cans, Nick went in to tell the mess sergeant.

The mess sergeant came outside and inspected the cans.

"Good job, guys. Thanks. Someone saw a rat out here the other day, so the cans needed a thorough cleaning. Okay, you guys can go. You better check in with the CQ — I'll tell him you did a good job."

Nick and Danny went to the orderly room to tell Crawford they had finished their detail.

"He said you did a good job? What does he know? He's always lying through his ass."

Nick turned as if to leave.

"Where do you think you're going? I'm not through yet with you sorry excuses for soldiers."

Nick realized that Crawford was probably going to play this game until chowtime — or maybe into the evening as well. So be it. Nick knew that he could take whatever

Crawford dished out to him. Nick wasn't sure Danny could take it, though.

"There's a kraut who walks his dog outside the fence around the tank park. There's so much dog shit out there it stinks. So, you guys go and pick up a couple of gunny sacks from Tank Section's maintenance shack, and then go outside the wire and pick up every dog turd you see."

* * * *

Danny whined and moaned and sighed. At times, he was on the verge of crying. At one point, Danny crumbled and sat down in the weeds.

"Nick, it's never going to end, is it? He's going to give us one dirty job after another. What's the use?"

Nick gave up trying to cheer up Danny. The truth was that Nick was tired of Danny's problems — he was tired of listening to Danny's complaints.

"Nick, why does he pick on me? Huh? Nick? And Ben and Joe and Ned and the others — what did I ever do to them? Huh?"

"You didn't do anything to them, Danny. Some people are just mean. You just have to get used to it, as long as you're in the Army."

"But what am I going to do, Nick? I don't think I can take any more of this."

Nick didn't reply.

"Huh, Nick — huh?"

"Danny, will you just shut the fuck up? I'm tired of your pissing and moaning and whining and complaining. Just do your fucking job and quit pestering me with your wimpy bullshit."

Nick stretched the time out on their detail so that it was almost chow time when they reported to Crawford.

To Nick's surprise, Sergeant Crawford didn't give them another job.

After chow, but before Danny was to start sweeping streets, Danny asked Nick for the key to their tank. He said he had left a box of Oreo cookies in the turret, and wanted to go and get it.

It was almost an hour later when Nick decided to go out and check on Danny. He heard the gas heater running inside the turret. The hatches were closed.

He had closed the hatch and started up the gas heater. The heater was not vented to the outside. Carbon monoxide was trapped inside the turret.

When Nick opened the turret hatch and looked inside, he thought Danny might just be sleeping.

"Danny? Danny, wake up."

Nick climbed inside and felt Danny's wrist.

He slapped Danny's face several times.

"No, Danny — no. Come on, wake up. For God's sake, Danny. Wake up."

He cradled Danny's head in his arms.

"No. Oh, no, no, no, no."

"Danny, Danny, Danny."

"HELP," Nick screamed.

17

No Regrets

Sunday, 18 September

Earl Crawford sat in a comfortable chair at the U.S. Army's Criminal Investigation Division (CID) office in Munich's McGraw Kaserne. He had finished a big breakfast, Maguire was gone, and he was ready to take on the bulls.

Two CID men, Ray Jones and John Thompson, were there to hear Earl's statement about Danny Maguire's death. A woman stenographer sat at a table on one side of the room. An MP stood at ease near the door to the room.

"Sergeant, please state your full name, rank, serial number, and date of birth," Ray Jones asked.

"My name is Earl Dellmar Crawford — that's Dellmar with two ls," Crawford said as he looked at the stenographer.

"My rank is Sergeant First Class, E-7; my serial number is RA11897353; and I was born on January 2nd, 1929."

"What were your duties yesterday — Saturday, 17 September 1960?"

"I was CQ for Headquarters Company on Saturday — that is, I was in charge of quarters."

Earl smiled.

"And when did you first see Private Daniel Maguire on that day?"

"I saw him in the morning during our routine Saturday inspection."

"And after the inspection, when did you next see Private Maguire — after lunch?"

"I had to find two soldiers for a work detail, so I went to my own Tank Section's quarters and found Private Maguire and Specialist Holloway."

"What was the work detail you assigned Private Maguire and Specialist Holloway to?"

"I told them to report to the mess sergeant — that he had some cleaning work he needed done."

"Did you know that the work involved cleaning garbage cans?"

"Yes, I did."

"Did the two soldiers report to you when they had completed their work for the mess sergeant?"

"Yes, they did."

"And did you then talk with the mess sergeant?"

"Yes, I did."

"And what did the mess sergeant tell you?"

"He said the job was completed."

"Is that all he said? Did he say anything about the kind of job the two soldiers did?"

"He said the job was done to his satisfaction, but what does he know?"

"Okay. Did you then release Private Maguire and Specialist Holloway for the rest of the afternoon?"

"No."

"Why not?"

"I knew that Captain Elliott, our company commander, was upset because a German civilian was walking his dog every day just outside our tank park's perimeter fence. The dog poop was starting to smell. I thought it would be a good thing to get that mess cleaned up before springtime, when it would really stink. So I told Private Maguire and Specialist Holloway to get some gunny sacks and go outside the fence and pick up all those dog droppings, which they did."

"Those were two pretty nasty jobs you gave Private Maguire. Didn't it ever occur to you that Private Maguire would feel humiliated to have to clean garbage cans and pick up dog crap?"

"No — it didn't occur to me. In the Army that I know, the Army the way it was, in the brown shoe Army, the way it should be, a soldier has to do a lot of unpleasant things. That's part of what a soldier's life is all about. A good soldier learns to deal with it. I call it good training — opportunities for growth."

Earl leaned back in his chair and grinned.

"What did you say to the two men when they reported to you that they had finished the second work detail?"

"I told them that was all — that the rest of the day was theirs."

"What time was that, sergeant?"

"It was about 1730."

"Did you go out and inspect the work the two soldiers did?"

"No, I didn't. I think I should be given some credit for trusting my men. I knew Holloway, anyway, was a stickler for doing good work."

"When was the last time that you saw Private Maguire?"

"I saw him just after evening chow. It was probably five after six — about 1805. He was leaving the mess hall. I assumed he was going up to his room."

"Did you realize that Private Maguire still had to spend two hours sweeping streets as part of his previously administered company punishment?"

"Yes — so what?"

"Sergeant Crawford, do you think that the two dirty work

details you gave Private Maguire and Specialist Holloway on Saturday had anything to do with Maguire's death that evening?"

"Hell, no. Excuse my French, but I don't see it that way at all."

"Do you have any regrets, sergeant?"

"No — no regrets — none whatsoever."

Sergeant Crawford was contemptuous of the two CID men. He thought their interview of him was of no use at all. An amateur job. All they had accomplished was to verify facts that they already knew. They learned nothing. They apparently knew nothing about the dirty laundry incident with his boys and Danny Maguire. Nor did they ask him anything about the hang fire incident, and his demand that Private Maguire be court-martialed for cowardice, or the permanent KP duty that he insisted the captain give Maguire if not a court martial.

Earl was ready to respond to any and all inquiries about those — he would have told those CID jerks all about Private Daniel Maguire. And then he would ask them what they would have done with him. Wouldn't they have tried to run the twerp out of the Army as he tried to do? No, maybe they wouldn't have, but they were not warriors like he was. No doubt they had never been in combat.

Earl Crawford was sure of himself. He knew he was doing the right thing. He had no regrets.

"Please wait out in the hall, Sergeant Crawford. We are going to bring in Specialist Nicholas Holloway and ask him some questions. After that, we might have more questions for you."

"Holloway?"

"That's right — Specialist Delvecchio suggested that Holloway had something to say to us, about your treatment of Private Maguire."

Shit, Crawford thought, as he left the room.

* * * *

Nick Holloway was called into the room and asked to take a seat. He was asked for his name, rank, serial number, and date of birth for the record.

"Well, Specialist Holloway, you had a rough day yesterday, didn't you?"

Nick shrugged his shoulders.

"One day you're the dog, the next you're a hydrant."

Jones and Thompson looked at each other.

"Now, Specialist Holloway, we understand that you were with Private Maguire on Saturday, and that you were the one discovered his body. Is that correct?"

"That's correct."

"Your buddy, Specialist Delvecchio, told us that we should talk to you, He said you had some strong opinions about how Sergeant Crawford had been treating Private Daniel Maguire, and that that might have contributed to Private Maguire's alleged suicide. Well, this is your chance."

"Danny should not have been in the Army at all — his draft board made a mistake."

"But, Holloway, what do you have to say about Sergeant Crawford's treatment of Private Maguire?"

Nick looked at the two CID men, and then his eyes focused on a framed photo of President Eisenhower on the wall. Nick didn't say anything.

This went on for another five minutes. Jones and Thompson asked Nick questions — and Nick didn't answer them.

* * * *

The door opened and Nick came out of the interrogation room. Nick didn't look at Crawford as he walked by him.

Earl was called back into the room.

"Well, that was pretty much an exercise in futility,

sergeant. The only thing he said was that Private Maguire should not have been in the Army at all. He said that if there was any blame to be assigned at all, it should be levied against his draft board in Illinois. We didn't think it was necessary to press him any further, since whatever he said would just be hearsay. Nevertheless, I'm not sure what just went on here."

The questions continued for Crawford. They were all pussy questions, in Crawford's opinion. They added nothing to the CID's understanding of the real situation.

These guys are not Sam Spades, just amateurs. They know as well as I do that Danny killed himself. They know the Army will whitewash the whole affair because officially the Army doesn't make mistakes. They know the Army might go so far as to lie to Danny's parents and family — in fact, he was sure of it — to tell them that his death was an accident rather than a suicide. Crawford had seen all this bullshit before. The CID has policies and procedures so that Jones and Thompson — and we all know those aren't their real names — they have to ask questions and fill out forms and write reports, just to comply with needless regulations. Those two keystone cops have no skills — and, more importantly, no desire to get to the bottom of the matter — to understand what I have to put up with from weak and marginal soldiers. But Holloway now — he surprised me. He passed up an opportunity to try to cause me trouble and he hadn't take it. He's a smart one — maybe he saw through the CID guys like I did. Still, I'll need to keep an eye on him. Well — keep your friends close, and keep your enemies closer.

18

ENGLISH GARDENS

Sunday, 18 September

Carol and Nick had arranged to meet at 2 o'clock in front of the art museum called the Haus der Kunst. The museum was located at Prinzregenten Strasse 1. The park called the English Gardens were directly behind, to the north of the museum.

Carol looked at her watch — 2:15 p.m. Where was Nick?

Carol paced back and forth for a while, and then sat down on the front steps of the museum. She wondered about Nick. She had met him only once, and admitted to herself that she was attracted to him. But she didn't know him. Would he stand her up? No, she didn't think so. Not without a good reason. She hoped he wouldn't. Then again, was he habitually late? If he was, how could he be late in the Army? Carol understood the Army to be strict in their discipline — and showing up on time was surely part of that.

Carol resumed her pacing. She studied the façade of the Haus der Kunst. She had read that it was built during the Hitler era, sometime in the 1930s. As she looked up, at the ceiling of the portico, she saw swastikas — lots of them. Since the swastika was the symbol of the Nazis, and the crooked cross was now illegal in West Germany, how was it that these ceiling tiles were still in place?

She walked to the edge of the museum and looked at the trees that formed the southern border of the English Gardens.

Carol had purchased and read a pamphlet about the park, called the Englischer Garten — the English Gardens — created almost 200 years before by Count Rumford, an Englishman. At 910 acres, the English Garden was larger than New York's Central Park.

Standing there, waiting for a man named Nick, Carol's senses were keen. The air, the sunlight, the sounds of people and cars passing by, all were registered in her. A baby crying — the mother leaning into the pram to comfort her child.

Carol looked at her watch again, it was now 2:30. Should she wait, or should she leave? She finally concluded that it was more likely that Nick had stood her up, rather than that something had happened to Nick, although she thought she would be sad if something had happened to him. She decided to wait another fifteen minutes.

A few minutes later, Carol saw a man get out of a taxi in front of her. At first, she wasn't sure that he was the Nick she had met. He looked different, somehow.

He waved to her.

When Nick approached Carol, he put his arms around her and held her firmly. Carol responded in kind.

After a few seconds, Carol relaxed, and let her arms fall at her side. Nick continued to hold her tight. His face was buried in the scarf at her neck.

Carol put her hands between her and Nick, and gently pushed him out of the embrace.

"Nick, you look … you look so … what's wrong? Tell me, what happened?"

Nick looked down at the sidewalk, and then he looked up at the sky. His feet fidgeted. Finally, he looked Carol in the eyes.

"Danny killed himself last night. It's terrible. I didn't sleep at all, and then this morning I was questioned by sergeants, lieutenants, the captain, and even a major and the colonel from battalion headquarters. Then they drove me to McGraw Kaserne where the CID guys — that's the criminal investigators — wanted me to blame Sergeant Crawford for Danny's death. We didn't get back to the barracks until 1400, that's two o'clock. I hurried and got here as soon as I could."

"Was the sergeant to blame?"

"Yes — he was a big part of it. But I've always thought that suicide was a personal decision, and that, in the end, the person who does it has no one to blame except themselves."

"It's okay, Nick. I understand. I'm glad I waited, it would have been even worse if you had come here only to find that I had gone."

Nick hugged Carol again, but this time he let go after a few seconds.

"Should we go into the park?" Nick said.

"Yes, let's. I've been reading about the English Gardens — actually there's a fascinating history to this place."

Carol sensed that Nick wasn't listening to her.

They walked in silence for a while. When they reached the lake — the Kleinhesseloher See — Nick suggested they rent a rowboat and go out on the lake. Carol agreed.

The weather was beautiful, with blue skies broken by only a few cotton ball clouds. The sun warmed them. With only a slight breeze, the lake surface was almost smooth.

This should have been one of those romantic times when a girl and her boyfriend could revel in dreams of perfection in each other. Instead, Nick looked like he was a million miles away. He was calm — his face showed no emotion. Carol studied him. She felt physically attracted to him, even though he was hurting. It was an awkward moment.

"Tell me, Nick. Tell me what happened. How did Danny die?"

Nick told Carol what had happened that week. He told her about the shakedown inspection, and how Danny's dirty underwear was found in his alert pack. He told her he was sure that some of the bullies in Tank Section had put it there. He told her about the punishment Danny received for the dirty laundry incident.

"And then, yesterday — just yesterday — Danny and I were put on a couple of dirty job details by Sergeant Crawford. I don't know — I'm not sure that could have been what pushed Danny over the edge."

Nick went into detail describing to Carol each event of the afternoon and evening.

"Carol, I can see it all happening again before my eyes. Think of it, just yesterday, Danny was still alive."

Laughter reached them from two people in a nearby boat.

"I'm at fault also, Carol. I snapped at Danny a couple of times. I even swore at him. Oh, if I could only push the clock back, and take those words away ...."

"What did you say to him, Nick?"

"I told him to quit whining. I said I was getting tired of his being such a weakling. I swore at him."

"That doesn't sound so bad. It just sounds like you were fed up. You were being honest with him."

"Maybe. Yes, I was being honest, but I wasn't being smart. He was Danny, just being Danny."

Carol didn't know what else to say to Nick.

"And then, this morning, all those officers, asking all those questions, afraid they would somehow be found responsible for causing Danny to kill himself. They didn't care about him. They're just scared for their own skins, their precious Army careers."

"Oh, Nick — that must have been hard for you."

"And then the CID — they're also trying to find someone to blame. They seemed to me to think Crawford was to blame. They want to pin it on someone, so they can nail him to a cross — that way they can say they've done their job. What a bunch of assholes. Oh — I'm sorry, Carol. I shouldn't talk that way to you."

"No, it's okay. They do sound like a bunch of dicks."

Nick laughed.

"But I didn't give them any satisfaction. I didn't tell them anything."

"But, Nick — you said it was Sergeant Crawford's fault — well, mostly his fault."

"Yeah — that's right — it was mostly his fault. But I'm not a snitch. I'm not going to be a rat and tell on anybody, especially another soldier."

"Why not, Nick? If it's something really bad, such as driving another person to kill himself, then I would think it's perfectly all right to let someone in authority know about it."

"Carol, you don't understand. Men have a code of honor. I learned about that way back in the fourth grade, when I was still a boy. A guy does not tell on another guy. And among us soldiers, it's an unwritten law. You just don't do it."

They docked the boat, and walked to the Seehaus — the lake house — which had a terrace overlooking the lake. They ordered coffee and sweet cakes.

"Do you know what bothered me the most, Carol? It's that the whole tragic thing wasn't necessary. Danny shouldn't have been in the Army to begin with. And then, once the Army found out what he was like, they should have sent him home. They should have given him a section eight, or whatever. This all could have been avoided."

"Why do you care so much, Nick? Why did you try to protect Danny?"

Nick was silent for a few seconds.

"You know, Carol, I'm not sure. Most guys — almost all the other guys — didn't care. They couldn't have cared less. Vince cared. Sergeant Cervenka cared. Lieutenant Anderson and Lieutenant Dolan cared. But what could they do? I was there — I was with Danny a lot, and I did care about him. What else was I supposed to do?"

Carol revealed the time a neighbor girl was hit by a car and killed on a street in Monticello.

"Neve didn't go to school. She lived with her parents. People called her slow. My friends and I never said mean words to Neve, but we never included her in any of our play."

After they left the Seehaus, they walked in the park along the Isar River.

"You know, Carol, I feel better now. I don't know why. I just do. Nothing's changed, but just talking about this with you was good."

Carol leaned over and kissed Nick on the lips.

19

Cigarette Ration Stamps

Wednesday, 21 September

Nick got the dreaded summons to the company commander's office. It was like the time he was called into the principal's office in high school for bringing his dog into the school; or like when his mother told you that your father wanted to speak to him about what had happened at school.

It was Wednesday — about mid-morning. Nick had been cleaning the leaves and other debris out of the battery well under the turret floor in the tank when the company runner came.

"Captain Elliott wants to see you right away."

"What for?" Nick asked.

"Don't know. He's got a couple guys in civvies in his office."

Nick climbed out of the tank and told Vince where he was going.

"You better clean up, Nick — you smell like a gas station."

Nick washed up and went to his room to put on a clean fatigue uniform and to change his boots.

When he went into the captain's office, he saluted and reported.

"Specialist Fourth Class Nicholas Holloway, reporting as ordered, sir."

"At ease, Holloway. These men want to talk with you. This is Ray Jones and John Thompson — they're with CID — the Army's Criminal Investigation Department."

Nick's face flushed and he felt hot. These were the same guys who questioned him about Danny's death. Was this about that again?

"Sit down, specialist. Relax, we just want to ask you a few questions," Jones said.

The other man — Thompson — held a small black address book in his right hand. He was slowly slapping it against the palm of his left hand.

"Do you recognize this book, Specialist Holloway?"

"No, sir, I don't."

Jones looked at Thompson.

"Well, what do you know, he speaks."

Nick sat with a stoic face.

"Well, your name is in it — see — right here: Nick Holloway, HQ Company."

Thompson pointed to a page in the little book.

"Yes, I see my name there, but ..."

"Can you explain why your name is in this little book?"

"Whose book is it? Maybe I know the guy."

"Oh, we think that you do know whose book it is. What is most important is that the guy was up to no good, and he knows you."

Why would his name be in someone's little black book? Someone who was up to no good? Anyway, what's the big deal? Selling ration stamps for a quarter? The Army certainly likes to make mountains out of molehills, Nick thought.

"I'm sorry, sir — I have no idea why my name is in that book — and I have no idea who that book belongs to either."

"Holloway, you better not lie to these gentlemen — you could be in deep trouble if you lie to them," Captain Elliott said.

Trouble? Sure — lying can get anyone in trouble, but Nick knew that he wasn't lying. Why would the captain think he was lying?

"No, I swear to you, sir — I'm not lying. I've never seen that book in my life."

"Do you smoke?" Ray Jones asked.

"No, I don't smoke — except for once or twice in high school. I didn't like it."

"Well, let me ask you a different question. What do you do with the cigarette ration stamps that you are issued?" Thompson asked.

"I sell them to smokers," Nick answered.

Now, things were starting to become clearer in Nick's mind.

"Who?"

Nick would never reveal names to the authorities — not about anything. He wasn't a stool pigeon.

In 1960, the U.S. Army rationed cigarettes to soldiers because of the difference in prices — a carton of cigarettes that cost two dollars in the PX could bring ten dollars if sold to a German on the black market.

The going rate for one ration stamp, which, with two dollars, could be used to buy one carton of cigarettes at the PX, was twenty-five cents. Nick had never had any problem selling the stamps to other soldiers.

Nick remembered that about three or four months earlier, a soldier who Nick didn't know had approached him soon after the new ration books were issued. The stranger offered to buy Nick's entire book of stamps at the going rate of a quarter per stamp. Nick said okay — why not?

Nick thought it was likely the stranger owned the little black book. Nick felt a chill in his spine. He knew that technically it wasn't legal to sell Army-issued ration stamps, even to other soldiers. In a way, Nick knew, it was a form of black marketeering, just as if he had sold the cigarettes to a German. But, really, it was small potatoes, in Nick's opinion.

"Did you sell them to the owner of this book?" Thompson asked as he held the book up again.

"I don't know. It's possible. The last time we got the ration books this guy came to me and bought the whole book from me."

"What was his name?"

"I don't know."

"Can you describe the guy?"

"Not really. I wasn't paying close attention. It didn't take long."

"Was he a white guy or a black guy?"

"He was a white guy."

That was true. Nick didn't want to lie, but he didn't want to get anyone in trouble either. There were more white guys than blacks in his unit. And, anyway, so what?

"Was he tall or short?"

"I don't remember."

"What unit patch was on his arm? Twenty-fourth Division? Seventh Corps? Maybe Seventh Army or USAREUR?"

"He wasn't in uniform — he was in civvies."

"Where was he from?"

"I don't know."

"Did he have an accent — like, was he a southerner? Or was he a New Englander?"

"No, he didn't have an accent."

Jones and Thompson twisted in their chairs. They looked at each other, and at Captain Elliott.

"You are aware that it is illegal to sell your own ration stamps?" Jones asked.

Nick didn't answer. Sure, he knew it was against regulations, but it was such a minor thing in his mind.

"Holloway, you better answer the man's question," Captain Elliott said.

"Yes," Nick answered.

Oh no, here it was. Nick's goal of getting an honorable discharge was going to be snuffed out because he violated some provision of the Uniform Code of Military Justice (UCMJ) that said he couldn't sell his cigarette stamps for a measly twenty-five cents a pop?

Nick remembered hearing soldiers joke about the UCMJ. It was called the *Variable Code of Military Injustice.*

"It's a serious offense to participate in black marketeering, soldier," Thompson said.

"Yes, sir," Nick replied.

Racing through Nick's mind was what he had heard — that Sergeant Crawford was involved in the black market. Nick had heard that Crawford had stolen some hand tools and sold them to Germans. Sergeant Crawford — the guy who thought it was okay to bully Danny until he killed himself.

"Are you aware of anyone who might be involved in the black marketing of cigarettes?" Jones asked.

"No, sir," Nick said.

What was Crawford up to? Nick was curious — no, he was more than merely curious — he felt compelled to know what was going on when it came to Sergeant Earl Crawford. Was he behind the guy with the little black address book?

"Okay, Specialist Holloway. We have no more questions for you. Just don't sell your ration stamps anymore," Jones said.

"You can count on that, sir," Nick said.

Nick vowed to himself that he would not sell his stamps — he would give them to his friends, starting with Vince. Vince had been upset when he learned that Nick had sold his entire book of stamps to a stranger. That won't happen again, *Vince — you'll get nibs from now on.*

Ray Jones and John Thompson stood up, shook hands with Captain Elliott, and walked out of the office. They ignored Nick.

20

BOBCATS

Friday, 23 September

They called themselves *Bobcats* because they had served in the Korean War together as part of the 5ᵗʰ Regimental Combat Team (RCT) — the "Bobcats." They had been tankers, in the 5ᵗʰ Tank Company.

Earl Crawford, Al Richards, and Frank Hairston. The reason they were together in 1960 was due to the fact that Charles Elliott, the commander of Headquarters Company, 3/34 Armor, had also been a Bobcat in Korea.

In the battle of Kunu Ri, in November 1950, Crawford, Hairston, and Richards had saved Elliott's life. Elliott, a young second lieutenant and tank platoon leader at the time, had his tank destroyed by a direct hit from a Chinese anti-tank rocket-propelled shell. His crew dead and his tank on fire, Elliott owed his life to Crawford and the others. They had risked their own lives to rescue Lieutenant Elliott and get him away from the burning tank.

In ensuing combat actions, Earl Crawford received a battlefield commission in the reserve Army for his leadership abilities and bravery under fire. Charles Elliott was instrumental in his promotion.

After the Korean War, the Army reduced the number of reserve officers, and Crawford was effectively demoted to his previous status as a noncommissioned officer.

Richards continued his career as an armor NCO. Hairston went to the Army Finance School.

Captain Elliott had used his influence to have these men assigned under him in Headquarters Company, 3/34 Armor, in Munich. The latest to arrive was Earl Crawford, who had been serving as an instructor at the Armor Training Center at Fort Knox, Kentucky.

However, his bitter resentment at losing his commission was stronger than any gratitude or loyalty he may have felt towards Captain Elliott.

On a sunny afternoon in September, the three men were at a corner table in a gasthaus near Henry Kaserne called *Die Drei Junge Erten* — the three young ducks. Joining them was Sergeant First Class Ralph Guzman.

Guzman was Headquarters Company's maintenance sergeant. He was not a Bobcat — in fact, he had not been in the Korean War. Nevertheless, Earl had already befriended Guzman, and learned that he was of a like mind in that he saw his job as an opportunity to make some money on the side. Guzman had a goal of buying a nice house — a very nice house — in Tucson, Arizona, when he retired, and he surely wasn't going to be able to save the money he'd need — not from his Army pay.

Earl had bought the beers.

"Frank, thanks for the liquor ration stamps. I got over on that dipstick Neumann with that last delivery. He was giddy when he saw the case of Johnnie Walker."

The other men laughed at that, even though they had never met Manfred Neumann.

"Also, he took both cases of cigarettes, so, that market hasn't dried up yet."

"How long do you think you can keep this going, Earl?" Al Richards asked.

"I think we've got a really good thing going here, guys. And I've got some ideas that could make us all rich — really rich."

Earl took a long swallow from his beer, and then rubbed the foam off his lips with his sleeve.

Just then, Nick Holloway and Vince Delvecchio entered the gasthaus.

"Hey, Sergeant Crawford — how you doing?" Nick said.

"What do you two animals want?"

"We thought we'd start the afternoon with a cool one here, before we head downtown."

"Guys, this here's Nick Holloway, and that's Vince Delvecchio. They're in my Tank Section. They're two of the best tankers we got in the whole battalion."

Richards, Hairston, and Guzman each shook hands with Nick and Vince. They knew the two men, or knew of them.

"So long, boys," Earl said.

Nick and Vince took the hint and left. They would have to drink their first beer someplace else.

"I thought you said Holloway was the biggest trouble maker you had in Tank Section," Frank Hairston asked.

"He is."

"Do you want me to get him out of your hair, Earl?" Al Richards asked.

"What do you mean — get him out of my hair? What can you do?"

"Well, the arms room is part of my Supply Section. I could easily make one of Holloway's weapons disappear, or get damaged."

"I'll keep that in mind — but for now, I can handle Holloway. My plan is to keep him close — to get him so involved in what I'm — in what we're doing — that way he'll be as guilty as we are if anything goes sour. The problem is that he really is the best tanker I've got. I need Holloway, or nothing would get done right in Tank Section. We could have used a guy like him — and Delvecchio — in Korea, I can tell you that much."

"Come on, Earl — let's get back to business. Why did you ask me to join you guys today?" Guzman asked.

"Okay, here's my idea. Neumann asked me if I could get him some gasoline — and oil too. That's when I thought of you, Ralph. What do you think? Is it possible?"

"Anything is possible. It's only a question of risk and reward."

"The risk is low if we do it right, and the reward is great."

Guzman leaned forward in his seat.

"I think it would be easy. Gasoline isn't like other stuff such as cigarettes and liquor — you can count cartons of smokes and bottles of whiskey. But gasoline — we could siphon off a thousand gallons from a nine-thousand-gallon load and no one would be the wiser."

The bar was quiet.

"I see what you mean," Crawford said.

"How would you transfer the gas from our truck to Neumann's truck, or trailer, or whatever he's got?" Frank Hairston asked.

"Well, the gas we get comes from a supply depot in France, and ends up at an Army depot in south Munich. We'll just divert a truck — you know, have the driver get lost for a while — and hook up with Neumann's truck. We set up a transfer hose — it wouldn't take long at all. No one will ever catch on."

Earl sat in silence. Then his face lit up in a big smile.

"The best thing about your plan, Ralph, is that it will bring in all profit. There's no cost to us — not like taking ration stamps to the PX and having to shell out some cash to buy cigarettes and booze. I love the idea. Now, Ralph, what do you have to do to fix the records?"

"No problem. I sign a receipt for nine thousand gallons, we lose one thousand, and no one's the wiser."

"This is great. Next time I talk with Manfred, I'll set up our first gasoline transaction."

Frank Hairston was the only one of the four who was not excited or smiling. He kept tapping his Zippo cigarette lighter on the table, turning it around on each tap.

"Frank — what's wrong? You don't think Ralph's idea is a good one? What gives?"

"Oh, I think Ralph's plan sounds good. In fact, it sounds like it's a lot less risky than what I'm doing — skimming off a few ration stamp books, then fixing the books to cover it up. But that's just it — I'm the one with my hand in the till. And now people are starting to ask questions."

Earl drained his beer.

"What people? What questions?"

"Yesterday, I saw Lieutenant Dolan talking with the head of Battalion Finance — warrant officer Gray. They asked me if I knew anything about someone going around to the non-smokers in the battalion and buying their ration stamps for a quarter a stamp. I said no, of course."

"Dolan, huh? He's already caused me problems — he convinced the captain that he shouldn't court-martial Holloway and Maguire," Earl said.

"Do you want me to cut the brakes on his jeep?" Guzman asked.

"Jesus Christ, Guzman. You leap immediately to murdering people? No — only if absolutely necessary, I'll think of something less drastic that will get him out of our hair completely," Earl said.

When they were finished, Earl asked Guzman to stay to discuss the profit sharing arrangements for his contributions of gasoline. Earl was determined to squeeze the man.

21

DEUTSCHES MUSEUM

Saturday, 24 September

"Did you know that the full name of this place is the German Museum of Masterworks of Natural Science and Technology?" Carol said.

Then Carol said the name in German.

"Now, that's a mouthful — I like plain old *Deutsches Museum* better," Nick said.

Nick kissed her.

Carol put her arms around him.

"Where should we start?" Nick asked.

"My only must-see are the 16th century workshops. Other than that, Nick, you can decide."

Nick laughed.

"What do you like about those old workshops?"

"Oh, I love seeing how things were done back in history. I think we've lost a lot of the practical ways of doing things. You know, with all of our machines these days."

They wandered through the many rooms and exhibits of the museum. This was Carol's first visit, and she was impressed. She had always before put down science, and the creations of technology, thinking they were inferior in some way to the fine arts of painting, sculpture, music, and literature. Now she was intrigued by the exhibits concerning science and the development of technology.

"Nick?" Nick? Where are you?"

Carol looked around her, but Nick had disappeared. Then she saw his foot wagging from behind a wall. She walked towards him.

"Shh," Nick whispered, as he took her arm and gently pulled her towards him. He was standing in an alcove, out of sight of other museum visitors.

Once they were both in the shadows of the space, Nick and Carol kissed, passionately.

She laughed — surely, he wasn't serious — but he kissed her more deeply. She leaned into him, filling her fists with the fabric of his shirt. Only when a crowd of Swedish tourists approached did they break apart.

"Whew. Let me come up for air," Carol said.

She looked around the corner, and saw the people walking toward them. She straightened her clothes, and put a hand to her hair.

"Let's go, Nick. People are coming this way."

Nick played several other games with Carol over the next hours. He went behind a display case and bent his legs so that only his head appeared above the case as he moved by, winking at Carol. And then he borrowed a docent's official-looking cap, walked up behind Carol, and in an affected German voice he said, "Please, *Fraülein, bitte*, do not touch the glass — it is *verboten.*"

Carol did not complain. It was as if Nick wanted her to know him as unpredictable. She had to admit to herself that she liked his attention and his spontaneous humor, even if it was, at times, in childish forms.

Nick showed Carol the exhibits of cars and airplanes, and then they went to the 16th century workshops.

"Would you like to go with me to the Oktoberfest next weekend?" Nick asked.

"Yes — yes, I would. It will have to be Saturday, though. Our class has a day trip to Chiemsee planned for Sunday."

"Saturday it is, then. I could pick you up sometime in the early afternoon — we can be together until the wee hours, well, at least until twelve-thirty or so. Vince is going to ask Barb as well."

They took a break, bought ice cream cones, and sat at a small table in the lobby.

"How are you doing with your feelings about your loss of Danny?" Carol asked.

Nick didn't answer immediately. He ate his ice cream, and he looked everywhere but at Carol.

"Nick?"

Nick looked at Carol.

"What?"

"I asked you a question. How are you doing? It must be strange and hard to have your friend Danny gone. Gone forever."

"Geez, that's an awful question."

"But he was your friend."

"He wasn't my friend."

"Okay. But you were his friend, maybe you were his best friend, his only friend. I can't imagine how you must feel, after what happened to him."

"I'm okay. I'm trying real hard to forget about him and the whole sorry business. I don't want to remember him, and I sure as hell don't want to remember how I feel about it all."

"Okay. If that's the way you want it. I won't ask you about it."

They spent the next hour going through the mining exhibit and the musical instruments collection. Nick was quiet, and he didn't play with Carol at all, not like he had done earlier.

"You know, Carol — they didn't even have a memorial event to honor him. They just shipped his body back to his folks — back to Illinois. It's as if he hadn't existed — hadn't been one of us."

Carol didn't blame Nick. She was sympathetic toward him, but she knew it wasn't good for him to go on denying his feelings about Danny's death, or about the role the sergeant played — that Sergeant Crawford. Carol wanted to help Nick, but she knew it wouldn't help to push him about it. He would just resent being pushed.

Nick had been bragging to Carol about his favorite restaurant in Munich, the Café Figaro, ever since they first met. Now she would be able to see it for herself.

They took a taxi from the museum to the café.

"Lola Montez Strasse 33, Café Figaro," Nick said to the taxi driver.

"This is going to be great. You have to have the Hungarian Reisfleisch. It is heavenly. And wine, we'll get a carafe of the Villany red wine."

"Fabulous. I can't wait."

Carol was basking in the fact that Nick was taking her to his special place in Munich.

"Good evening, Nick. And a special good evening to you also, *Fraülein*. Let me show you to your table," said the maître d'.

The man lifted Carol's hand to his lips and kissed it softly.

When they were seated, Carol said, "All right, I'm impressed. Who is that man? And have you been here so many times that he knows who you are?"

"That's Bela Varga — he owns this place. I've been here several times, not many. I think Bela is one of those people who just has a knack for remembering people. He's eastern European — Hungarian."

Then a waitress appeared at their table.

"Nicky, *Schatzi*. How nice I see you again. Hey, this must be my lucky day."

"Roza, *mein süsses*. And my lucky day also. How have you been?"

"Oh, you know, Nick, I've been so lonely not to see my Nicky for so long time. You should come see me more often, Nicky baby."

Nick laughed.

Roza the waitress left menus with them, and then she walked away to another table.

Carol watched Roza. She may be almost thirty, but she knows how to get younger men to drool over her. Black hair, done in a curl set. Red lipstick smeared on her lips. Too red. Too much. Way too much bosom showing above her low-cut, colorful, peasant dress. Oh, yes, Roza. You would love to have a romp in the hay with my Nick, wouldn't you?

Carol watched Roza as she moved from table to table.

"And who was that, if I may ask?" Carol said.

"Oh, that's Roza — Rozalia Varga, Bela's daughter. They came to Munich in 1956, after the failed rebellion in Budapest."

"She seems to be quite familiar with you. How well do you know her?"

"You mean, have I dated her?"

Nick laughed.

"Me? Roza? Date? No, no, not at all. We just have a lot of fun together. I mean — you know what I mean — when Vince and I are here. You should see how she flirts with Vince. He's talked about asking her out, but he thinks she's too old for him. She must be almost thirty."

They studied their menus for several minutes.

"Are you going to try the *Ungarisch Reisfleisch?*" Nick asked.

"No. I think I'll have the stuffed peppers — the *töltött paprika* stuffed peppers. That sounds good to me."

"Not the *Reisfleisch*, then?"

"No — stuffed peppers."

"And for the wine, Carol, I recommend the *Villany* red. It's very good."

"You know, Nick, I'd like to try the *Taschner* red. That looks good."

They gave their order to Roza, the waitress.

Rozalia looked at Carol with a hint of disdain. Carol returned the look with a slight movement of her eyebrows.

Carol watched again as Roza walked away. String sandals. Toenails painted bright red.

"Gypsy show-off," Carol muttered.

"How are your classes going?" Nick asked.

They talked this way until their food and wine arrived, and then continued to talk — without saying anything — throughout their meal.

As soon as they left the restaurant, Carol stopped, took hold of Nick's arm, and turned him to face her.

"Don't you ever tell me again that this is your favorite place. That woman is evil — watch out for her, Nick. She only wants to …"

Nick took Carol in his arms and kissed her.

* * * *

Later, in the taxi, Nick finally put it all together. Carol was jealous of Roza. That was all.

"Oh, wow," Nick said as he laughed.

He held Carol close to him.

* * * *

25 September

A dozen roses were delivered to Carol on Sunday. The note with the flowers said:

> *You're adorable and very sweet but there's nothing between me and that waitress, and also, you are incomparably beautiful. Don't forget about Saturday, all right?*

22

OKTOBERFEST

Saturday, 1 October

Nick had seen Carol twice since they first met — once at the English Gardens park, and then they went to the Deutsches Museum the following week.

Nick couldn't believe how natural he felt when he was with Carol. She looked better to him each time they were together. She smiled and laughed a lot, and was easy for Nick to talk with.

Except for Roza, Carol had never asked him about other girls he knew, or had known, and he hadn't asked her about her other boyfriends either. Nick was thankful for that, and he didn't know why, since he didn't think he had any secrets about his old girlfriends. He certainly didn't want to hear about Carol's former dating life. One thing, though, he had to ask Carol what her middle name was. Nick realized that he knew none of the middle names of his previous girlfriends.

Nick and Vince met Carol and Barb at the Stachus streetcar stop. From there they went to the Theresienwiese — the Oktoberfest grounds.

The Oktoberfest began as a wedding celebration in 1810 for Crown Prince Ludwig and his bride Teresa. All the citizens of Munich were invited to help the couple celebrate on the fields in front of the city's gate. That place became known as Theresienwiese — Teresa's meadow — or *wies'n* for short.

In 1960, the seven major breweries of Munich had constructed large beer tents on the wies'n. At the end of the grounds, opposite from the main entrance, were carnival rides and other attractions.

Soon after entering the grounds, Carol and Barb met some of their classmates from JYM. The other girls looked and smiled at both Nick and Vince as they chatted with Carol and Barb. The JYM men were disinterested.

Nick tried to look as normal as he could. So, now that Carol's classmates knew that she and Barb were dating GIs, they didn't look surprised, but Nick definitely felt that he was being judged. He was confident, that wasn't a problem. But he did need to stop and think so that he didn't say anything inappropriate to the girls, or to be sarcastic when talking to the JYM males. Vince had no difficulty relating to anyone — friend or potential foe.

"Carol, what is your middle name?" Nick asked.

Carol looked at him.

"That's an odd question. For what it's worth, though, my middle name is Anne. Carol Anne Benjamin. Now, what is yours?"

"William. Nicholas William Holloway. My grandfather was a William, so that's where it comes from."

As they wandered through the grounds, taking in the sights and sounds and smells, Carol asked Nick a question.

"Vince told Barb that he and you were going to reenlist and make the Army your career."

"He did?"

"Yes, he did. Is that true?"

Nick hesitated. How could he answer her honestly?

"Yes, that is true. But I think it's more true for Vince than it is for me."

"What does that mean, Nick? Is it true for you, or isn't it?"

"It's not that simple. You see, for almost a year and a half, we had the best section leader and section sergeant — they might have been the best in the whole United States Army. I wanted to be just like Sergeant Cervenka. He's the one who suggested that Vince and I reenlist. He wanted me to apply for the NCO Academy."

"And did you?"

"Yes. I did apply."

"You're going away to school? When?"

"I don't know, Carol. Captain Elliott is holding my application until I prove myself more."

"Prove yourself? How?"

"Good question."

Nick did not look Carol in the eye.

"What's the answer?" Carol asked.

Nick looked directly at Carol.

"I don't know. I think about it a lot. But now, with this situation with Sergeant Crawford … I just don't know."

"If you don't reenlist, what would you do when you get out of the Army?"

"I've thought about running a greasy spoon truck stop on the new freeway in Ohio," Nick said with a smile.

"No — come on now — get serious."

"You know, Carol — if I don't re-up, I've made no plans. I have to decide soon — my tour of duty ends in a little over three months. I think I'd like to go to college if I don't stay in the Army — I think, maybe … — I just don't know."

At the carnival site on the festival grounds, they went on several of the thrill rides, and then they rode in the bumper cars. Finally, they went to the big beer tents that dominated the grounds.

Nick led them to a table inside the large Paulaner-Salvator-Thomasbrau beer tent. A Bavarian band was playing from a raised platform in the center of the tent. Strong women hurried around the tables with arms full of liter-sized glass beer mugs, large pretzels, and platters of fried chicken, sausages, cheeses, and other Bavarian culinary dishes. The delightful odors of food and tobacco smoke, the light music, and the friendly faces — all gave meaning to the German word *gemütlichkeit*.

Carol wasn't sure about the beer — Nick had ordered them each a liter mug of the light-colored beer. He explained to Carol that his strategy was to drink the first one as he wished — to just enjoy it. Then he would order a second and let it sit — taking only a sip once in a while.

"I think I'll treat my first one like you do your second," Carol said.

They sang along with the crowd — Carol and Barb were able to translate many of the words for Nick and Vince. They hooked arms together with the Germans sitting next to them and swayed back and forth to the music.

Carol leaned in closer to Nick, a huge pretzel hooked around her neck, and her half-finished mug of beer before her on the table, explaining breathlessly in his ear the lyrics to the songs.

Nick laughed heartily as he hummed along with the singers.

Then the good mood was interrupted.

Nick saw them sit down at a table not ten feet away from where he and Carol were sitting. At almost the same time, Ben Bartlett recognized Nick and Vince. Bartlett was the gunner on Sergeant Crawford's tank.

Ben got up and walked over to Nick.

"Well, lookee here. If it isn't Mr. goody-goody and his wop mafia buddy Delvecchio. Who let you apes out of your cages?"

"Cool it, Bartlett," Nick said.

"And who are these two lovely Fraüleins?" Ben said.

Bartlett turned his attention to Carol and Barb.

"Hubba hubba, ding ding — *Sprechen Sie English, Schatzis?*"

Carol gave a puzzled look at Nick, and then she let loose with a stream of German words aimed at Ben. Carol then turned to Barb.

"*Nicht wahr, Inga?*"

"*Ja — bestimmt, Erika,*" Barb replied.

Both girls had spoken in their best country bumpkin German voices.

Ben smirked.

"Just as I thought, Holloway — a couple of dumb farm girls. They probably don't even shave under their armpits."

Nick stood up, ready to tangle with Ben.

Vince then stood up quickly and stepped between Nick and Ben.

"Okay, Ben — that's enough of that kind of talk," Nick said.

Nick took Ben's arm and smoothly turned him around. Vince followed quickly to block Ben from going back and getting closer to the girls.

Nick steered Ben back to his own table.

Nick wondered what he should do next. He wanted to punch Ben in the face — to make him hurt and bleed, but Ben had three of his buddies with him. That would mean Nick and Vince would have to take on all four. They'd probably all end up in a Munich jail if they fought on or near the festival grounds. And then what would happen to Carol and Barb? What would Carol think? Would she ever want to see him again?

Vince had already decided what his next step should be. He laid a one hundred Deutsche Mark bill on the table in front of Ben. That was a lot of money — about twenty-five dollars in 1960.

"Here you go, boys. Have a good time on me," Vince said.

Nick thought he either had to fight Ben because he had dishonored Carol and Barb, or they had to stay where they were in order to save face with Bartlett and his pals. On the other hand, he could sense Carol was upset, from the way her smile came and went regularly as she looked anxiously over at the Bartlett group.

"Thanks, Vince," Nick said.

"Oh, no," Carol said. "How horrible."

Nick looked to see what Carol was looking at.

Ned Lafontaine, the loader on Ben's tank, was standing on a table. He had combed his black hair down and across his forehead and was holding the black comb under his nose. He was giving the Hitler salute to the crowd.

"That's it — let's go," Nick said. "We can go to another tent."

"Watch out, Holloway. That kraut heifer could give you the clap," Ben said.

Ben and his friends laughed.

Vince restrained Nick and pushed him towards the exit.

As he looked back, Nick saw several burly Bavarians pull Ned off the table.

23

MERGERS AND ACQUISITIONS

Monday, 3 October

Why not?

Those two words had been bouncing around in Earl Crawford's brain since he heard the news that his competitor for cigarette ration stamps at Warner Kaserne was rotating on permanent change of station assignment back to the States. Why not take over his business? The scheme was working so well at Henry Kaserne — even the business with liquor ration stamps — why not absorb the business at Warner as well? And, to kill two birds with one stone, this was a good opportunity to pull Nick Holloway into his schemes. Get Holloway involved — that's the way to take that self-righteous young soldier down a peg or two.

"Holloway — you busy? I need a driver for an hour or two."

"Gee — I don't know, sarge. Let me check with my secretary to see what appointments are set up for this afternoon."

"Smart ass — here's the keys, go get the lieutenant's jeep."

Nick and Earl drove to Warner Kaserne to meet with Sergeant First Class Maurice Banyon. Mo Banyon was the supply sergeant for Headquarters Company of the Second Battalion, 28th Infantry — the Black Lions of Cantigny.

"Mo — glad to finally meet you," Earl said as he shook Banyon's hand.

"And this is Specialist Nick Holloway, my driver."

Nick shook hands with the other sergeant.

"Nick — why don't you go over to the snack bar and have a Coke, or whatever you want. Here's a buck — maybe get yourself something to eat too. I'll come and get you when we're done here."

Nick left.

Earl watched Nick as he walked away. Where was that cocky swagger he usually saw? Was he still thinking about that little shit Maguire packing himself in? How pathetic.

"So, Mo — you're going back to the land of the round door knobs and the big PXs — lucky you," Crawford said.

"Yeah. I'm ready to go back — been here since '58. The Mrs. is absolutely looking forward to seeing the good ole U.S. of A. again."

So, this was the mighty Mo Banyan Earl had heard so much about. He looked like a small-time operator. A man with no vision.

"So, all I need is your list of the nonsmokers in the 28th and we can wrap this business up."

Banyon handed a small notebook to Earl, who flicked through it.

"Is this up-to-date?"

"As far as I know, it is."

"Do you have a handle on any of the other units here at Warner, other than the 28th?"

"Afraid I don't, but I don't think anyone else has moved in on this scam, so if you can find some willing souls in those units, I'd say give it a try."

"Do you have anybody in your Battalion Finance Office? You know, someone who has access to the undistributed ration books?"

"I'm afraid not — at least I never tried to talk to anyone over there."

"Can you give me some names, just in case I might want to give it a shot?"

"Sure, here — I'll write down the names I know of in personnel and finance."

Mo Banyon tore a blank sheet out of another notebook he carried, and wrote down four names. He handed the sheet to Earl.

Sergeant Crawford gave Banyon a twenty-dollar bill.

"Thanks, Mo — it's been a pleasure doing business with you. Is there anything else I should know about your operation so that I can keep it running smoothly?"

Mo was silent. Finally, he spoke.

"Earl, the kid I had doing the contacts with the non-smokers quit on me. He said that as long as I was leaving the battalion, and that I never paid him enough for the risks he was taking, he was done with it. You'll have to find someone else to do that for you."

"No problem — I'll have Holloway — the kid you just met — he'll be good at the job. I'd better pay him well, though, huh?"

Both Earl and Mo laughed.

Earl Crawford was pleased with himself. He patted his field jacket pocket where the little red notebook was. The names in that book were like money in the pocket for him. He was realizing the importance of volume in business. And what an opportunity to get Nick Holloway implicated into his illegal operations. Nick would be an active participant in a criminal enterprise — then he won't dare to go blabbing to people he shouldn't, about the Bobcats and the black market. Nick had kept his mouth shut when the CID asked about

Danny. Now, if Earl's calculations were correct, Nick will keep his mouth shut about Bobcats, Inc. as well.

Earl walked over to the snack bar. Nick was sitting by the jukebox, sipping a Coca Cola and reading a paperback book.

"Whatcha reading there, Holloway?"

"It's called *Lolita*, by Vladimir Nabokov."

"Written by a commie, eh?"

"No. Nabokov came from Russia, but now he lives in the States."

"Once a commie, always a commie, I say."

Earl laughed at his own attempt to make a joke.

Nick closed his book and put it into a deep field jacket pocket.

"Are you ready to go, sergeant?"

"Yeah — let's go."

It was a short drive from Warner Kaserne back to Henry Kaserne.

"Nick, how would you like to make some extra money?"

"That depends."

"That depends on what? Either you do or you don't. It's a simple yes or no question."

"Well — it depends on what it is — on what I have to do to earn some extra money."

"Look here, Holloway — we're getting nowhere. Do you want to hear me out, or should we just forget the whole thing?"

"Okay, sergeant, what do you want me to do?"

"I have a kid here on Henry who goes around to nonsmokers — like yourself— and buys up their cigarette ration stamps."

Nick's look turned serious. It was Crawford after all.

Nick kept his eyes on the road.

* * * *

Earl waited until Nick had parked Lieutenant Jensen's

jeep near the maintenance shops before he again approached the subject of Nick working for him by contacting the nonsmokers at Warner Kaserne.

Nick gave his undivided attention to Sergeant Crawford.

Earl took the little red notebook from his pocket.

"This book contains the names of all of the current non-smokers in the Second Battalion of the 28th Infantry at Warner Kaserne. It's like gold. With one cigarette ration stamp I can go to the PX and buy a carton of Luckies for two bucks — and then I can sell that carton to the Germans for nine or ten bucks. That's a good profit on each and every ration stamp. Are you with me, Holloway? We can make some real money — and I will be more than generous with you for your cut."

Nick was motionless — his eyes fixed on Crawford.

Nick thought about the risks involved in doing what Crawford asked. He had just been caught illegally selling his own cigarette ration stamps — why would he want to get any deeper into this business? On the other hand, Sergeant Crawford was mean, and he had the power of a non-commissioned officer. He could make life miserable for Nick. It wasn't about the money. It was about survival and going home with an honorable discharge.

"Look, Nick — you think it over. But be quick about it — I won't ask you again. But I can tell you this — you'd be a fool to turn this down."

Earl tried to look as serious and threatening as he could to Nick. He wanted Nick to know that if he wasn't all in with him on this — there would be hell to pay for Nick.

"Look, Nick. This is easy money, and it isn't really wrong. It's small potatoes. So what if we sell a few cartons of cigarettes to the Germans. Who cares? It really is no big deal. And each time you go over to Warner Kaserne, I'll give you ten bucks. And as a bonus for doing this for me, I'll give you a tenner right now."

Earl held out a ten-dollar bill.

Nick reached over and took it.

Crawford stepped out of the jeep and walked towards the Headquarters Company barracks.

Nick waited until Crawford entered the barracks before he followed.

* * * *

That evening, Earl ate dinner at the NCO club on Will Kaserne.

His dinner guest was Master Sergeant Joe Teale, the top NCO in S-4, the supply section of the Third Battalion, 34th Field Artillery. Part of Teale's job responsibilities was disposing of empty brass shell casings for the battalion's howitzers. Crawford had already recruited Master Sergeant Eugene Laycock, who held the mirror position in the Third Battalion, 34th Armor. Laycock was in a position to facilitate the stealing of empty brass shell casings from the tanks' ninety millimeter main guns. Crawford was actively looking for a fence to dispose of the brass in case Manfred couldn't handle the sale.

After eating, Crawford ordered a bottle of champagne for he and Teale.

"What's this for, Earl — are you trying to get me drunk or something?"

"Or something, Joe — we're about to celebrate our new partnership."

Earl poured them each a glass of champagne. He held his glass up.

"Here's to prosperity."

Earl downed his drink.

Teale sipped on his glass — he looked straight into Earl's eyes.

"What's going on here, Earl? What are you playing at?"

"No playing, Joe — I'm as serious as I can be. So, here's the deal. You are going to supply a ton of empty brass shell casings for me every three months. I have the contacts on the outside — I will sell the shells to a German civilian who will pay us top dollar. You will receive a share of the proceeds. That's what we're talking about, Joe. It's just business — strictly business."

Joe Teale put his glass down on the table so hard that champagne slopped over and onto the tablecloth. He looked at the people sitting around them, and then he leaned over the table toward Crawford.

"You can't be serious. That's strictly against the law and Army regulations. Why — what you are suggesting would land both of us in Leavenworth."

"Yes — can't argue with you on that, Joe. But that ain't going to happen. We're too smart for that. You know, Joe — don't you — that at least ninety percent of the people in the Army are incompetent. And most of the other ten percent aren't very smart. So, we've got nothing to worry about."

"You sound pretty certain that I'm going to go along with your criminal scheme."

"Oh, I am certain, Joe. You and me are partners — that's for sure."

"No, no, no — I won't get involved in any of your harebrained scams — no sirree, bob, you can count me out."

Earl took an envelope out of the inside pocket of his dress green jacket. He opened it, and took out about a dozen photographs. He spread them out on the table in front of Teale.

"What have you got there — Earl? What are those pictures?"

"Pictures of you and Katrina Klaussner. Oh, and this one of your son Dieter — it is Dieter, isn't it? What a little cutie he is — Dieter Joseph Klaussner."

Crawford looked at Teale, and then back again at the photograph.

"Yes, I do believe he looks like you, Joe."

The color had drained from Teale's face. His shoulders drooped, and the wrinkles in his forehead were deep and red. He leaned back and slumped down in his chair. To Crawford he looked small.

"Where did you get those pictures?"

"Does it matter, Joe? I've got more if you'd like to see them."

"How much do you want, Earl? For the photos — and the negatives?"

"It's not going to be that easy, Joe. If all I wanted was money, I'm sure your wife Eleanor would pay handsomely for these pictures. She'd pay more than you would. But I'm not that kind of guy, Joe. All I want is a little cooperation from you. I want your help in making a little money by selling a few empty brass shell casings to the Germans. That's all."

Neither of the men said anything for a few minutes.

"It's your decision, Joe. What's it going to be?"

"Eleanor must never know about Katrina and Dieter," Joe said.

"They won't, I swear. Joe, you've got to trust me."

24

FRUSTRATION

Wednesday, 5 October

Nick's room looked like an olive drab, white, and yellow painting by Piet Mondrian. A dark green wall locker, and a footlocker of the same color resting on a metal stand, stood lined up straight, both with sharp corners. The olive drab bunk's metal foot and head rails were the only rounded objects in the room. No pictures or posters were allowed on the white walls trimmed in yellow. The door and the rectangular window frame were white. The towel, on which Nick's black boots and low quarter shoes rested upon the open shelf under the footlocker, was tangerine yellow. Yellow was the Army's color for cavalry and armored forces.

Nick Holloway sat on the edge of his bunk, spit-shining his boots. He had already hung a clean and starched fatigue uniform on the door of his wall locker. He would be ready to go in the morning when reveille sounded.

Nick had used Brasso to polish his belt buckle bright. As he buffed his boots, Nick's head bobbed to the beat of the music playing on the armed forces radio evening show, *Bouncing in Bavaria.*

"There you have it, listeners, April Stevens and *Teach Me*

Tiger. I love that song — it makes me want to ... oh, never mind."

Someone knocked on Nick's door. It was the CQ's runner.

"Specialist Holloway — you've got a phone call in the orderly room. It's a girl."

Nick was worried. He had asked Carol to never call the company, unless there was an emergency. Otherwise, she could leave a message for him at the service club. That was where Nick usually called from because there were several enclosed phone booths there.

Nick buttoned his shirt and tucked it into his trousers. He shut out the competing sounds of voices, country music, rhythm and blues, and rock and roll, coming from the open doors along the hall.

I wonder what happened? Why is she calling? What's the emergency? I hope she's okay.

He ran down the hallway, and descended the stairs two at a time.

Nick was accustomed to the loud adolescent banter of young men on free time. Although he didn't smoke himself — his chain-smoking parents caused Nick to see the folly in getting the habit — he was used to the ubiquitous tobacco haze that surrounded soldiers in the barracks.

In the orderly room, there was a tapping chatter from a typewriter as the runner worked on some report or another. Two soldiers from Ben's crew in Tank Section sat near the orderly.

"What are you two eight balls doing here?" Nick asked. "Go outside if you have to pick your nose."

Joe Flores and Ned Lafontaine stared back at Nick — they didn't leave.

Nick picked up the black telephone receiver.

"Hello? Oh, Maria, it's you."

Nick relaxed his body.

"No, I don't know where Vince is right now. He might be over at the gym playing basketball."

Nick listened. Maria was upset, sobbing and, at times, talking in German.

"Maria, calm down, please don't cry — I can't understand what you're saying. Now, tell me again."

Joe and Ned had stopped talking and were actively listening to Nick.

"But, Maria — how can you be so sure? Maria, please, honey — don't cry. It doesn't help to cry. Maria, try to get hold of yourself and calm down. What? What did you say? You haven't been to a doctor yet — but still you're certain …?"

Nick looked at Joe and Ned, and then turned away from them. He lowered his voice.

Joe and Ned got up and left the orderly room.

"Okay, Maria, I've got to go now. Yes, certainly I'll tell Vince that you called. And yes, I'll ask him to call you back as soon as possible."

Nick held the phone to his ear.

"Well, I know that Vince has been awfully busy lately — maybe that's why he hasn't called you."

Nick hung up the phone and stood still for a moment, looking at the desktop. Looking at nothing. He slowly traced his finger through the sweat on the telephone receiver.

Nick knew the situation immediately — Vince had not broken off yet with Maria Schuhmacher after he met Barb Milner. Vince told Nick that he really liked this Maria. But he also liked Barb. Nick had met Maria before, and he liked her — he could see how Vince could fall for her. But now Vince needed to take the next indicated step — especially if Maria was pregnant.

"Is everything okay?" The orderly clerk asked.

"Look, private, it's none of your business. If it were, I'd tell you. Now, just forget everything you heard here."

The private first class held his hands up.

"Hey — be cool — it don't make me no nevermind."

Nick walked slowly back to his room on the second floor of the barracks. The pungent smells of fresh white paint and newly varnished floors were the only things that disturbed his concentration.

Joe Flores and Ned Lafontaine came into the hallway from Ben Bartlett's room. They glanced at Nick and giggled.

"What's so funny?" Nick asked.

The smiles on the two men's faces were gone — they stopped and faced Nick.

"We just thought it was funny that you — Mr. goody-two-shoes Specialist Holloway, has knocked up some kraut girl," Joe Flores said.

Nick grabbed Joe's shirt below his chin and pushed him up against the wall.

Just then Ben Bartlett came into the hallway.

"What's going on here? What are you doing to one of my men, Mr. Big Shot?"

Nick released his hold on Joe.

"Only a little behavior correction, Ben. If you'd teach these clowns some manners and discipline, this wouldn't be needed."

Ben looked at Joe and Ned.

"Squirrel, young 'un — you don't have to take any crap from this turd machine," Ben said.

Ben turned to face Nick.

"See here, Holloway — you mess with my men, you mess with me — you got that?"

"Spec four Bartlett — Big Ben Bartlett — gunner on Sergeant Crawford's tank — tank numero uno. You're a sorry ass specimen of a tanker, Bartlett. No wonder we call you the last with the least," Nick said.

A small group of men, all from Tank Section, now stood around Nick and Ben.

Vince Delvecchio had just returned from the gymnasium. He reached out and touched Nick on the arm.

"Nick — how about you and I going over to the snack bar and talk about the plan for getting the tank ready for going to Hohenfels next week."

Nick stared at Vince, but didn't say anything.

"Nick, it's not worth it — he's not worth it. It can only mean trouble," Vince said.

"Stay out of this, Delvecchio — this is between asswipe Holloway and me," Bartlett said.

"Listen, Bartlett — you've been cock-of-the-walk here for too long, and I don't know why," Nick said. "You suffer from delusions of competency. Your tank is broken down more often than any of the other three. Your crew's scores on the firing range are always the lowest — you guys haven't passed the tank crew proficiency course lately, and you and your crew look so scruffty most of the time — people think you're grease monkeys — not warrior tankers. You guys are a disgrace to the Army. You need to be busted down to recruit and sent back for basic training again."

Bartlett clenched his fists.

"Now you hold on there just a minute, Holloway. You're so self-righteous and so goody-goody — well, that don't cut no ice with me," Ben said.

"Mr. Big Ben Bartlett — you're even shaped like a pear. If you had half a brain in your head, instead of that itty-bitty thing that lives up your ass — or is your brain in your skinny little pecker? Yeah, that's it — that must be it. That must be why you're such a royal fuckup, Bartlett. But your day in the sun is over. You see, things are going to be different around here from now on."

Nick caught himself. *Why did I say that? Where did those words come from? If anything, it's going to be worse now, with Crawford as section sergeant.*

"Come on, Nick. Let's take a walk and cool off a bit," Vince said.

"Take a hike yourself, Delvecchio. This doesn't concern you," Bartlett said.

Ben Bartlett was about three inches taller than Nick, and outweighed him by at least twenty-five pounds. But Ben had a heavy, thick, flabby look about him — in contrast to Nick's fit and muscular body.

"Holloway, let's settle this thing here, right now — just you and me, and we'll see who is the senior man in Tank Section here in the barracks."

"Fine — that's just fine with me, lard-ass, let's do it; but maybe you're not up to it — maybe you don't have the guts to tangle with me," Nick said.

Ben's face turned red.

"I hear you knocked up your girlfriend, Holloway. That don't sound so smart to me," Ben said.

Vince looked at Nick with wide eyes.

Ben's face returned to its normal color and he smiled. He turned to the men standing around.

"So, Mr. stud here, the lady's man, can't keep his pants zipped up. So, what are you going to do now, Mr. oh-high-oh buck nuts? Are you going to marry your kraut whore and move off post? Then I won't have to even look at your pathetic mug in the barracks. Ha!"

Nick lunged toward Ben, but Vince and one other soldier stepped between them.

"Why don't you two settle this out in the tank park instead of here — the CQ could come by here at any minute," Vince said.

25

ALPHA MALES

Wednesday, 5 October

The group moved down the hall, down the stairway, and outside of the barracks. The tank park was a short block from the barracks — with machine shops, supply storerooms, and various offices and garages in between. Those buildings were all dark now. Just before the group reached the tank park, they passed the line of wash racks where the muddied tanks were hosed down after field training exercises.

There were ninety-nine tanks in the battalion tank park. Each of the hulks loomed dark in the evening dusk. Each tank was covered with a dark olive drab tarpaulin. The tank park looked like a field of sleeping monster elephants, tucked under their regulation Army blankets. Damp wisps of fog were thick, and filthy with lingering odors of gasoline, oil, and grease solvents.

When the men got to the open gravel space behind Tank Section's four tanks, the men formed a circle around Nick and Ben. Nick took off his cap and field jacket and put them on the cold fender of his tank. Ben did the same.

"Let's go, motherfucker — I've been waiting for this," Ben said.

The two faced each other and moved slowly in a circle, their fists at the ready. Then Ben stepped in and swung his fist, connecting with Nick's face.

Nick's eyebrow was split open and bleeding profusely. In spite of that — Nick sent a quick left jab that hit Ben's nose with a cracking sound. Both of Ben's hands went up to his face. Nick followed by driving his right fist into Ben's solar plexus, and then he fired a salvo of fists to Ben's face, followed with a knee to Ben's groin. With Ben groaning and doubled over, Nick kicked Ben's shin with the edge of his boot heel. Ben went down and rolled from side to side on the ground.

Nick caught his breath — then breathed deeply.

"Had enough, Bartlett?"

Ben didn't say anything. Nick kicked him twice in the ribs.

"C'mon, tubby – is that all you've got?" Nick said.

Ben yelled an animal-like sound — then he reached out and grabbed Nick's ankles. Now both men were down on the gravel. They grappled each other and rolled — stopped — and rolled again, and stopped again. They were both expending their strength in this isometric struggle, each trying to break out of the grip of the other, or to find a way to hurt the other.

Nick found himself looking close in at Ben's ear. Nick bit the ear — hard — and then spat a chunk of meat out of his mouth. Ben screamed and loosened his grip on Nick. The two men scrambled to their feet. Ben held his bloody ear and bobbed his head as he stumbled around in a daze.

Nick shook his tight muscles, and watched Ben. *I could do it — I could kill the son-of-a-bitch — now — right here.*

Nick spat twice to get rid of the metallic taste of Ben's blood.

Ben looked at Nick — it was a look of hate without words.

Ben's face was red, and it was streaked with blood from his nose, his lips, and his ear. Ben's eyes were bloodshot red and opened wide — he not only looked bloodied but also like he had been on a three-day drinking binge.

"Why you ...," Ben said as he charged forward.

Ben pounced on Nick. Ben's hands went around Nick's head — he put a choke hold on Nick.

Nick started to go limp. He went down on his knees. His eyes closed.

"Dammit, Ben — let him go," Vince yelled. "You'll kill him."

"He hasn't given yet," Ben replied.

"Yes, he has — just look at him. He can't talk."

"He ain't said quit yet."

"Then I'll say it for him — I quit — he quits," Vince said.

"He gotta say he sorry."

"Oh, for crying out loud, Ben, let him go before you really hurt him. I'll say I'm sorry for him. And you're the better man — tonight."

"Ben — let him go — you could get into real trouble from Crawford," Joe Flores said.

Ben released his hold and let Nick fall to the ground.

Flores and Lafontaine gave Ben their handkerchiefs.

"Come on, Ben — we'll take you to the dispensary. Damn — he bit a piece of your ear off," Joe said.

Vince bent down to attend to Nick.

"Billy, go to the mess hall and get some water and paper towels. Some water to drink too," Vince said.

Vince held Nick's head in his arms. Shortly, Nick opened his eyes and spoke.

"What was that? What happened to me?"

"Ben put a choke hold on you. You passed out."

"The son-of-a-bitch. I had him — I had him beat."

"For sure you did, Nick."

"Big Ben? Where is he?"

Nick moved to get up, but winced and put his hands to his head and neck.

Billy Dryden returned with water and towels.

Vince gave Nick a drink of water, and then cleaned his eyebrow and face with a damp towel.

Nick struggled again to get up — he used Vince and Billy as supports.

"We should get you over to the dispensary to have that cut looked at, it might need stitches — but Ben and his pals might still be there. Here, Nick — walk around 'til you feel a little better."

They walked around the tanks for about five minutes. Nick finally walked without holding on to Vince and Billy. Finally, Nick jumped up and down a few times, did a few jumping jacks, and jogged in place. He swiveled his head from side to side.

"Okay, I'm ready. Let's go to the dispensary. If Bartlett's still there — so be it. Billy, will you get my cap and jacket — it's over there, on tank two — on the fender."

They walked slowly across Patton field to the other side of Henry Kaserne, where the dispensary was located.

Ben and his friends were still there — a medic was working on Ben's ear. Ben also had a broken nose.

Another medic was on a telephone, calling for an ambulance — Ben was going to spend the night in a hospital.

Ben had a pained smile on his face.

"I guess that's settled then — I'm the chief enlisted man in Tank Section," Ben said.

"What do you mean?" Nick said.

"What? Didn't your wop friend tell you? He gave in and apologized for you."

Nick looked hard at Vince.

Vince looked at Nick, shrugged his shoulders and held his hands out — palms up.

"He would have killed you, Nick," Vince said.

The medic left Ben and walked over to Nick. Then he yelled through a door for the other medic to come help him.

"The ambulance will be here in a few minutes for the other guy," the medic said.

"Great, Dennis — here, this guy just needs a couple stitches in his eyebrow."

The medic called Dennis didn't say anything while he worked. He cleaned Nick's eyebrow, applying generously an antiseptic, and then put in the stitches to close the cut.

An ambulance came and took Ben away. His boys left.

With a bandage over his eyebrow, the medic said Nick could go.

"You guys won't need to report this, will you? How important can it be — two guys ran into the same door — pure coincidence — you don't have to report small stuff like this, do you?" Nick asked.

"And the piece missing from the other guy's ear — how did that happen?"

"Oh, yeah — I think there was a mad dog hanging around that dangerous door, just waiting for an opportunity to present itself."

The medic laughed out loud.

"Don't worry, we won't report this so that you guys get into trouble. Your imagination is priceless. Also, I've been where you are, several times."

Nick tried to laugh also, but his face hurt too much.

"Now, let's hope that Ben keeps his mouth shut," Vince said.

With a bandage over his eyebrow, a black eye, and a fat lip, Nick asked Vince to join him for a Coke at the snack bar. Billy said he was going back to the barracks.

"Vince, what gave you the right to quit for me? You know I would never want you to do that."

"I had to do it. He would have killed you with that choke hold, or given you brain damage, at least. And what if he'd used a sleeper hold? Huh, what then? For sure I'd be planning your funeral right now."

"You don't get it, do you? How long have we been friends now? Long enough for you to know there's no honor in quitting — none at all. It's like there's no honor in snitching, or lying, or cheating — and for sure — none in quitting."

"Nick, try to understand. I wasn't going to let him kill you, or make you into a vegetable. I knew you'd never stop it. I'd think you'd want to thank me, Nick."

Nick didn't say anything. He kept turning his Coke bottle around and around.

Finally, Nick looked Vince in the eyes.

"You're right — I owe you one — thanks."

Vince leaned in over the table.

"What did Ben mean when he said you had knocked up your girlfriend? Is Carol pregnant?"

"Oh, I almost forgot. No, no way — Carol isn't pregnant — not by me anyway."

Nick's face winced as he talked.

"Earlier — actually, that is how this whole business got started. You were at the gym, playing basketball with those guys from the 724th — Maria called the orderly room. She's upset that you haven't seen or called her for a while."

"Maria? She called here? At the company? I told her to never call me at the company."

"Well, she did. She cried a lot. She misses you. Vince — she thinks she's pregnant."

"What? But that's not possible," Vince said.

"Well, she said she thinks so. She hasn't been to a doctor yet — who knows."

"You know, Nick, I thought I was in love with Maria. I really did. This summer when she had me up to Geiselhöring to see her parents — and grandparents and uncles and aunts and cousins — it was great, Nick. But then, you know, Barb came along, and Nick … I'm confused. What do you think I should do?"

"I don't know, buddy. The first thing I would do is to call Maria and find out what the truth is."

26

ARNDT AND FRIEDA MEIER

Friday, 7 October

Ben Bartlett was released from the Army hospital on Friday. He was put on light duty by Sergeant Crawford. Nick avoided seeing him as much as he could. Joe Flores and Ned Lafontaine gave Nick dirty looks — Nick ignored them.

* * * *

Saturday, 8 October

On Saturday morning, Headquarters Company marched to Patton Field for a command inspection. This meant that the battalion commander and his senior staff walked through the ranks and personally inspected the soldiers.

After the inspection, and after noon chow, Nick and Vince prepared for their dates. Vince had lied to Barb, so that he could see Maria again. Nick went downtown.

Nick knocked on the apartment door and waited. He had bought a new claret red crewneck sweater to go with his sky-blue shirt and gray dress trousers. He had polished his black oxfords so that he could see himself in the toes. He got a fresh haircut. He made sure he had a clean, pressed hankie in his pocket — and breath mints. This was the day he would have dinner with Carol and the German family she lived with — Arndt and Frieda Meier. He had already met them, briefly, but Nick wanted to know them better, and especially, he wanted to make a good impression on them — and Carol, of course.

He cleared his throat and focused on what he was doing and what he was going to say.

The door opened and Carol greeted him — her big smile quickly disappeared. Nick wondered whether she was concerned for him, or was she upset that he had been fighting again.

"Nick — you're here."

Carol hugged Nick politely, and then she stepped aside and Nick walked into the apartment.

"Frieda, Arndt — you remember Nick Holloway? Nick — Arndt and Frieda Meier."

"I'm very pleased to meet you again, Mr. and Mrs. Meier."

"You look so — ah ...," Frieda said.

Arndt nudged Frieda.

"Oh, I'm sorry — I mean your eye, your lip — your face looks .... Are you okay, Nick?" Frieda said.

Nick shook hands with both Arndt and Frieda.

"Yes, I'm fine now. As they say — time heals all wounds — or something like that."

Nick had checked himself in a mirror earlier, and didn't think he looked that bad.

Both Arndt and Frieda stared at Nick's face.

"Come in, come in, and sit down," Arndt said.

"Can I get you something to drink, Nick?" Frieda said. "We have beer, wine, brandy, and soft drinks."

"And schnapps," Arndt said with a grin.

"Beer would be fine," Nick said.

"I'll get it, Frieda. And Herr Meier, do you want another brandy?" Carol asked.

"No — I'm okay," Arndt said.

Frieda and Carol went to the kitchen.

Arndt lit a new cigarette.

"Soldier Nick. I see you have not stayed out of trouble at your kaserne? Was it the Russians?" Arndt asked, with a smile.

"No — not the Russians. Just practicing for when we do tangle with them."

Arndt flicked the ashes from his cigarette into the ashtray.

"So, then — how are things going for you?" Arndt asked.

"Oh, things are going good — well, as good as can be expected — you know, it is the Army."

Arndt didn't respond. He just looked at Nick. He puffed on his cigarette, not looking at much of anything.

"I'm sorry, Nick — here, would you like a cigarette?"

"No, thank you."

Arndt reached over to a small table beside his chair and picked up a box.

"Are you a cigar smoker? If so, it's okay to smoke here."

"No, I don't smoke at all. My parents are both smokers, and I never got into the habit."

They both leaned back in their chairs and sat in silence.

Nick felt warm. He twisted in his chair to find a more comfortable position. He could hear Carol and Frieda in the kitchen preparing the dinner meal.

"Arndt — if you don't mind my asking — how is it that you speak English so well? Where did you learn?"

Arndt flicked the ashes from his cigarette into an ashtray. Then he looked at Nick.

"I learned my English in the United States."

Nick slowly shook his head as he chuckled, softly and briefly.

"In the United States?"

"Yes — I was a prisoner of war there from June 1943 until August 1946."

Nick straightened in his chair. So, Arndt had been in the U.S. during the war. Nick had never heard about, or thought about, German POWs being in the States. He made a mental note to learn more about that. How many? Where? Any problems? Escapes?

"Like — where in the States?"

"North Carolina — mostly. I was at a POW camp near Shelbyville."

Nick turned to face Arndt directly and leaned in.

"Do you mind my asking? What was it like in the POW camp?"

"It was good. We had such good food — you see, we had poor food and not much of it in North Africa."

"North Africa? So, you served under General Rommel in the *Afrika Korps*?"

"That's correct."

"What was he like — Rommel? Did you like him as a commander?"

"Oh, yes. We thought we would never lose with Rommel leading us. We were very disappointed when he left us. You know — he kept the SS out of Africa. We were very grateful to him for that."

Nick couldn't help but wonder what it would have been like to have served under General Rommel. Obviously, Arndt idolized the man. So, then — there were some good men who were in the German Army. How would Sergeant Crawford have fit in with Rommel's Army? No doubt, Crawford would have been in the SS.

"What did you do in the *Afrika Korps*, Arndt?"

"I was a tanker, like you, Nick — a *Panzer Soldat*. I was a tank driver most of the time."

"What type of tank were you driving?"

"Panzer IIIs and IVs. I liked the IIIs best because they were fast — and they had a powerful engine. The IVs had a bigger gun, and were heavier, but they had the same engine as the Panzer IIIs, so they were slower."

"Did you fight against the British or the Americans in North Africa?"

"Both. We were in the battle for the Kasserine Pass against the American Army. We defeated them. I don't think you want to hear about that, Nick."

"Oh, but I do want to hear about it. What unit were you in?"

Nick chided himself.

Arndt looked at Nick. Finally, he spoke.

"I was in the 6th Company of the 7th Panzer Regiment of the 10th Panzer Division — actually, I was in the same unit from the time I volunteered in 1939, until I was captured in May 1943."

Nick was fascinated to hear Arndt's stories as a tanker in World War II.

"Well — you were lucky you never had to go to Russia."

Arndt drank down his brandy, and sat there turning the glass around in his hand without looking at Nick. He refilled his glass.

"Oh, but I was in Russia. We were there from June 1941 until May 1942."

"You were? Wow — what was that like? Did you see any combat action there?"

Arndt snuffed out his cigarette into an ashtray, lit another cigarette, and then took another drink of brandy. He stared straight ahead.

"It was hell, Nick — utter hell. You see, tank soldier Nick, you are lucky — you have never lost a close soldier friend."

Now it was Nick's turn to be quiet. He drew within himself and stared at nothing.

They sat like that for several minutes.

After dinner, Nick and Carol went for a walk around

the neighborhood. It was a beautiful evening, and the two of them walked hand-in-hand.

"Nick, I haven't asked you this yet, but I need to know. What was this fight about?"

Nick walked on without answering. Finally, after several minutes, he spoke.

"Carol, I don't know how to tell you — what to say to you."

"Just tell me this, to start with, who did you fight?"

"Do you remember the big guy that was so rude at the Oktoberfest?"

"Yes, I remember him."

"That's Ben Bartlett — we call him Big Ben."

"You had a fight with him? Why?"

"Well, you remember the stupid and mean things he said to you?"

"Yes, but I've actually heard worse from other guys."

"You have?"

"Yes, I have. But that's not the point here. Why did you think you had to fight him?"

Nick thought for a moment.

"Well, I did think I had to fight him for that. I couldn't let him get away with talking to you and Barb like that. And ..."

"And what?"

"Well — Ben and I are seen as the leaders among the guys in Tank Section that live in the barracks. When Sergeant Cervenka was here, he looked to me to provide that leadership. Now, with Sergeant Crawford in charge, it's up in the air whether I or Ben are in charge. It seems that since Ben is the gunner on Crawford's tank, he thinks he's the man. It has split the section. On one side you've got me, Vince, Hal Washington, and Billy Dryden — on the other hand, there's Bartlett and everyone else."

"So?"

"Well, it seemed like a good time to settle both issues."

"Both issues?"

"Yeah — to punish Ben for the way he treated you and Barb, and then to settle once and for all who's in charge in the section."

"Who won?"

"I did, on the punishment part. I punished him real good."

"And the other part?"

"He did."

They walked in silence back to Carol's apartment. They stood outside the door and kissed. Carol's hand accidentally hit Nick's stitched up eyebrow.

"Oh, no — Nick, did I hurt you?"

Nick reached up and felt something oozing out from his stitches.

"I don't know — it's not supposed to bleed or whatever it's doing, is it?"

"Come inside. I'll clean it, and see what I can do."

Nick sat on the sofa while Carol got some warm water in a pan. She looked in the medicine cabinet, reading the German labels, until she spotted one that served the same function as Mercurochrome. She washed Nick's wound, and then applied the antiseptic.

It looks like the Meier's have gone out," Carol said.

"Ouch — that stings," Nick said.

"That must mean it's working."

They sat there with Carol playing with his short hair.

They kissed — gently at first because of Nick's bruised lips — and then hard and long. The feeling of desire, of pleasure, was stronger than any pain Nick felt. Nick moved his hand to her breast — she pushed his hand away.

They lay together on the sofa and kissed until they fell asleep.

The Meier's clock chimed on every quarter hour, and bonged on each hour.

Arndt and Frieda returned late.

Nick cried out and sat up quickly — Carol almost fell off the sofa.

Nick looked at his wristwatch — it was twelve-thirty. Nick's class A pass was only good until 0100. He had a half hour to get back to Henry Kaserne.

"Oh, no — bed check is in half an hour."

"Bed check? What does that mean?"

"It means I'll be a private again if I'm not in my bunk at one o'clock. Sorry, but I've got to go. I've got to find a taxi — *mach schnell*. I better call the company CQ first and tell him I'm on the way."

Arndt and Frieda came into the living room.

Arndt was tipsy. He took a quick step to regain his balance.

"What is all the fuss about?" Arndt asked.

"Oh, I'm sorry, *Herr Meier*. We fell asleep, and now Nick needs to get back to his kaserne soon — before one o'clock. He's going out to get a taxi to take him back."

"No — I'll take him back," Arndt said.

Frieda gave him one of those looks.

Arndt put on a leather jacket. He had car keys in his hand.

"Come, soldier Nick — I'll get you back in time."

Nick looked at Carol with the question. She shrugged her shoulders.

Nick made a quick phone call to Headquarters Company, to tell the CQ that he was on his way.

"Thanks so much for the delicious dinner, Frau Meier," Nick said.

Arndt and Frieda owned a two-door 1956 Opel Rekord. Arndt kept it clean and in top running condition.

"So, Nick — you are at the Henry Kaserne. In my day, it was called *General-Wever-Kaserne*. I know just where it is."

The wheels of the Opel spun in the gravel as they left the

alley and headed for Leopold Strasse. Nick could smell the fruity schnapps on Arndt's breath.

"So — how do you like the Army, Nick?"

"It's okay — better some days than others."

Nick looked at his watch.

"Do you like being on the tanks?"

Arndt slurred his words.

"Yes — yes — I do like the tanks."

Arndt drove fast and he knew exactly where he was going. It was like he'd been to the kaserne before.

The Opel's tires squealed as Arndt turned off of Leopold Strasse onto Ingolstadter Strasse. Eventually, Arndt turned off of Ingolstadter Strasse onto Kollwitz Strasse. From there it was only a quarter mile or so to the front gate of Henry Kaserne. Barely fifteen minutes had elapsed.

As soon as Arndt stopped in front of the main gate, Nick got out of the car, with his pass card in his hand.

"Nick," Arndt said.

"Yes?"

"Carol is like a daughter to us. She is like perfection to Frieda and I."

"I agree with you."

With Nick looking into the open car window, close to Arndt's face and his brandy and schnapps and tobacco breath, Nick wondered if he should say something else.

Arndt pointed at the American flag above the guardhouse.

"Nick? What I said earlier, about being in the Army — don't believe a word of what I said — it was all shit. Armies are shit. War is shit. People die."

Arndt choked back a sob.

"I hated every day of it — even being a prisoner of war. It's all shit, Nick — no good."

"Yes, sir."

"I mean it."

"I know you mean it — I believe you."

Nick looked at his watch and then through the front gate.
"No — I really mean it. Do you really unnershtand me?"

"Yes, sir, I understand you. And, I agree with you."

Nick showed his pass and his ID to the gate guard, and
then he went back to Arndt's car.

"Thank you for driving me here. Are you okay, Arndt?
Maybe you should have a cup of coffee before you drive
home?"

"I'm chust fine, no worries."

Nick hesitated. Should he do something? Should he let
Arndt go like this?

Arndt waved for Nick to go — to hurry.

Nick looked back as he started to sprint towards the
Headquarters Company barracks. Looking back, he saw
Arndt was still there — watching him.

27

Courtesy Patrol

Saturday, 15 October

"Sergeant Crawford — you wanted to see me?" Nick asked.

"That's right, Holloway — I've got courtesy patrol duty tonight and I need a driver. Are you up to the job?"

Nick's response belied his true feelings.

"Yes, sergeant."

Carol had a JYM event that night, so Nick was spending a rare Saturday night without a Class A pass to go off the kaserne.

It was Saturday night, and Headquarters Company was assigned to provide the courtesy patrol in downtown Munich as a way of keeping its men out of trouble. That was impossible, of course, but at least the courtesy patrol could help some of the men. Usually, a noncommissioned officer lead the patrol, assisted by an enlisted driver. A truck driver was also assigned along with a deuce-and-a-half truck (two-and-a-half ton).

"Here are our keys, Holloway — go get our jeep. Make sure it's got a full tank of gas. Also, don't forget the Courtesy

Patrol sign for the jeep. Then meet me back here in ten minutes."

Nick got the jeep — actually it was Lieutenant Jensen's jeep, but Crawford seemed to run Tank Section for the lieutenant, so it made sense to Nick that they used his jeep.

There was a small tarp covering something in the back of the jeep. Nick looked under the canvas and saw that there were two boxes full of cigarette cartons.

That's odd, Nick thought.

The truck from Headquarters Company's Transportation Section was waiting on the street beside the barracks. Nick pulled in front of the truck and parked. Sergeant Crawford got into the jeep.

"We'll hit the bars on Goethe Strasse first, Holloway — do you know how to get there?"

"Yes, sergeant."

"Okay — let's go."

Crawford turned around and gave the truck driver an arm signal to follow them.

Nick headed the jeep through the front gate and out of Henry Kaserne — one-quarter mile down Kollwitz Strasse, then left onto Ingolstadter Strasse, which eventually became Leopold Strasse and then finally Nick turned onto Ludwig Strasse, past the Karlstor-Stachus into the oldest part of downtown Munich. Nick recalled watching old newsreels showing columns of Nazi troops goose-stepping through these same streets.

"Do you know these bars, Holloway?"

"I've been down here once or twice," Nick said. "Sergeant — can I make a suggestion?"

"What is it?"

"I think it's best if we not park the truck or the jeep right on Goethe Strasse. That could be inviting trouble. Some of these guys get pretty rambunctious when they get drunk, and they could cause some trouble for us that we don't need."

"You think so? You know, Holloway, you're not as dumb as you look. Park us wherever you think is best."

Nick had felt relieved since the end of the Warner Kaserne ration stamp affair. He was glad he was done with that business. He was upset with himself for even agreeing to do it in the first place. He had gone to Warner and discovered that Mo Banyan's little book was out of date — full of names of guys long gone. Now, he felt he was walking through a minefield when it came to Sergeant Crawford. Nick had to get along with him — had to keep on his good side. In less than three months Nick would be out of the Army. He just had to leave with an honorable discharge.

"Thanks, sergeant. The truck also — I know just the place to put these vehicles."

Nick turned onto Schiller Strasse and found a parking spot for the jeep. Then he got out and guided the truck driver to the space behind them. The truck would provide a ride back to the kaserne for any soldiers too drunk to make it on their own.

Sergeant Crawford told the truck driver to wait by the truck, and then he and Nick walked around the corner and soon were on the Goethe Strasse, a street of cheap bars that U.S. soldiers called *Gertie Strasse*.

Crawford and Nick went into the Atlantic Bar first. The noise was loud. A jukebox blared. Tobacco smoke filled the air. Laughter, insults, and glass on glass, glass on thick wooden tables — the soldiers were enjoying themselves. But it was already midnight, and the Saturday night curfew was extended by one hour only — to 0100. Any soldier not in his bunk at 0100 could be busted down one full pay grade level, unless he had called in ahead of time with a valid excuse, or was on an approved overnight pass, or on vacation leave. A private first class would be a mere private again. A specialist fourth class would find himself a private first class, and so on.

Sergeant Crawford moved among the men, gruffly

reminding them that there was a truck available to take them back to their kaserne if they needed. Nick greeted those men he recognized, and reminded a few to tuck their shirts in because he didn't want Crawford to cause a scene over something that minor.

Nick noticed that most men showed their fear of Crawford, except those who were already passed out or close to it. Crawford was a large man. He looked at people as though he wanted to hit them. His five stripes on each arm also intimidated others.

Next, they went to the Texas Bar, and then to the Hollywood, and then across the street to the West Side Bar, and to the Paradise. Finally, they came to the Dolly Bar — Nick's usual hangout.

Inside the Dolly Bar, Nick found Ursula Schmidt, a barmaid, and greeted her.

"Ooshie, baby — how you doing?" Nick asked.

Ursula looked like she was in her thirties, but Nick knew she was only twenty-four. Blondish and attractive, she had a child by an American soldier who never told her when he went back to the States, and he never let her know where he was.

"Nicky — Nicky honey — I'm happy to see you. Where have you been keeping yourself?"

"Oh, you know — we young guys gotta keep moving — lots of girls to keep happy, you know."

Ursula laughed with him.

"And how is your new American girlfriend?"

Nick looked at her with a changed expression.

"How do you know about that?"

"Word travels fast, Nicky — but don't worry, I'm not mad at you."

Nick relaxed.

"I see you and sergeant sourpuss over there are on the courtesy patrol tonight. So, you can't come home with me?"

Ursula had a seductive smile on her face.

Nick laughed heartily again.

"Nicky — I'm happy to see you again — I really am. There are two guys on the floor over there in the corner who have passed out. Their buddies just left them there."

Ursula pointed to a corner at the back of the room.

Nick took two dollars out of his billfold and gave them to Ursula.

"Here, Ooshie — give them some coffee and try to wake them up. Then the sergeant and I will help them get to our truck."

"Okay, Nicky — you know you're still my favorite GI, don't you?"

Nick laughed.

"And you, Ooshie — you're my favorite Fräulein."

They both laughed at that.

Nick caught Crawford's attention and nodded toward the back of the bar where Ursula and another barmaid were using cold washcloths and serving coffee to the now conscious, but still inebriated soldiers.

Crawford and Nick helped the drunks get on their feet, then put the men's arms over their shoulders, and walked with them out of the bar and to the truck that was parked on Schiller Strasse.

They helped several other men as they stumbled out of the bar onto the sidewalk on Goethe Strasse. At the truck, Sergeant Crawford gathered information as to which kaserne each of the men was from.

Their first stop was at Henry Kaserne.

Then they made the rounds of Will and Warner Kasernes. When all the men had been delivered, Crawford directed the truck driver to return to Henry Kaserne.

"Okay, Holloway — now you and I've got one more mission yet tonight. Go back to Ingolstadter Strasse and turn north. We're going out past Schleissheim. I'll tell you where to go."

Nick did as he was told. What other choice did he have?

Nick guessed this had something to do with the two cases of cigarettes in the back of the jeep.

They went past Schleissheim and were soon in an area where there were still bomb-damaged buildings — and no streetlights.

"Pull in over there — and drive behind that warehouse."

There was a black BMW already there — with a man standing beside it.

Nick studied the man. He had that same sneer on his face that many mean sergeants had — even Sergeant Crawford at times. The man had a grey fedora on, with a ring of sweat and hair oil stain. A long, black overcoat. The man had his hands in his coat pockets.

"Manfred — this is my associate, Nick Holloway — and he's one mean and tough fellow. Nick — this is Manfred Neumann — a business customer of mine."

Nick just stared at the German.

Manfred held out his hand for Nick to shake.

Nick ignored him.

Now he thinks I'm his associate — well, we'll see about that.

28

Doubts

Saturday, 15 October

"Where did Vince take you?" Carol asked.

"A cute and cozy little hotel on Starnberg Lake," Barb answered. "Called the Tutzinger Hof. It was great — so great."

Barb raised her eyes and rolled her head, as she pursed her lips and blew out her breath.

"Oh, Barb — you're so bad — what am I going to do with you?"

"You know what they say, Carol — good girls go to heaven, but bad girls can go anywhere."

They both laughed.

"What did you do there?"

"We stayed in the room, mostly."

They both laughed, hysterically.

"We did go out for dinner, and then we took a walk along the lake. In the moonlight — so romantic. It's a beautiful place, Carol. You and Nick should go there sometime. I know you'd love it."

Carol looked out the window of the study room.

"How about you and Nick? Have you …?"

"Not yet."

"Why not?"

"I don't know — it's been one drama after another with him. Fighting. Grief over his friend's suicide. Complaining about his sergeant. Frustration with the Army. I don't know where I come in. You know how it is. For once, I'd like to think that I'm number one in his life."

"Oh, Carol — from what Vince tells me, he does think you are number one. Nick adores you. He's madly in love with you."

"I still don't know. I guess I don't know him very well. Who is he? Who is the real Nick? Is he just the happy go lucky soldier man, going through some rough times? Or is it deeper than that? I can't see a future with an emotionally unstable man — not at all."

"Oh, come on, Carol. I know you — probably better than you know yourself. Admit it. You don't believe he's emotionally unstable. Nick is an exciting guy, and you like that. You like the drama. Vince said he's known Nick for almost two years. He speaks so highly of him, I wonder sometimes, like you do — do I come in second to his best friend Nick? According to Vince, since this new sergeant arrived, things have gone to hell in a handbasket."

"But … I don't know, I just don't know. Sometimes, I think I should end it now. Maybe that would be for the best. Let Nick deal with his problems by himself. I'm not helping him anyway, that's for sure."

"Carol, Carol, Carol — will you stop talking like that."

"Oh, you only want me to continue seeing Nick because that will somehow be good for you and Vince."

"Carol — I can't believe you said that. I don't think you really feel that way. If you do …"

"I'm sorry. I shouldn't have said that. But, Barb — what should I do.?"

"It would be a big mistake for you to break up with Nick now. Give him some time to get through all of this."

29

SNAFU

SNAFU. *Situation Normal — All Fucked Up.* That phrase summed up the usual course of events in the Army at its worst. Nick Holloway knew that, but it still irked him, especially now in the third year of his three-year enlistment term. What happened at Hohenfels on 24 October 1960 was a classic SNAFU.

Field training exercises for the Third Battalion, 34th Armor, included such activities as day and night road marches, attacks in tank formations such as line, wedge, and in echelon; finding, occupying, and setting up bivouac positions with defensive fields of fire; and firing weapons — at stationary and moving targets, at night as well as in daytime — and on the tank crew proficiency course at Grafenwöhr. Small arms and machine guns were also fired. Each tank crewman was issued an M1 Garand .30 caliber rifle and a .45 caliber M1911 semi-automatic pistol. Also, each tank carried a .45 caliber M3 submachine gun.

There were two major field training areas used by the battalion in Bavaria, both had been previously developed and used by the German Army until the end of World War

II — Grafenwöhr and Hohenfels. These were large land areas with rolling hills, valleys, woodlands, creeks and rivers, and abandoned farmsteads and villages. Grafenwöhr was the larger, at 53,000 acres. Hohenfels covered 40,000 acres. These were ideal for training combat units that might be called upon to fight the Soviet Union's Eighth Guards Army and the First Guards Tank Army that waited just beyond the Iron Curtain — the border between East and West Germany.

The battalion's tanks were loaded onto railway flatcars — one tank per flatcar — that rolled on narrow tracks into Henry Kaserne in Munich. The M48A1 tank was about twenty-four inches wider than the flatcar, so driving skill and the help of ground guides, i.e., soldiers who walked in front of the tanks and gave the drivers hand signals as they carefully guided the drivers onto the train, were important in getting the tanks positioned properly on the flatcar. German railroad workers walked alongside with measuring sticks — when they were satisfied that a tank was positioned correctly, they would signal the ground guide, who in turn signaled the tank driver.

The engine of the tank was then shut down, the turret hatches were locked, and the tank was fastened to the flatcar with wedge-shaped chock blocks and steel cables.

When the destination was Hohenfels, as it was on 24 October 1960, the tanks were driven off the train at Parsberg, a village about midway between Nuremberg and Regensburg. Trucks and jeeps would be driven on highways from Munich to the Hohenfels training area. A road march procession of tanks and other vehicles would then drive from Parsberg to their bivouac sites inside the Hohenfels training area.

Nick Holloway's tank was directly behind Section Sergeant Earl Crawford's tank. Then followed a long string of Headquarters Company's vehicles. At the tail of the column were Tank Section's other two tanks. The first training exercise was to be a night road march — from Parsberg to somewhere in the middle of the Hohenfels training area chosen to be the company's bivouac.

It was still daylight when the company stopped on the road inside the training area until it became dark. The men were given a meal consisting of boxes of World War II -vintage C-rations. Cooks and kitchen police (KP) helpers served coffee carried in insulated containers from vehicle to vehicle.

When darkness came, men mounted their vehicles and the column started moving again. Lieutenant Jensen lead the procession in his jeep. Captain Elliott and Lieutenant Dolan had gone ahead to find the company's bivouac site and to select positions for the command post (CP) and the various sections.

Jensen was the one who knew the map coordinates of the company's destination, and it was his responsibility to lead the column to that place.

All vehicles were to run without lights. That was part of the training. Each tracked vehicle, jeep, and truck had a narrow slit with a white light showing in the front — a similar small red light was mounted on the rear of the vehicle. The purpose of these small lights was to avoid collisions in the darkness. Also, those blackout lights were hooded, so that they would not be visible to aircraft. The only interior lights allowed were dim red lights. Once the soldiers' eyes had adjusted to the dark, any bright light would negate their night vision. The road ran alongside a river, and drivers needed to be extra careful driving in the dark with a river embankment close by.

Nick's crew was in good spirits — they had been excited about coming to the field, away from the monotony of the everyday maintenance and training routine of being in the kaserne.

A soft rain began to fall.

An hour went by, and the only disruptions were the

occasional stops and starts caused by the accordion effect of single-file movements of vehicles and men. It got cooler, then cold — the men put on their field jackets and leather gloves with woolen liners.

The rain came down steadily, and a little harder.

At about 2330, the signal was given for the column to halt. After a few minutes, Nick and Sergeant Stark got down from the tank, and walked up to where Crawford had just returned from the lead jeep.

"What's happening, sergeant?" Stark said.

"The lieutenant fucked up — he thinks he missed a turn off the road a while back. If you ask me, he couldn't find the latrine even if there were billboards to show him the way."

The jeep with the lieutenant turned around and sped back past the stalled column. Men were not in good spirits any longer, as the truth and the rumors ran down along the string of tanks, armored personnel carriers, five-ton trucks, two-and-a-half ton trucks, three-quarter ton trucks, ambulances, and jeeps.

"Nick, what's going on?" Hal Washington asked.

"Lieutenant fucked up — missed the turn — got us lost," Nick replied.

"Geez, he must not be very smart," Hal said.

"Yeah — he'd probably try to sell bras to the women on Tahiti," Nick said.

The men were cold, wet, tired, and frustrated. They were also angry — angry at being inconvenienced, and angry at the truth in the Army acronym SNAFU. But what could they do but grumble and wait?

Nick huddled with Sergeant Stark, Vince, and Hal Washington, the loader who had replaced Danny Maguire. Nick knew the situation was out of his control, and there was nothing he could say or do about it. Lieutenant Jensen screwed up — maybe he couldn't read a map. Nick thought about how it would have been if Lieutenant Anderson and

Sergeant Cervenka had been leading them. They wouldn't have gotten lost.

As they waited, Nick thought about Sergeant Crawford and that creepy-looking German criminal — Manfred — Manfred Neumann. The two of them made a sinister pair — partners in crime. Nick thought about his own role in Crawford's schemes. Nick had no doubt that Crawford could cause him trouble — could get him a dishonorable discharge — or worse. And there was something between Crawford and Captain Elliott that Nick couldn't put his finger on. He didn't trust either one of them.

After about twenty minutes, the jeep with Lieutenant Jensen returned. He had found where he should have led the company in the first place. The order came over the tank's radio for all vehicles to do a 180-degree turn and head back in the direction from which they had come.

Now Nick's tank was at the very tail of the column instead of near the head.

By the time his tank turned off the road, and headed up the hill toward the wooded bivouac area, Nick could see a muddled mess. All vehicles now had their full lights on. Vehicles were stuck in the mud, facing this way and that, all over the hillside. One of the three-quarter ton trucks and its trailer had turned over on their sides.

Lieutenant Jensen came to Nick's tank and told Sergeant Stark that the tanks were needed to help make order out of the chaos. The four tanks of Tank Section were to be used to pull the trucks and jeeps up the slippery hillside, into the woods, and onto dryer ground.

Nick and his crew of Tank 2 went to work. It took at least an hour to get all of the company's vehicles and equipment up off the muddy slope and into the dryer woodland above.

Once they had taken up their defensive positions in the perimeter around the command post, Sergeant Stark went off to meet with the other tank commanders. Nick volunteered to stand guard so that Vince and Hal could go to the mess truck and get some hot soup. Later, they would divide up the night guard duties — one man for each tank had to be awake on guard all night.

Nick sat on the back deck of the tank, feeling the dying warmth emitted by the now idle engine. He sat there, numb tired, and he dreamed.

Nick dreamed about making love with Carol Anne Benjamin. They were not memories of what had been, but rather dreams of what could have been — and, hopefully, would still be. Nick hadn't seen Carol for two days, but he dreamed about her often. After this long night, after the tank had been hidden in the woods, high above the road and the river, and the trip wires put in place — now he could sit on the tank and dream. He planned romantic dates with Carol. He would take her to the Spatenhaus, at Residenz Strasse 12, famous for its good food. And, if she wanted, they would go to the Osteria Italiana Lombardi — her favorite. He would take her to the noisy Karl Valentin Tanzlokal where they would dance for hours. He would then take her to the intimate and quiet Zigeuner Keller for a nightcap. And when she trusted him enough — he would take her to Garmisch on a weekend — for skiing and après-ski. They would stay at the Goldenes Hart Hotel, and they would make love until dawn. He was ready for all of that.

Carol was young, and she hadn't slept with a man yet — Nick was almost sure of that. They had kissed passionately. He had tried to go further but she wouldn't let him. Nick dreamed about what it would be like.

When the rest of the crew came back with his chow, Nick ate — he also continued to dream. He then set up his pup tent near the tank with Vince, and tried to go to sleep.

Had she ever slept with another man?

30

NEVER EXPLAIN — NEVER APOLOGIZE

Thursday, 27 October

One thing that Earl Crawford's father drummed into his head was that not only must a military leader be competent and confident — he must also appear to be so. His subordinates must assume that he knows all — that he can do anything — and that he never makes mistakes.

That trait, combined with his natural meanness, and his lack of empathy for the sufferings of others, made Crawford a bully. A case in point was his treatment of Sergeant Hollis Stark. Now that Danny Maguire was gone, Stark was Crawford's next target.

Crawford resented Stark's World War II veteran status — that he had served under General Patton; that Stark had even received a letter of commendation from Patton; and that he had earned a Bronze Star for bravery in the Battle of the Bulge.

Stark was a competent tank commander. He also was a man who was not impressed by those who flaunted their authority in front of, and toward, their subordinates. Stark never worshipped the ground his superiors walked on, or even pretended to do so. So, it was inevitable that Stark and Crawford would co-exist in Tank Section in a thinly veiled state of antagonism. This was not okay with Sergeant Crawford.

"Stark — where are you going?" Crawford said.

Tank Section was still at Hohenfels. Hollis Stark was holding his duffle bag, ready to walk to the mail truck that was about to leave for Munich.

"Munich. I've got a three-day pass to go home to Munich for my wife's birthday."

"Forget that — I need you here."

"But you signed off on my leave request — you knew I was going."

Several tankers stood nearby, listening to the exchange between the two sergeants.

"No matter. Now I'm telling you to forget that nonsense."

"Sergeant Crawford, it's Charlotte's birthday tomorrow. I promised her that I would take her to her favorite restaurant to celebrate. She's expecting me."

"Don't you talk back to me, Stark. I'm your superior here, and I say you stay."

"Okay, if that's the way you're going to be, I'll go talk with Lieutenant Jensen.'

Crawford had a self-satisfied look on his face. He puffed up his chest, put his hands on his hips, and posed for the men looking at them.

"Go right ahead — but I've already cleared it with the lieutenant. He said he'd back me up all the way."

Stark wilted like a balloon when a hole is punched in it. Defeated, he put his duffel bag on the ground and sat on it. He put his head in his hands.

31

NICK WRITES TO CAROL

Hohenfels
2 Nov. 1960

Miss Carol Benjamin
c/o Arndt Meier
Isabella Strasse 6
Munich 80798

Dear Carol,

Greetings from the Bavarian hinterland and the life of a tank soldier in the field. I would much rather be in Munich and spending time with you!

I would have written to you earlier, but we've been busy with training and maintenance. Over the weekend, we had a 3-day field problem that was exhausting. Our tank broke down during the second night, and we all had to stay awake and work on it until it was fixed. Actually, we didn't get any sleep for 3 days and nights!

Hey, what am I doing, going on like this, complaining? You know how much I detest complaining and whining and using excuses as reasons.

Here's something funny that happened today. We got up this morning, ate breakfast, and then lined up for formation before we started the day. First Sergeant Dixon, he's the top non-commissioned officer in the company, scolded us because someone had left a sandwich and some cookies inside his sleeping bag. Dixon said, "Food left in your tents will attract insects and rodents. When I inspect your tents tomorrow, I want to find them neat and tickety-boo." It was hilarious! What made it so funny was the tone of voice he used — "…insects and rodents …neat and tickety-boo…" I'm still laughing inside at that. I'll try to imitate him for you the next time we are together.

Did you know that there are wild boars in the woods here at Hohenfels? I haven't seen any yet, but I can sure smell them, and last night I heard one grunting somewhere near my tent.

Forgive me, Carol, I've been going on and on about myself again. How have you been? How are your classes going? How did that German grammar test go, the one you were worried about? How are the Meiers? And Barb, how's she?

You probably know by now, Vince said he talked with Barb about it before we left Munich, that he has broken off completely with … she who will not be named … and wants to date Barb only. I think it was an easy decision for him. He really likes Barb.

I keep thinking about the good times we had together. And there will be more!

We're scheduled to return to Munich on the 18th. After that … let the games begin!

Thinking of you often,

Nick

32

EBERSDORF FARM

Despite that Warner Kaserne thing, which was that bastard Mo Banyan's fault, Earl had not given up on drawing Nick Holloway into his schemes. That was the only way he could see to control Nick, and to prevent him from exposing the black-market operation to higher authorities — short of murdering Nick, and that was out of the question.

Earl wondered why Nick hadn't already exposed the black-market operation? Whatever the reason was, it worked to Crawford's benefit.

About a week after the SNAFU, Tank Section had a day devoted to tank maintenance. Crawford told Nick that he would be his driver for the day, and that he should get Lieutenant Jensen's jeep. Then they would be off on a little trip.

Nick was pleased that he would no longer have to be the point person in buying up cigarette ration stamps among the non-smokers in the 28th Infantry at Warner Kaserne. So far, Crawford hadn't pressed the matter by asking Nick to do something similar in other units. His guess was that Nick would refuse to do it if forced, but that he didn't want to have to actually say no. Maybe Nick was afraid that he would be charged with disobeying a direct order again. But that didn't make sense to Earl. Nick had already disobeyed a direct order, when that cowardly Danny Maguire wouldn't evacuate the tank during the hang fire. Surely in this case, Nick knew that what Crawford had asked him to do was illegal? The answer must be that Nick wasn't sure what the consequences would be, so he decided to be cautious and not say anything. Nevertheless, Crawford thought he had to keep a close eye on Nick — and, who knew — he might still relax and get involved in a way that Earl wanted him to. Earl didn't care if Nick hated him. Maybe, just maybe, he could use Nick's hatred and turn him into an enterprising young man like himself. Like he did with Johnny Foreman at Fort Bliss. But Nick was smarter than Johnny, a lot smarter. Johnny ended up getting killed on one of their business trips into Mexico. Crawford firmly believed that everyone — each and every single person, even Nick Holloway — was attracted to the idea of getting more money — by hook or by crook.

Nick drove and Crawford held a map. Earl directed Nick to drive to Schwandorf, and then to Cham, and finally on lesser and lesser roads to the village of Ebersdorf, about 12 kilometers from the Czech border.

In Ebersdorf they found the gasthaus Arbeiter's Ruhe — Worker's Rest. Inside they sat down at a table with Manfred Neumann.

"Manfred — you remember my associate, Nick Holloway?"

Manfred held out his hand for Nick to shake. Nick ignored the gesture.

"Aw, c'mon Nick — just a friendly handshake," Crawford said.

Nick took Manfred's hand. Manfred made a display of rigorous up and down hand shaking motions as though he were pumping water.

They ate sausages and hard rolls and drank beer, while Earl and Manfred talked business.

Nick listened carefully to their conversation. Devil number one sparring with devil number two. Which one would win?

Many of the others in the place were staring at Nick and Earl. Of course, they stood out in their U.S. Army uniforms. Both soldiers carried their standard issue Army pistols in holsters at their sides.

Finally, it was time to move on. Manfred went to his car, and Nick and Earl followed him with the jeep.

They drove east out of Ebersdorf. From a paved road to a gravel road, then a turn onto a dirt road into a forest and up a rather high hill. On the other side of the hill, at the edge of the woods, stood a stone house and a long L-shaped stone barn.

Nick followed Manfred and parked in the middle of the yard.

"There it is, and there is my brother, Aldo," Manfred said.

Manfred waved — Aldo stood motionless awaiting them in front of the barn.

To Earl, Aldo looked older than Manfred — maybe as much as ten years older. He was dressed in dowdy and dull brownish corduroy trousers and a blue workman's jacket. He wore calf length rubber boots. Manfred had told Earl that Aldo worked for the public works department for the city of Regensburg — mostly cleaning and repairing the sewers of the city. Unlike Manfred, Aldo showed no expression on his face. Earl couldn't tell whether Aldo was glad or unhappy to see them.

Earl shook Aldo's hand.

"Aldo — it is so good to finally meet you. Manfred has told me so much about you. All good, of course," Crawford said.

Manfred and Earl both laughed at Earl's joke. Aldo didn't laugh - he remained stoic.

Then they toured the large and empty barn.

"This is perfect," was Crawford's verdict when they finished going through the building.

"I'm glad you are pleased," Manfred said.

"We could actually drive a truck in and hide it if we had to. And we can build some bins to hold the different sized brass shell casings."

"It is okay then?" Manfred asked.

"Prima. Perfecto mundo. Ichiban," Earl replied.

"Good. Let's go into the house then and get down to brass tacks, as you Americans say," Manfred said, grinning widely.

Earl Crawford stood looking at the vista before him.

"So, this is your family's farm, Manfred?"

"This was our farm. Most of our land was sold by dad when he fell on hard times."

Manfred pointed to beyond the clearing.

"That was all our land. Someday, when we have enough money, we will get our farm back."

"Yes, yes — it is too bad," Crawford said.

Aldo Neumann had not said a single word yet. As he held a coffee pot he looked at Earl and spoke.

"Do you want cream and sugar?" Aldo asked, in English.

So, he does have a tongue. Earl said to himself.

"Ah — no, black is fine."

Nick sipped his coffee and looked and listened.

"Five hundred marks each month — that's a little high, isn't it, Manfred?"

"Look at it this way, sergeant. I have to give Aldo a piece of the action now. He deserves it."

"True — but 500 marks a month just to rent that old barn?"

"I should ask you for a thousand a month — we — Aldo

and I — we could lose the whole farm if this doesn't work out."

They went back and forth like that for about ten minutes. Finally, Crawford yielded.

"Okay, Manfred. You've got a deal. Five hundred a month, and here's my payment for the first month."

"Thank you, Sergeant Crawford — and here is the key for the barn. Aldo and I prefer that none of your men come into the house."

Crawford took the key.

"No problem about the house — nobody's going to stay overnight here. Just deliveries and pickups. Have you had any success in finding buyers for my brass yet?"

"I'm talking with two or three. I'll let you know when they agree to talk to you," Manfred said.

"In the meantime, we'll store the goods here. The first truckloads should be here in two or three days."

Aldo didn't wave goodbye. He just stood outside with his hands in his pockets.

Nick and Crawford drove off towards Ebersdorf, and then they headed back to Hohenfels.

Crawford tried to converse with Nick, but Nick responded only with one or few word answers to Earl's questions. Finally, Crawford decided to try something new.

Earl took a one hundred mark note from his wallet, folded it twice, and put it in Nick's right side field jacket pocket.

Nick looked down at Earl's hand as he put it into Nick's pocket.

"What's that for?"

"Oh — it's nothing — just a token of my appreciation for all that you've done for me lately."

Nick looked at Crawford with a pained expression.

"Look, sergeant, this is bullshit — I'm not your associate, or your partner, or anything of the sort. I just drove your jeep."

Nick took the bill out and handed it to the sergeant.

Crawford smiled, and then put the money back into Nick's pocket..

The next morning, Earl Crawford heard that Nick had treated all the men in Headquarters Company — he had taken a three-quarter ton truck into Parsberg the previous night, and bought one hundred marks worth of beer in snapper capper bottles.

All that next day, men were coming up to Sergeant Crawford and saying thank you for the party the night before.

33

CAROL WRITES TO NICK

Munich
Nov. 9, 1960

Specialist 4th Class Nicholas Holloway
HHC, Third Battalion, 34th Armor
Munich, APO 29

Dear Nick,

How nice it was to get your letter and to hear a little of what you are doing while training in the field. I can't imagine what it must be like to go without sleep for 3 whole days and nights! You must tell me all about it when you return to Munich.

Classes are good, and the grammar test went swimmingly, I even got an A on it!

The Meiers are the same. Frieda worries about Arndt's drinking. He says he doesn't drink too much, he just drinks often. From what I can see, he does both.

Ah, yes — Barb. She was so happy when Vince told her that it was over 'with that other girl.' I think Barb and Vince make a delightful couple. They both have really weird senses of humor, maybe that's why they get along so well. I'm happy for them.

I also think of you often, Nick. I understand that what you do can be dangerous, and I pray that you will be okay and not get hurt.

The only humorous things that happen here are about our director, Dr. Kienetz. He likes to be called Herr Professor Doktor Helmut Kienetz. He dresses very properly, in the old German style. He always wears a conservative bow tie, and has these ugly little wire-rimmed round glasses. He never smiles. Our nickname for him is *der Kalte*. He does know his German, but he's not a very good teacher. Good for laughs, though!

Some of us girls are cooking an authentic American Thanksgiving dinner, at the apartment of one of the host families. I would be so happy if you would join us on the 24th. What do you think? Can you make it that day? Let me know.

Stay safe!

With love,
Carol

34

SHOWDOWN

Saturday, 12 November

A wet snow had been falling all afternoon — now, as night approached, it was colder — the road was slippery in places. The jeep's headlights reflecting from the large snowflakes made it hard for Nick to see the road. He slowed down.

Sergeant Crawford was quiet after his tirade when they started out. He had gone on and on about the Neumann brothers — how much they had cheated him — how much they lied to him — how he should not have trusted them in the first place. Nick knew that the theft of empty brass shell casings had started — some had already been delivered to the farm for storage.

But he was totally wrong when he said that Nick was in with him on all of his crimes — stealing, selling stolen goods. Nick had nothing to do with any of that. He believed in honor in how one lives, and loyalty to the oath he took when he enlisted in the Army. Stealing and selling U.S. property was certainly not honorable.

So, why am I here? Why am I driving this jeep for this psychopath hiding behind the flag and his uniform? Because, Nick, you know why. In the Army, you do as you are told, or you will be in serious trouble — that's why. It's called disobeying a direct order, and that can get you a dishonorable discharge, at least. And you know you can't go home with that label pasted on your forehead. You wouldn't be able to hold your head up, to look your dad in the eyes. No, that can't happen. Sure, I disobeyed Crawford when Danny froze in that hang fire incident, but I hardly knew him then. I assumed he would be as understanding as Sergeant Cervenka would have been.

"Are you lost, Holloway?"

"No — didn't you see that car in the ditch back there? I just slowed down to see if anyone needed help."

"Forget it. I'm in a hurry."

It was dark, and still snowing when they got to the farm past Ebersdorf.

Crawford touched Nick's arm and signaled to him to stop just before where the road emerged from the trees.

"Shut off the lights," Crawford whispered.

The barn door was open wide, and light poured out from within. A large truck — a German truck — was there — backed into the barn.

Crawford had Nick back the jeep under the trees. They walked along the edge of the road until they reached the farmstead. Lights were on in the house as well as in the barn.

Crawford had his pistol in his hand as they approached the barn. Manfred Neumann was talking with his bodyguard Oskar. Another man was atop the bin that held the large empty brass ninety-millimeter shell casings. He was tossing them into the truck — one at a time.

"What's going on here?" Crawford asked, as he stepped into the light.

Manfred and the other two men looked at Crawford and Nick with wide, frightened eyes.

"What's the matter, Manfred — has the cat got your tongue?"

"Sergeant Crawford — my dear sir — I can explain this. Let me explain this to you."

"Good — I want to hear this. Start explaining. Those are my shell casings you're stealing."

He made a circular motion with his gun hand.

"I've got a buyer for you in Nuremberg. He needs the metal quickly, so I hired Erni and this truck to haul a load of brass tonight. Then I was going to contact you and give you the money."

"Bullshit. I don't believe you — you lying piece of scum. Why didn't you talk to me first? You're a crook, pure and simple, and both you and I know it. What I'm wondering is how much else you've cheated me out of."

"No, no — sergeant. I wouldn't cheat you. You are one of my best suppliers — why would I cheat you?"

"You'd cheat your own brother if there was a pfennig in it for you."

"No, he wouldn't," a voice behind them said, in English.

Aldo stood behind Crawford and Nick. He was holding a shiny nickel-plated pistol — pointed at Crawford.

Aldo walked closer.

"Manfred, my brother, would cheat me never."

"Naturally not, Aldo. Because blood is thicker than water," Manfred said.

Manfred, Oskar, and Erni relaxed.

Nick's mouth was dry, his knees felt like jello, and the muscles in his neck and shoulders were as tight as a bowstring.

"Put your pistol down, Sergeant Crawford," Aldo said.

Crawford dropped the Colt on the ground.

"Now, kick it off to the side."

Crawford complied.

"Now, sergeant, it looks like the shoe is on the other foot," Manfred said.

Manfred used German to tell the others.

The four Germans laughed.

"An American expression I learned from one of your crooked predecessors. *Auf Deutsch sagen wir, das Blatt hat sich gewendet.* The paper has turned itself over. Now what are we going to do?" Manfred said.

"Why don't you give me the money you owe for stealing from me?" Crawford said.

Manfred again used a German expression for the benefit of the others.

The Germans all laughed again.

Nick noticed that Aldo had relaxed, to the point of being open to an attempt by Nick to get the pistol out of his hand.

"Now, why should I give you back the money that I stole from you, fair and square," Manfred said.

Manfred seemed so sure of himself that he felt he could say anything, and do anything with impunity.

Nick interpreted Manfred's bravado, and Aldo's steady hand with the pistol, to mean that he and Sergeant Crawford were not going to leave the farm alive.

Aldo walked forward closer to Crawford, and pointed the pistol at the sergeant's head.

"You always thought you Americans were so much smarter than me," Manfred said.

Aldo was ignoring Nick.

"You talked to me like you were the great captain giving orders to a private. Well, sergeant — now it's my turn to give you some of your own medicine."

Manfred held his head back, and closed his eyes as he roared laughing.

He was having a good time.

Manfred slapped Crawford on the face — hard.

"Sergeant Crawford — I've not told you that Aldo and I fought against your cowardly American brothers in the shameful last war that we never should have lost. We were in the Ardennes — in December, 1944. Yes, we were there. I saw how weak the Amis were. They didn't follow orders, because they mistakenly believed that each man is an individual and should think for himself, and make his own decisions."

"Oh, yeah? Who won the fucking war?" Crawford responded.

The Germans laughed heartily.

"You bastards," Crawford said, as he took a step toward Manfred.

"Tut, tut, sergeant — Aldo has killed American soldiers before also, and he won't waste a second to send you to the cemetery as well."

"*Ich auch*," me too, a grinning Erni said from atop the pile of shell casings.

All eyes, including Aldo's, looked up, at Erni.

Nick quickly used his hand to chop Aldo's wrist — the shiny pistol fell to the floor. Crawford picked up the weapon, and Nick retrieved Crawford's .45.

Crawford signaled for Aldo to join the other Germans.

"You killed American prisoners of war — you bastards. I had a cousin who was murdered by you fucking animals at Malmedy."

Crawford shot Manfred in the heart. Then, in quick succession, he did the same to Oskar and Erni. Finally, he walked up to Aldo, stuck the snub-nosed gun barrel into his mouth, and pulled the trigger.

Aldo fell backwards. Blood spattered over the wooden bin behind him. After his body came to rest on the barn floor, there were no sounds — none.

Nick pinched his nostrils together in an attempt to stifle the bitter smell of gunpowder. His stomach roiled. His eyes were fixed on the four bodies in front of him.

Crawford stood like a statue, holding the shiny gun in the same place as when it entered Aldo's mouth. Finally, he lowered his arm and held the pistol at his side. He looked at the four bodies. He walked to each one. Looked carefully at each one, checking to see if any had a pulse. He stood as if ready to shoot again if any of them moved.

"You shot them — you killed them — you murdered them all," Nick said.

Crawford stared at Nick, and then back at the bodies.

"Shut up, Holloway. Here's what we're going to do. You saw what just happened here, didn't you? Aldo shot his brother and henchmen, and then he killed himself. You saw it happen — right?"

"Bullshit."

"Give me my .45 Nick — calm down, get your head straight, and hand me my .45."

Nick handed Crawford his pistol. Crawford returned it to his holster.

"Now, here's what we're going to do. Give me a hand here."

Crawford grabbed Aldo by the jacket and lifted his torso up. He wiped his fingerprints off of Aldo's gun, and put it in the dead man's hand.

"Holloway — give me a hand."

"Hell no — you're on your own now. You just shot four men — you murdered them."

"We can talk about that later. Now, we need to remove anything that would point to us being here."

Nick's thoughts were muddled — he couldn't understand how any man could shoot four others — in cold blood. He wondered how Crawford could be so calm about it. At least he seemed calm. It was normal, of course it was a normal thing Crawford had done. An enemy threatened you and you killed him before he killed you. That's what war was like.

Maybe, Nick wondered, maybe Crawford was like him in that he seemed calm on the outside when he was under stress, but inside, he was a mess?

No, the two of them were in no way alike. Nick knew Crawford was not right in his head. Maybe all that killing in

Korea had messed him up — screwed up his brain — really good.

Crawford walked around the scene — making sure there was nothing to indicate he and Nick had been at the scene.

"You shouldn't have done it. You shouldn't have killed them like that," Nick said.

"What are you going on about? You yourself know it had to be done. Aldo, or Manfred, would have killed us if we hadn't done what we did."

"We? What do you mean we? You shot these guys — not me."

Crawford let out a clipped laugh.

"Holloway — I owe my life to you. I just might put you in for a medal."

Sergeant Crawford laughed louder, and longer.

"But, sergeant — we had the guns, you could have got your money, and then we could have just left. You didn't have to shoot them."

"Hell, Nick — we'd be the bodies lying there if you hadn't put the hatchet on Aldo's arm. Funny how it's the little things that can mean so much in matters of life and death."

Crawford laughed. He sat down on a box and took out his handkerchief to wipe his eyes.

"It was murder, and you know it. I saw it. I saw it all — from start to finish. What are you going to do now, Crawford? Are you going to make it look like I shot them? Are you going to kill me too? You'll have to, you know. Because I saw it all — and when I report you, you're going to Leavenworth for the rest of your life — unless they fry you in the electric chair first."

"No — no — you're wrong. Nick — you won't report me. Because you're not a ratfink, for one thing — I know that — and because you are as involved in this as I am. You never turned me in before — why, I'll never understand. But now, you are my accomplice. No — Nick — you won't report me.

I think you have the guts to do it — but you're so smart and logical and you know how to weigh the pluses and minuses and see what they add up to. What you want them to add up to. I'm not worried about you, my boy."

"Don't call me your boy — and, I'm not your accomplice."

"But you still won't report me, will you?"

* * * *

Nick and Crawford were both silent for most of the drive back to Hohenfels.

At the company area, Nick parked the jeep and walked back to Tank Section's bivouac. Earl sat in the jeep. He held his head in his hands.

Nick could not get to sleep.

35

FÜRSTENFELDBRUCK

Monday, 14 November

Nick's mind, his conscience, and even his soul, had not given him any peace since the murders. He had stayed in his sleeping bag during the soldiers' free time on Sunday. At one point, he woke up with a start. He was in that barn, with those bodies, and all that red. And then, there were those red thumbs flying through the barn, like those bats that were also there. The red thumbs swooped around, steeply up and down, and then landed on each of the corpses — Manfred, Erni, Aldo, and Oskar. Nick sat up and shook his head to remove the pictures inside.

Vince came into the tent with a canteen cup of coffee and some food for Nick.

"Crawford just said we're going to some place called Fürstenfeldbruck air base, for a special assignment."

After World War II, U.S. armed forces took control of a German airfield at Fürstenfeldbruck — west of Munich. In November 1960, this airfield was being used to fly U.S. troops to Mediterranean bases to be ready to intervene, if needed, in the Congo crisis.

Seventeen African nations had gained their independence in 1960 — including the Belgian Congo.

The Congo had been a Belgian colony since the 1880s, and on 30 June 1960, Belgium gave the Congo its independence. Immediately, there was trouble. On 11 July, the country's richest province — Katanga — declared itself independent from the rest of the Congo. Belgian paratroops went in to protect Belgian citizens from the chaos, and on 12 July the United Nations decided to send in a peacekeeping force. The United States was afraid of the Soviet Union becoming involved to exploit the uncertain political situation, and the valuable copper mines in Katanga.

The Second Battle Group of the 28th Infantry — stationed at Warner Kaserne in Munich, was ordered to be part of the U.S. force. They were told to prepare for combat. They moved to Fürstenfeldbruck to be flown to Africa.

Tank Section — Nick Holloway's unit — was ordered to Fürstenfeldbruck to help in processing the infantry soldiers for their journey. Some of the other men of the Third Battalion, 34th Armor, were also involved.

Nick drove Lieutenant Jensen's jeep with the Lieutenant. Sergeant Crawford followed in a three-quarter ton truck with the other men of Tank Section.

At the airfield, they went to a large unused hangar that was now bustling with soldiers being processed for deployment. There were personnel people, medical people, small arms people, cooks, mechanics, and even a couple of chaplains.

Tank Section's main assignment was to help the cooks who had set up a kitchen and a serving line in one corner of the hangar. Vince Delvecchio and Hal Washington were part of that work detail. Nick was instructed by Crawford to sit at a table and help several small arms experts as they checked over weapons.

Each infantryman's M-1 rifle, or carbine, and/or pistol,

was quickly inspected, and coated with an oil-like substance that would inhibit rust once the men landed in a tropical setting. Any weapons needing repairs or adjustments were also taken care of.

Nick's job was simply to sit with a box of weapons receipt cards in front of him, and verify the weapon and its owner by looking at the man's weapon and identification card. A simple task, Nick thought.

Sergeant Crawford stood by — watching Nick. Instead of overseeing the kitchen and serving line, he stood against the wall, where he could keep an eye on Nick.

Neither of them had said anything on the drive from the farm back to their bivouac at Hohenfels. Nick had decided that he had to tell somebody about the murders, and he could feel that Crawford sensed it.

Shortly thereafter, Crawford told Nick to take a break. Paul Becker came from the kitchen to take Nick's place. Crawford crooked his finger to have Nick follow him.

Uh-oh. Here it comes, thought Nick. *Should I refuse to go? Should I fake a fainting spell? Should I run over to Captain Elliott and tell him everything?*

They went outside.

They walked into the shadows, about twenty feet away from the cement sidewalk and the light over the entrance door.

Crawford pushed Nick up against the hangar.

"I'm warning you, Holloway. If you so much as breathe one word of what happened … Believe me, I'll have your balls fried and served on a platter to a court-martial board. You know I can do it. I've got Captain Elliott wrapped around my little finger, it will be so fucking easy. You got away with disobeying me once, but that was because that piece of shit Dolan got in my way. But, next time you won't be so lucky. I'll make sure he's nowhere around. So, just keep quiet, okay?"

Nick had not looked at Crawford once. Nick stared into the distance, at nothing.

"Holloway — you got that? I'm asking you a question, soldier — do you understand me?"

"Sergeant — you murdered four men, four German civilians. When the police discover the bodies, they're going to come after you."

Nick didn't want to get into any trouble. He wouldn't be able to face his parents, other relatives, and friends back home if he were court-martialed. But this was murder.

"If they do, numb nuts, they'll be coming after us, you and me," Crawford said.

What madness.

"Sergeant, what you did, killing those men — it was wrong, and you know it was wrong."

"Holloway — what the fuck is the matter with you? You know it had to be done. It was them or us. Simple fact. Of course, the Army won't see it that way. And the German courts wouldn't see it like that. But, you and I know it had to be done. Now, I'm giving you a direct order — you keep your fucking mouth shut. You hear me?"

Nick was breathing hard, and he knew his face was flush. If he said no to a directive from Sergeant Crawford — the word *no*, in and of itself, could put him in trouble with the Army. Nick certainly couldn't argue morality with Sergeant Crawford — Nick wasn't sure where Crawford's moral base was, or even whether he had a set of moral values. Were Crawford's values based on immorality? Nick didn't know. All he did know was that he was stuck in the middle of a minefield of ethical eggshells.

Of course, Nick knew he should report the murders, but maybe Crawford was right, and in that case, he shouldn't report Crawford for the murder he committed. Like Crawford said, maybe Nick was as guilty of murder as if he had pulled the trigger himself.

"Maybe you're right, sergeant. Still — it was wrong — it was murder. The law says it's wrong, the Army's UCMJ says it's wrong, the Bible says it's wrong."

Sergeant Crawford looked like he was about to lose control of himself.

"You ... you smart ass shithead. I saw guys like you in Korea, and they — like you — were worthless on the battlefield. You hear me? Worthless sacks of shit — that's what they were. Always thinking about what is right and what is wrong. Don't you doubt for a fucking minute that I can't get you. Don't you ever forget — you're a fucking accomplice to the killing of four krauts."

Crawford had a tight, evil look on his face. He relaxed the expression, momentarily, and then he moved his face closer to Nick.

Crawford's fists were flexing as he raised his right arm. Then he opened his fist, and slapped the fatigue cap off of Nick's head.

Nick's mouth was dry. His body felt taut and jelly-like at the same time. His instinct was to fight — to smash Crawford's teeth in, and to bloody his face — to break his nose and punch his eyes out. But something inside him told Nick not to do that. The voice said that he was in a no-win situation, and that he had to remain passive. Crawford reached up and grabbed Nick's hair and smashed his head against the wall — twice.

"You understand me now, Holloway? I own you, and don't you forget it. I won't let you forget it. I'll make your life so miserable that you'll wish you could climb into the tank, turn on the gas, and end it all — just like your fucking yellow little buddy, Maguire."

Crawford spit in Nick's face. The spittle ran from Nick's forehead down— onto his nose and into his eyebrows.

Just then a colonel and his aide appeared on the sidewalk.

"What's going on over there? Is someone there?"

"It's okay, colonel. We're just taking a break and having

a friendly chat here, sir. You know how it is, sir— always educating," Crawford replied.

Crawford grinned at the colonel.

Nick rubbed the back of his head as he bent down to pick up his cap.

He wiped the spit off his face with his handkerchief, and followed Crawford back into the hangar.

I've got to talk to someone about this, or I'll go nuts.

36

SERGEANT CERVENKA

Tuesday, 15 November

Live with Honor — Die with Dignity. Those words, tattooed under a waving American flag on Cervenka's upper arm, impressed Nick Holloway. It was one of the first things that drew Nick to Sergeant Steve Cervenka. He had been Nick's section sergeant from when Nick arrived in Tank Section until recently, and then he was transferred to another company in the battalion.

Sergeant Cervenka was for Nick what an Army noncommissioned officer (NCO) should be. He had honor, courage, integrity, loyalty, and competence — all qualities that Nick admired and tried to live by himself. Nick thought that Cervenka's calm manner of dealing with all situations came from the confidence the sergeant had in his own ability to deal with anything that came up. There was no doubt in Nick's mind that Cervenka would be an excellent leader if they ever had to go into combat.

It was natural that Nick would seek out Cervenka, a man he trusted, to talk to about Sergeant Crawford and the murders at Ebersdorf. Nick felt a twinge of guilt that he hadn't confided in his best friend Vince, but then, he thought he knew Vince well enough to predict that Vince might do something rash, and that would only make things worse.

Nick walked to Sergeant Cervenka's tank and tent in Alpha company's bivouac.

"Nick — Nick Holloway. What a pleasant surprise. Long time, no see. How you been, Nick?"

"Oh, you know — picking 'em up and putting 'em down, one foot at a time."

"Good, good. How're you and Sergeant Crawford getting along?"

"Well, um, ah, actually — that's what I wanted to talk with you about."

"That bad, eh?"

A frown replaced Cervenka's happy face.

"Let's go sit under that tree, and you can tell me about it."

Nick was having second thoughts about confessing all to Steve Cervenka. What good could possibly come of it?

"Okay, what's going on?" Cervenka asked.

"Sergeant, I need some advice."

"I'll try. No promises, mind you — it all depends on what it is."

"Well, first of all, it is about Sergeant Crawford."

"What has he done?"

"Uh, let's slow down a bit. What I have to say would get him in a lot of trouble. And me, it could get me in trouble, too — trouble I don't need."

Cervenka's eyes looked for answers in Nick's. That was another thing Nick admired in him — Nick felt like the sergeant was paying total attention when he listened to you.

"And ..."

"And I don't know what to do about it." Nick said.

"Can you give me any details? Anything at all? It would be easier for me to advise you if I knew what has happened."

Nick picked up a small stick and used it to play with the dead leaves, twigs, and pine cones in front of him.

"Nick?"

Nick looked at him.

"Nick, I can't help you if I don't know what the problem is."

Nick stood up and brushed the leaves from his field pants. He paced back and forth. He was as confused as he had ever been. It wasn't fair, he thought, to bring a good man like Sergeant Cervenka into a mess like this.

"It was a mistake for me to bother you like this, sergeant."

"No bother, Nick. I would help you, if I could. But, I respect your right to find another way. Have you thought about talking to someone in your chain of command?"

"Well, Crawford is my immediate superior."

Both Nick and Cervenka laughed at that.

"And then there's Lieutenant Jensen. But I don't trust him. I don't think he's very smart, and I sense that Crawford manipulates him. There is Lieutenant Dolan, the executive officer, but I don't know, he's a good man, but he's so close to the CO ..."

"To your company commander, Captain Elliott."

"Yes, Captain Elliott. I don't really trust him either. Crawford seems to have something on the captain — I don't know what, though. But Crawford is his responsibility, and when the fit hits the shan on this, the captain is going to be right in the center of it."

"There you go, Nick. Captain Elliott's your man. If you feel you must get this out in the open, he's probably the best place to start."

"I guess."

Nick was sure he had made the right decision to not confide in Cervenka. After all, there was little that he could do about it. He would go to Lieutenant Anderson with the information, and then Anderson would go to... No, it was best to not go in that direction.

Nick walked back to Headquarter Company's bivouac and went directly to the command post tent.

"Sergeant Dixon, is the captain here?"

"Yes. What is it you want to see him about, Holloway?"

"It's personal."

"Ohh-kay. Let me ask if he can see you now."

Nick felt sweat beads on his forehead.

Dixon went through the door flap to the captain's office, and then he returned.

"Okay. The captain said he'd see you now."

Nick saluted the captain.

"At ease, Holloway. What's on your mind?"

Nick told him about Crawford's thefts and black market activities, and then he went into detail about the murders at Ebersdorf. When he had finished, Nick felt good, clean almost, in an odd sort of way.

"Sit down, Holloway. Make yourself comfortable."

Nick wondered why the captain didn't seem alarmed — why he hadn't put in calls right away to the MPs and the CID.

"Nick, I know you've been under a tremendous amount of stress lately, especially since your good friend Private Maguire died. Now, I'm no head shrink, but I can understand how such stress can play tricks with your mind. My best advice for you now is to try to relax, as much as you can."

The captain wrote on a piece of paper, and then handed the note to Nick.

"Here, take this to our medic, he'll give you something that will help you to relax. When we get back to Munich in a few days, I want you to arrange to see a psychiatrist at the Army hospital. They are good at dealing with cases such as yours. They'll help you get through all of this."

Nick wanted to vomit — the smells of stale cigar smoke and lingering farts didn't help.

Nick stood up and saluted his commanding officer.

"Thank you, sir."

"Quite all right, soldier. Take care of yourself now, you hear?"

Nick left the tent, went into the dark among the trees, and sat down. He crumpled the captain's note and threw it into the night. He realized that he had not cried since he joined the Army, almost three years before.

37

PARSBERG

Wednesday, 16 November

Sergeant First Class Crawford was losing his patience with Sergeant Stark. Okay, he had served in combat during World War II. But now he was an old man — just putting in his time until he could retire. Crawford preferred youth over experience in his tank commanders. He wouldn't admit to himself that combat veterans like himself and Stark were alike in many ways. The other tank commanders in Tank Section were still in their twenties. They submitted more readily to Crawford's ways than Stark did.

"Sergeant Stark — come here. How many times do I have to tell you not to use gasoline to clean the machine guns? Is your brain as burned out as your body is? It's against battalion policy — and it's not safe. You moron."

Crawford unloaded this criticism against Stark in front of Nick, Vince, Hal, and four other men of Tank Section.

Sergeant Stark stood with drooped shoulders, staring at the ground. Finally, he looked up at Crawford.

"Sergeant, you know that Battalion Maintenance is so stingy with the regulation solvent that the little they give us is not enough to do the job right. Also, you know that gas does a better job. We've been using gasoline for years. You must have used gas in Korea?"

"Don't tell me what I know or don't know, old man. I know this much, that if you don't follow my instructions — to the letter — instructions that are backed up by the battalion's Standard Operating Procedures (SOP), then I get into trouble. No one, not even old geezers like you, are going to get me into trouble."

Crawford looked at Nick with a long gaze, and then he walked away.

Nick went to Sergeant Stark and put his arm around the man's shoulders.

* * * *

Friday, 18 November

On the day the battalion was scheduled to return to Munich, Crawford picked out Hollis Stark for ridicule once again.

The men of Tank Section had struck their tents, and packed their personal belongings in their duffel bags.

"Stark, get over here — with your duffel bag."

"Here you are, sergeant," Stark said.

Crawford opened Stark's duffel, tipped it upside down, and shook it until all the contents were in a pile on the ground.

"You call that a neatly packed duffel bag? Holy cow, Stark, didn't you learn anything in that big war of yours? What kind of example are you setting for your men?"

All the muscles in Stark's body seemed to go limp.

Nick watched as this humiliation of his tank commander played out, once again.

Crawford used his foot to paw through Stark's things.

"What a fucking mess you've got here. You're a sorry ass excuse for a tank commander. I've often wondered how it was that a big war hero like you never got past E-5. Now, I understand."

You son of a bitch, thought Nick. You thief, you murderer, you mean son of a bitch.

"Get your shit and your crew together, Stark. We're moving out to the railhead in five minutes," Crawford said.

"But, Sergeant Crawford. Cut me a little slack here."

"What the fuck, Stark. Quit your fucking whining and get with the program. We can't wait all day on the likes of you."

* * * *

Nick sat on the back deck of his tank, leaning against the turret. The four tanks of Headquarters Company's Tank Section were parked along a hillside street in the village of Parsberg, waiting to be loaded onto a train for the return trip to Munich. The battalion had just completed one month of field training at the Hohenfels training area in eastern Bavaria.

"Hey, Holloway — you want to sit in on a game of five card stud?" said Phil Pavek, the new loader on tank three, and a protégé of Ben Bartlett.

"Fuck you," Nick said.

"Hey, a simple yes or no was all I wanted. Who put the burr under your saddle?"

"Forget it Phil. His Schatzi probably broke up with him — and he's angry at the world," Joe Flores said.

"Yeah — forget him," Ned Lafontaine said.

Nick wondered at the stupidity of the men around him. Not only their stupidity, but also their meanness. Joe Flores would cheat his own mother at cards if he could. Nick didn't wonder any less at the stupidity of the so-called leaders in his chain of command. All the way up the chain of command, it was the same, he thought.

My God, he thought, was he, himself, as stupid as all these people? He must be, because he was one of them.

Nick turned and spit on the turret — right in the middle of the big white star. He watched the phlegm dribble down, like a river flowing to lower ground, like piss flowing downward in the Army's hierarchy.

Okay, Vince was an exception. And Sergeant Stark was okay — he was competent, and he wasn't mean, not by nature at any rate. And Sergeant Cervenka, he was tops. Also, Nick had to exempt Lieutenant Dolan, the executive officer of Headquarters Company, and First Sergeant Dixon. But that's what — only a handful of the many who had the power of life and death over young soldiers like Nick and the others.

Nick's head was swimming in a sea of negatvitity.

For instance, the field training the battalion had just completed. The first exercise was that night road march to Headquarters Company's bivouac area. It turned out to be a real SNAFU. Nick had griped about the incident for several days. He finally quit complaining when Vince reminded him that things would have been worse if Sergeant Stark hadn't directed them so well and so fairly. Vince told Nick that he was taking Sergeant Stark for granted. Nick conceded that Vince was right. He had to admit to himself that he had more than grudging admiration for Stark.

Then there was the broken track on their tank. Vince had gone back to Munich for a few days to have a wisdom tooth pulled. Hal Washington, the loader who replaced Danny Maguire, was filling in as driver until Vince returned.

Nick agreed with Sergeant Stark's decision to have Hal drive — it would give him valuable experience.

The decision was a mistake. Hal's driving skills and judgment were poor.

Sergeant Stark had talked to Hal over the intercom as the tank sat astride a rutted trail under the trees a short distance up a hillside. Tank Section was hidden under the trees, with engines idling, waiting for the order to move out down to the valley. The trail in front of the tank took a sharp turn about thirty meters ahead, so Stark had pointed this out to Private Washington and cautioned him to not get the tank tracks into the ruts when he made the turn on the trail. The risk was high that a sharp turn while the tracks were channeled into ruts would break the track. That is exactly what happened.

Stark reamed Hal out loudly, and then the sergeant calmed himself and tried to make it an opportunity to teach Hal about driving a fifty-two ton tank over rough terrain. Here was a textbook example of how not to drive a tank. Also, Stark made sure that Hal learned what hard work it was to fix a broken track.

At least one of the section's four tanks had broken down every day. Broken tracks, broken center guides and lost track end connectors, broken torsion bars, engines that wouldn't start for various reasons, dead batteries, oil and hydraulic fluid leaks, broken or worn out linkages between the driver's compartment and the transmission at the rear of the tank, radios and intercom equipment that failed, fuses blown, and weapons jammed, machine gun barrels burned out, other weapon components broken, and radios that failed for no apparent reason. It seemed to Nick that many of these problems were not caused by operator misuse or abuse. The M48A1 Patton medium tank was just not a reliable machine. Nick found himself starting to use the phrase worthless piece of junk, but he caught himself after the first couple of slips because he didn't want to further hex the crew's luck.

Nick vowed to himself to pay closer attention to tank maintenance, and to be more insistent on bringing potential problems to Sergeant Stark's attention, and getting things fixed as soon as he spotted them.

One day, they had run the tank on field exercises supporting an infantry company. Nick got more and more anxious as the day wore on — he was becoming accustomed to asking himself when the tank would break down instead of if the tank would break down. When the infantry exercises were completed, Sergeant Stark told the crew they were heading back to the bivouac area for a hot meal and some needed sleep. They were within a mile of the bivouac area when the tank ran out of gas, unlike the other three tanks, which made it back to the bivouac.

The company's bulk gas tanker trucks were all being used to refuel the tanks of the line companies of the battalion — therefore, a five-ton truck was sent to bring fuel to Nick's tank. The truck was loaded with dozens of five-gallon jerry cans full of gasoline. Nick and the rest of the crew, including Hollis Stark, had to unload the heavy gas cans from the truck, schlep them about ten meters to the tank, and then hoist them up to the tank's back deck, where they were poured through a funnel into the tank's gas tank.

All of these memories, and visions of Carol Benjamin, filled Nick's tired mind as he sat there on the back deck of the tank, waiting for the order to load the tank onto the train.

Lieutenant Jensen drove up the street in his jeep to where Tank Section was lined up.

Curious German civilians — men, women, boys and girls — young and old — surrounded the tanks. Nick wondered — do they see us as conquerors or occupiers? Do we really represent their last best hope — saviors of a sort — a bastion protecting West Germany from the communists, as our leaders said?

"Let's go men — mount up — crank 'em up — be ready to move down to the loading ramp. I'll let you know when to move," Sergeant Crawford said.

"Where's Stark?" Vince asked.

Vince had been dozing on the back deck also — on the other side of the main gun tube from Nick.

No one had seen Sergeant Stark since they arrived in Parsberg over an hour earlier.

Tank engines turned over, coughed, and then roared to life.

Hal Washington was ready to climb through his loader's hatch on top of the turret.

"Oh, no — no, no, no," Hal said, as he motioned for Nick to take a look.

Nick stuck his head into the open tank commander's cupola hatch.

Sergeant E-5 Hollis Maynard Stark, of Senatobia, Mississippi, veteran of World War II, husband of Charlotte, father of teenagers Jeffers, Jackie, and Jordie, was unresponsive as he lay face up on the floor of the tank turret. An empty wine bottle lay beside him.

Nick climbed down into the turret — the smell of vomit caused Nick to gag. He pulled out his handkerchief and held it over his nose. Stark's face was covered with puke. Nick checked for a pulse but found none. He used his handkerchief to clean Stark's face as best he could.

Nick told Hal to keep his mouth shut about what he saw, and then Nick whispered to Vince.

"We've got to keep this quiet, at least until we get the tank on the train."

Vince drove and Nick acted as tank commander and ground guide. When Lieutenant Jensen gave the word, they drove the tank to the loading ramp and drove onto a flatcar. When the German railroad inspectors were satisfied, the crew put wedge-shaped wooden chock blocks in front of and behind the tracks, and tied the tank to the flatcar with steel cables.

This was serious. They couldn't just lock up the tank with Stark still inside. Nick told Hal to run and find a medic — it was possible that Stark was still alive, or could be brought back to life. Then Nick had Vince go to Billy Dryden and ask him to help them get Stark up and out of the tank turret.

Nick's mind was racing. He wanted to keep Sergeant Crawford and Lieutenant Jensen out of this for the time being. If they could only get Stark into the passenger car before Jensen and Crawford started their ranting.

Germans were watching them. A silent crowd, watching

the soldiers of Tank Section. Nick imagined he could feel them thinking: how could this mob of Americans and their drunken sergeant ever protect them from the Red Army? How had they lost a war to these guys?

Nick cut off a laugh at the absurdity of it all.

A medic arrived when they got Sergeant Stark into the passenger car. Hollis Stark was indeed dead. The medic's best guess was that he had aspirated — choked on his vomit.

Nick sent Hal to find Sergeant Crawford and Lieutenant Jensen.

"He was nothing but a drunk," Ben Bartlett said.

Ben and Joe Flores and Ned Lafontaine laughed.

Nick put Ben down with one punch. Then he knocked the wind out of Joe with a power punch to Joe's solar plexus. Ned cowered behind his seat.

38

CHAPLAIN REYNOLDS

Munich
Saturday, 19 November

The men of Tank Section spent Saturday morning cleaning the tanks and other equipment. The usual loud playfulness was subdued. Nick found himself going about his tasks without any sense of enthusiasm, or even joy at being home from the field — back in Munich. He had trouble even trying to think about Carol. The thoughts came, collided with many darker thoughts, and then faded.

First — all those guys who died at Grafenwöhr. Nick was still haunted by visions of red thumbs. Then Danny, poor Danny, who just gave up on life. Then four Germans, murdered. Now this — Sergeant Stark, gone.

"You'll see, Nick, everything's going to be okay," Vince said.

Hal Washington gave Nick a thumb up.

Nick repeatedly asked himself what he should do. What could he do? He had gone to the captain and told him about Crawford, but the captain thought Nick was crazy. Maybe it would be better to go higher, to someone at battalion headquarters? No, Nick rejected that idea. They'd go along with Captain Elliott. Okay, what to do then?

At the noon formation, the first sergeant announced that there would be a memorial service for Sergeant Stark on Tuesday, in the Henry Kaserne chapel. His body would then be flown to the States for a proper funeral and burial.

Nick remembered the chaplain who helped Danny Maguire back in September. Nick even remembered his name — Captain Reynolds, Bruce Reynolds. Nick felt that he could trust Chaplain Reynolds to keep his mouth shut, if Nick asked him to, and wasn't that a chaplain's duty? At any rate, Nick wanted to ask the chaplain if it would be okay for him, Nick, to speak at Stark's memorial service.

* * * *

Sunday, 20 November

"Now — Specialist Holloway — is it okay if I call you Nick? How can I help you?"

"Please, sir — I don't want to take up much of your time. If you're busy, I can come back some other time."

"No — no — this is a good time, and I'm not too busy."

Nick thought about what he wanted to say.

"First of all, I wanted to ask you if I could say a few words at the memorial service for Sergeant Stark on Tuesday? I was on his tank crew."

The chaplain made a note on a sheet of paper.

"Yes, Nick. That will be fine. I'll call on you at the proper time in the service."

"Thank you, sir."

There followed an awkward silence.

"Was that all, Nick?"

"Well, you see, sir — captain — chaplain, I mean — I've got these questions."

Nick's mind raced — he had to stall, he couldn't jump right into things. What if he couldn't trust the chaplain?

"Okay — fire away. I might be able to answer your questions — some of them, at least."

Chaplain Bruce Reynolds was a distinguished looking man of about forty. His Army haircut showed the beginnings of graying and his face was smooth and pink — signs of a man who didn't smoke, and who didn't spend a lot of time outdoors. He was about the same height as Nick, and his posture was the model of a military man.

"Okay. You have spoken about Jesus' message of love one another, love your enemies even, turn the other cheek, and all that stuff."

"Yes, Jesus did say that, several times — go on."

"Well — I was wondering — the Army teaches us to give tit for tat — and then some more — not to turn the other cheek."

"I see, and you can see the contradiction there, can't you?"

"Well, sir — I was just wondering — is there something I missed — something I don't understand?"

Chaplain Reynolds leaned back in his chair.

"Nick — that is a great question. I've asked myself that many times. I don't know the real answer, or even if there is a real answer. We are both soldiers in the United States Army. We know that soldiers are trained to kill and destroy — not to turn the other cheek and love our enemies. But, the fact remains — that is what Jesus taught us to do. For myself, I've tried to follow Jesus in my personal life, while still doing my job for the Army. I do refuse to carry a weapon, though."

Chaplain Reynolds raised his cheeks up to his eyes, and widened his mouth as though he was hurting.

"I guess that wasn't too helpful, huh?" Reynolds said.

"It's okay. I guess part of what I'm learning is that there aren't any easy answers."

"Well, Nick — I think Jesus did give us some clear and

easy answers — it's just so darn hard sometimes to follow what he taught was the right thing for us to do."

Nick hesitated as he gathered the words for his next question.

"Who needs religion, captain? Isn't it enough to just try and live a moral and ethical life?"

Chaplain Reynolds chuckled.

Now the chaplain stopped a few seconds, before he spoke again.

"That's another good question. I believe people do need a structured spiritual life in communion with others. Worshipping God together builds a special bond among seekers as well as believers. Also, it is a time of learning — a structured spiritual life involves constant learning and attempts to understand God, and what he wants for us. And you are right about living an ethical and moral life. Much of what we consider moral and ethical comes to us from the Bible — in the Ten Commandments, in the Beatitudes, and in Jesus' message of love one another."

Nick pursed his lips and furled his eyebrows.

"Was that helpful, Nick?"

They sat in silence for a while. Nick sensed that the chaplain was wrestling with some of the same questions that he was struggling with.

Finally, Chaplain Reynolds looked up at Nick again.

"Were those all of your questions?"

"What? Oh, no — no, I've got lots of questions."

"I've got time, Nick."

Nick twisted back and forth in his chair.

"Captain Reynolds, what is my purpose in life? What am I supposed to be doing with my life?"

"Well, the Bible has plenty of answers to that question. For example — Micah, chapter six, verse eight says: *He has told you, O mortal, what is good; and what does the Lord require of you but to do justice, and to love kindness, and to walk humbly with your God?"*

Nick fidgeted some more as he repeated the words to himself — *to do justice.*

It was like water building up behind a dam after a deluge, ready to burst forth. But ever since he bared everything to Captain Elliott. Nick had held back. Would the chaplain also think that Nick was crazy? Was he really under too much stress? How long before the dam would break, and he could talk about it again?

"Yes — no — I mean, what is my duty morally — to act on certain information I have regarding someone else's crimes?"

"What are you talking about, Nick? Can you be more specific?"

"No — I mean, yes — I mean, I could be more specific ..."

Chaplain Reynolds let Nick work through whatever was going on in his head — at least, that was what Nick thought was the reason why the chaplain didn't say anything.

Finally, the chaplain spoke.

"Nick, somehow I knew that your wanting to talk with me was about more than your religious questions. I'm not going to press you for details. I am worried about you, though. You seem to be carrying a lot on your shoulders right now. And the secrets you are protecting are causing you a great deal of distress. Have you been able to talk with anyone else about this? Someone you trust? A friend or buddy — or a girlfriend?"

That last word stung as Nick heard it. He wished he could talk more openly with Carol — really talk with her — talk about it all — and what he should do about it all. About Sergeant Crawford mostly, but also about losing Danny, and whether he should stay in the Army, which he doubted now — and if he didn't stay in the Army, then what should he do with his life — and how he felt about Carol — and what did all that mean?

"I've told my buddy, Vince. But no — no, I didn't — I just told him what he already knows. I can't talk with Vince about how I feel — how I really feel. We're men and we're soldiers — we don't do that. We don't cry, we don't whine — we just say yes, sir — and I'll try, sir. But Carol — my girlfriend — oh, how I do want to tell her, but I'm scared. I'm afraid she will think I'm weak — that I'm a scaredy cat — not a real man. I don't know — I just don't know."

"Do you love her, Nick?"

"Oh, yes — chaplain — sir. I love her — I'm sure of it."

"Then you have to tell her, Nick. It's okay to tell her. Then listen to her — listen to what she has to say. If she thinks you're weak for revealing your feelings — then she isn't the woman for you."

Nick sensed that Captain Reynolds knew there was something serious — something so deep, that Nick couldn't talk about it, not yet, even in confidence.

"Nick, I don't need to know the details of what is bothering you, but I am concerned about you. Something is eating you up inside, and I want you to think about this: be honest with yourself, and with others. As Jesus said, 'the truth shall set you free.' Hold to that, Nick, and when you are ready to step into the open, you will feel peace and freedom — more than you can imagine."

"Thank you, captain, sir."

39

MEMORIAL SERVICE

Saturday, 19 November

Nick called Carol as soon as he could on Saturday afternoon. It was good to hear her voice again. As much as he didn't want to be negative with her, one more time, as it were, he told her about Sergeant Stark. He hinted that there was more to tell her about Sergeant Crawford.

"Can you come for the Thanksgiving meal on Thursday?" Carol asked.

"Yes, yes, yes — I'm so looking forward to it."

"Oh, there will be good food, I promise."

"Now, I forget, where is it again?"

"The address is Wilhelm Strasse 11, apartment 3B. The family name is Osterheid — Werner and Ilse Osterheid."

"Thanks. When should I be there?"

"We plan to eat at about one o'clock, so any time before that."

"I'll be there."

* * * *

Tuesday, 22 November

On the day of the memorial service, Nick and Vince put

on their dress green uniforms and walked over to the chapel. Hal Washington had also dressed, and said that he and some friends were going to sing at the memorial service. None of the other soldiers in Tank Section went. Sergeant Crawford didn't go, and Nick heard that Lieutenant Jensen was going to a casino at Bad Wiessee for the afternoon and evening.

When Nick and Vince entered the chapel, the chaplain's assistant was playing the electronic organ. The music was *Abide with Me*.

The prelude finished, Chaplain Bruce Reynolds stood and faced the people in the pews.

"Good afternoon and greetings — Mrs. Stark and children, and to those who served with Sergeant Hollis Stark and are here to help celebrate his life. I would like to begin with a word of scripture. The gospel of John, chapter fourteen, verses one to three. *'Let not your heart be troubled: ye who believe in God, believe also in me. In my Father's house are many mansions: if it were not so, I would have told you. Now, I go to prepare a place for you. And when I go and prepare a place for you, I will come again, and receive you unto myself; that where I am, there you may be also.'* The Word of the Lord."

Chaplain Reynolds closed the Bible that he had read from the lectern, and walked down into the aisle between the attendees.

"Charlotte, Jefferson, Jacqueline, and Jordan — Colonel Strickland, Captain Elliott, Specialists Holloway and Delvecchio, and private Washington, and all the rest of you who knew and loved Sergeant Hollis Stark."

The chaplain exuded a sense of calm assurance, sincere kindness, and command of his goal of bringing comfort to the Stark family and to Sergeant Stark's colleagues.

"Hollis Maynard Stark was born in Cleveland, Mississippi, on 12 March 1920. He volunteered for the Army in September 1942, and served with bravery and competence as a tank soldier in North Africa, Sicily, Normandy, Luxembourg, and

Germany until the war ended in May 1945. When the war ended, he stayed in the Army. He would have been able to retire in two more years. Hollis and Charlotte were married in 1945, in Senatobia, Mississippi, which is their home now. Charlotte and the children will accompany Hollis back to Senatobia where he will be buried sometime next week."

Chaplain Reynolds paused and looked around at the people gathered. Nick had the sense that the chaplain had looked directly at him with eyes that said *don't worry – all is well with Hollis Stark*.

"I knew Hollis Stark somewhat – we had talked briefly several times. I know that at heart he was a dedicated soldier – he wanted to be seen as a soldier's soldier."

Vince jerked a little, and pulled out his handkerchief.

"I've talked with some of you who worked with him. I'm not breaking any confidences, or announcing any bombshell news, when I say that Hollis Stark was not a perfect man. Not a perfect soldier, and not a perfect family man. But then – who is perfect? Well – no one is perfect – does it matter to God? No, it doesn't. *Through many dangers, toils, and snares I have already come; tis grace has brought me safe thus far, and grace will lead me home.* Ah, yes – that amazing grace – that blessed gift of God called grace, that saves us even though we are not perfect. Don't worry about Hollis Stark, he is in good hands. Let me conclude by saying a prayer for Hollis. Dear God – we thank you for the life of this man – Sergeant Hollis Stark – the man we loved, and admired, and knew – for he was a child of yours – and in spite of his imperfections, he was still worthy of your compassion, and of our respect. Take good care of him so that we might see him again in time, and enjoy his company."

The chaplain paused.

There was silence in the chapel.

"*The Lord is my shepherd; I shall not want. He maketh me to lie down in green pastures. He leadeth me beside the still waters.*

He restoreth my soul: He leadeth me in the paths of righteousness for His name's sake. Yea, though I walk through the valley of the shadow of death, I will fear no evil; for thou art with me; Thy rod and thy staff they comfort me. Thou preparest a table before me in the presence of my enemies. Thou anointest my head with oil; my cup runneth over. Surely goodness and mercy shall follow me all the days of my life: And I will dwell in the house of the Lord forever."

Hal Washington and three of his friends stood in front of the chapel and sang *There Will Be Peace in the Valley* with such feeling that even Nick choked up. Hal sang the high tenor voice in the group that was called the Gospel Harmonizers. Nick wondered what was going through Hal's head right then. Hal Washington was certainly a young man with a richer and more complicated make-up than Nick had thought. Maybe it was because he hadn't had much opportunity to socialize with Hal. Although the Army was officially integrated, there was de facto segregation in many ways. For example, white soldiers frequented the bars on Goethe Strasse. Nick had never had seen a black soldier in any of the bars there. On the other hand, Nick had never been to the Florida Bar, or any of the other black bars. It never occurred to him what that cultural separation meant. Nick had observed that although a third or more of the soldiers in 3/34th Armor were black — there were no black officers in the battalion. He had also noticed that black soldiers were busted more often than whites, and that some of the Article 15 and court-martial punishments seemed to fall on the black men more than on the whites. Nick wondered if he could ever talk about some of that with Hal?

When the quartet finished singing, Lt. Col. Arthur Strickland stood and gave a short official offer of condolences to the Stark family. He was followed by Captain Elliott, who gave awkward excuses for the absences of Lieutenant Jensen — Stark's section leader, and Sergeant Crawford — Stark's section sergeant. The last tribute was to be given by Nick Holloway.

Nick appeared nervous, but he always tried to face whatever he had to do, and he did it in spite of nervousness, and fear, and whatever difficulty was involved.

"Mrs. Stark, Jeff, Jackie, Jordie — I'm so sorry for your loss. You must be hurting in ways that none of the rest of us can even imagine."

Charlotte Stark sobbed. Her oldest son Jeff put his arm around her, and rubbed her shoulder. The girl Jackie was doubled over. Jordan, the youngster, sat still.

"I knew Sergeant Stark pretty well — maybe as well as anyone else in Tank Section. Here's what I knew about him. He was a professional soldier — in the best sense of what that means. He tried. He tried his darnedest to do his best. He tried hard to do his duty. He was a man who lived with honor. I know also that he loved you — his family. He talked about you a lot, and when we were in the field, he couldn't wait to get back to Munich to see you all. I hope that you will remember the best side of your husband and father — love him and celebrate him for that."

Nick sat down.

Vince gave him a nudge and nodded his head.

The organ started playing, and the people sang "Rock of Ages." The chaplain had said Charlotte Stark told him that was Hollis' favorite hymn.

The service ended with Chaplain Reynolds saying a benediction.

Nick and Vince left the chapel quickly. They didn't want to observe what they expected to be the phony schmoozing going on between the officers and the battalion commander.

The two friends walked in silence across the Patton Field and parade ground toward the Headquarters Company barracks.

When they got to the second floor where their room was, they were met by Ned Lafontaine, Joe Flores, Phil Pavek, and a couple of their pals.

"So, you said your final goodbyes to that stumble drunk Stark," Ned said.

The others laughed loudly.

Nick made a fast move with his hands outstretched towards Ned.

"Why you, I'll ..." Nick said.

Vince grabbed Nick and pulled him back, as Ned stumbled backward.

"No, Nick — not now. Not today."

"Ha, ha, ha," Ned said.

"You haven't heard yet, have you? Crawford is promoting Ben — he's going to the NCO Academy in a month or so, after he re-ups. Ben will be TC on Tank 2 now — your tank. Now you'll be in for it, Holloway."

40

THANKSGIVING DINNER

Thursday, 24 November

Nick stood before the door to apartment 3B at Wilhelm Strasse 11, just off the main thoroughfare of Leopold Strasse. The door opened, and Werner and Ilse Osterheid, the hosts for the Thanksgiving Day dinner, greeted him. Carol came to the door also.

"*Es freue mich sehr, Sie kennenzulernen,*" Nick said, just the way Carol had taught him.

Carol kissed Nick on the cheek.

Werner shook Nick's hand vigorously, as he led him into the living room where a few other JYM students had already gathered. Werner gave Nick a small glass of cognac. Carol excused herself to help Linda and Nancy in the kitchen.

Nick was as relaxed as he could possibly be in the wake of Sergeant Stark's death.

"I'm so glad to finally meet you — Carol has told us so much about you," said a girl who introduced herself as Shirley Lundberg.

"And everything she said was good. Hi, Nick — John Cooper. I'm also glad to meet you. I want to talk with you about what it's like in the Army. You know — with the draft and all — all of us guys might have to serve, same as you are."

Nick liked John Cooper at once.

"I'm glad to meet you too, John. Hopefully, we'll have a chance to talk this afternoon."

"And, Nick — this is my roommate, Larry Connors," John said.

More handshakes and smiles and polite words.

Others came up to him and introduced themselves. John introduced Nick to David Monteath and Arthur Parsons, who were sitting in stuffed chairs by the bay windows that overlooked Wilhelm Strasse. They did not stand up. Their handshakes were limp. Nick decided he didn't like them.

After all the introductions, Nick reflected that his first impression was that he liked these people, except for the two wet blankets in the easy chairs.

The building was new — probably built in the 1950s, Nick guessed. It was plain on the outside, and the apartment was large on the inside. The Osterheid's apartment was spacious — with three bedrooms, and living and dining rooms that looked to have been designed for entertaining. Nick guessed that Werner Osterheid must have had a well-paying job to afford such a nice, large apartment.

Soon, the last guests arrived. JYM students Connie Maxwell and Ronald Nash — and then, Arndt and Frieda Meier. Carol had asked Linda and Nancy to ask the Osterheids if it would be okay if the Meiers joined the dinner group. The Osterheids agreed, and they had formally invited the Meiers.

Nick walked over to Arndt and Frieda. He gave Frieda a big hug and a kiss on the cheek, and held his hand out to Arndt. Arndt shook Nick's hand, and then, to Nick's surprise, Arndt hugged Nick.

Arndt looked terrible. Red eyes, filled with sadness — and he looked like he hadn't shaved that morning — several days possibly. Frieda looked at Arndt with a worried expression.

Nick smelled the sour smell of alcohol on Arndt's breath, and his ripe body odor. His clothes also emitted an unpleasant, stale tobacco smell.

"It was great of you to take a day off of work to help us celebrate our American holiday," Nick said to the Meiers.

Arndt grunted and moved heavily past Nick into the room, ashes falling from his cigarette to the floor.

It was then that Nick noticed the look on Werner's face. No smile — no judgment — but tightened muscles around his eyes — and a fixed stare at Arndt.

"Time to eat, everyone," Nancy Johnson announced.

Nick saw Carol, Nancy, and Linda standing just outside the door to the kitchen with Ilse. Nick thought Carol looked just as beautiful with an apron on, as she did with any other dress outfit. It was then that he realized that it didn't matter what Carol, or anyone else for that matter, wore — it was the person inside the dress that was most important.

The expression Nick saw on Carol's face as she stared at Arndt was what — worry? Concern? Disgust? No, Nick didn't think it was disgust. If it was, it was not from the Carol he knew, or who he thought he knew. Nick knew Arndt had a drinking problem. But was he just a sad drunk, or did he get violent? Nick would have to ask Carol.

"Okay — who can say the dinner prayer? Who will lead us?" Carol said.

"I'll do it," John Cooper said.

With God thanked, the group took seats at the tables. In the center was a large round table, around which were twelve chairs. Werner and Ilse protested that they should not be seated but would work in the kitchen, because there wasn't room for fifteen people at the table. But Linda and Nancy wouldn't hear of it. They had planned and prepared for this event, and the Osterheids were their guests. Shirley Lundberg was also on kitchen duty.

Carol had removed her apron, and was sitting next to Nick. She squeezed his hand under the table.

Turkey and dressing, mashed potatoes and gravy, candied yams, peas and carrots, hot dinner rolls and butter, cranberry relish and watermelon pickles, and a lettuce salad to start with.

Werner made sure everyone had an opportunity, at least, to have some German wine. Nick noticed that Arndt had a half pint flask of schnapps inside his suit jacket that he took out from time to time under the sad eyes of Frieda.

The conversations around the table went from the latest operetta performance in Munich, to the election of John Kennedy, to Fidel Castro's speech at the United Nations in New York, to the records of favorite professional sports teams, and also — a little gossip about one of the JYM teachers. They answered the Osterheid's questions about the American tradition of Thanksgiving, and about the influence of the many German immigrants on the development of the United States.

Finally, one of the girls suggested they go around the table and tell a favorite Thanksgiving story, with the caveats that it had to be funny, and — it couldn't be mean. Also, it had to be suitable for mixed company.

The stories were hilarious, in Nick's opinion. He kept looking in his past for a story he could share.

With visions of death trying to take over his conscious mind, Nick could not fully concentrate on the frivolity. There was Danny, cleaning garbage cans, and then inert on the turret floor; then gunshots, and four corpses in that barn; and Sergeant Stark, gasping for air; and also, those ever-present, nasty red thumbs flying through the air.

When it was Carol's turn, she told how one year when she was maybe seven or eight, her mother had set the turkey on the back porch so that it would thaw before she was ready to put it into the oven.

"But dad didn't know that, so he let Yippee, our Pekinese dog, outside, and of course the little dog got into the porch — and you know what happened then!"

Uproarious laughter resulted as Nick visualized the scene.

"What did your mom say to your dad?" Connie Maxwell asked.

"Well, she said that dogs need to eat, too."

"That's hilarious," Connie said.

More laughter.

"Okay, Nick — your turn," Connie said.

"Well, I can't come close to the stories you've all told. Maybe we should just let it be for now," Nick said."

"Oh, come on, Nick — go ahead," Carol said.

"Well, okay — this story happened last year on Thanksgiving Day, but it wasn't at dinner — it was at breakfast. We were in the field at Hohenfels — that's a training area up near Regensburg — and they got us up early — like 0400."

"0400 — did you guys get that? Don't you all like it — that Army talk?" Arndt said. "Nick is my friend."

"Okay — so it's really early in the morning and still dark. Pitch black — you could hardly see your feet in front of you. Because we were training, we had to sit at least ten meters apart, under the trees, in the darkness."

"You will all keep the proper interval, or you will be sent to the Russian front," Arndt said.

Nobody laughed with him this time.

"Next to me — ten meters away, that is — sat Billy, Private Billy Dryden — eating his scrambled eggs and soggy toast. All of a sudden I hear Billy cussing a blue streak — swearing loudly. It turned out that a dead leaf had fallen into his mess kit, right on top of his food. Billy couldn't see it, because it was still pitch dark, so he put it in his mouth — and that was when he let us all know that it had no taste."

The group was in a good mood, and predisposed to find

humor where they could. They laughed as heartily at Nick's story as they had at anyone else's.

"Well, it's a breakfast story — but it was on Thanksgiving Day," Nick said.

More laughter.

"Have you ever been shot at?" John Cooper asked.

"No — I haven't — thank God."

It was quiet around the table.

"But he's seen men die — haven't you, *Amerikanischer Soldat*?" Arndt said.

Everyone turned and looked at Arndt Meier.

"The rest of you *Amis* know nothing of death."

Arndt struggled to hold on to his dignity.

Frieda put her hand on Arndt's arm.

"Tell them about Private Daniel Maguire and Sergeant Hollis Stark, Nick. Tell them what it looks like when soldiers die. Tell them about the blood, and the shit, and the puke — tell them what it feels like when someone you know dies."

Arndt was sobbing. Frieda stood up and helped him to his feet. Werner also stood and went to steady Arndt.

"I'm so sorry — please — it's the war, you see — he can't forget it. It comes and goes. It's been bad lately. He visited an old Army friend at St. Johannes hospital last week. Kurt lost both legs in Russia. He died yesterday. Now Arndt can't sleep. He drinks too much. He smokes all the time. Please, forgive him — it's not his fault," Frieda said.

They finished the meal in silence.

After dinner, Nick and John Cooper talked for a while, until John said he had to leave.

Nick went to the kitchen, grabbed a dishtowel, and started wiping the dishes that Carol was washing.

After goodbyes and expressions of thanks to Linda, Nancy, and the Osterheids, Nick walked in silence with Carol to her home on Isabella Strasse.

They sat down on a bench beside an inactive fountain.

Germans, mostly older women, were out on their daily walks with their dogs. A Dachsund and a Chihuahua exchanged insults until they were pulled apart.

"Nick — I'm proud of you. David and Arthur can act like little boys sometimes. But John and Larry and the girls all liked you. I think I love you, but sometimes I feel that we are still miles apart. I want to know you better. I want to know what goes on in your life as a soldier. I want to know what you feel, and, how I can help you."

"I know, Carol — I know."

"I haven't told you this before, but now I feel I should."

Nick looked at her.

"When I was in junior high, one of my good friends died in a fire. Her family lived in an apartment above the café they owned. It happened one night — the only survivors were the dad and a small baby he saved. The funeral was so sad. I was one of the honorary pallbearers — she was only thirteen."

Nick let her cry as he held her tight.

"I know this isn't the right thing or the right time to say when someone you love has had someone else die …"

Nick kissed her. Now he knew what real love felt like.

"I know why you wouldn't want to tell me everything about Sergeant Crawford. I understand why you are being so careful about it. All I ask is that you finish it up, all right? Then you and I can move on with our lives together."

41

MARKUS ZIMMERMANN

Saturday, 26 November

Markus Zimmermann looked plain, like he could fit into any group of men in their forties — businessmen, truck drivers, electricians, or farmers. He dressed simply — in between a postal clerk and a bricklayer. There was nothing about him that would attract attention as being someone odd. About five feet ten, brown hair, blue eyes, and a pencil mustache above his upper lip. His bodyguard, Jürgen Mueller, could only be described as a man whose muscles were important in whatever line of work he was in. Rudi Wachter, Earl Crawford's new fence, looked a lot like his predecessor, Manfred Neumann. Rudi had told Earl how tragic it was that Manfred had been shot by his own brother, who then shot himself.

"Just a minute," Earl said. "I want you to meet my associate."

Crawford went outside and motioned for Nick to come in with him.

"Rudi, Herr Zimmermann, Herr Mueller — this is my associate, Nick Holloway."

At Earl's instruction, Nick was carrying an Army .45 pistol in a leather holster on his hip.

Earl didn't care what the three Germans thought about him bringing Nick to the table. For that matter, he didn't care what Nick thought about it, either.

As a rule, Earl didn't want to be seen as negotiating from a position of weakness.

"Okay, now that everybody is here, let's get down to business. Rudi tells me that you wanted to meet me. Well — here I am. Now, what is it that you can do for me, Herr Zimmermann?"

Zimmermann studied Sergeant Crawford — looking directly into his eyes, as if to play a game with him to see which one of them would blink first.

Zimmermann blinked and then he stared at Nick. Nick didn't flinch.

"Okay, Sergeant Crawford. Herr Wachter has told me a great deal about your activities here in Munich. Stealing from the U.S. Army and selling your wares to Germans — at a profit. The Black Market, I think you call it."

Earl stared at Rudi with eyes of ice.

"It's illegal, isn't it, sergeant?" Zimmermann said.

Earl could see that Zimmermann was a skilled negotiator. He used pauses and other timing devices to create a sense that he was the one in command of the business at hand, and his sarcasm could be used to catch an adversary off guard. He let Earl know that he had information that he could use against him.

"Never mind — we on this side are also involved in illegal activities. Herr Wachter here has told me what he will pay you for cigarettes, liquor, gasoline, tools, paint, and even the brass shells, and frankly, it's not that much. You will never get rich selling cartons of Lucky Strikes and Camel cigarettes, or fifths of Four Roses. The gasoline and the brass shell casings are more profitable for you — but they involve substantially greater risk. Selling a ton of brass is more complicated than a case of cigarettes — but you are aware of that, aren't you, sergeant?"

Earl was seething inside — to think that Rudi Wachter would tell this stranger the details of their business together. He vowed to himself that he would make Rudi pay for his betrayal — maybe in the same way that Manfred Neumann had been paid.

"Okay, let's say you're right — what can you offer that is any better?"

"Ah — now we get to the nub of the matter, as you Americans like to say."

Zimmermann looked around the room. He rested his gaze on Nick.

"He's okay. I trust him. Whatever you say to me you can say in front of Specialist Holloway," Earl said.

Earl noticed that Zimmermann's eyes had lingered on the holster on Nick's side.

"You are on active duty with the United States Army. You are in a position to provide much more than cigarettes and empty tank shells. I have contacts in the East who have needs for things that you can get your hands on."

"Wait a minute here — when you say the East, do you mean the commies? The Russkies? Are you asking me to do business with the Reds?"

"Oh, I don't know how many of them are communists — maybe …but what does that matter? We're talking business here. Money. Real money. A lot more money than you are getting from pushing 100 cartons of cigarettes a week, a case of whiskey or two, and some paint. My contacts have lots of money — and some of it can be yours, sergeant."

There was silence while Earl processed what he had heard. He really didn't care who bought his loot — just so they paid him well for it. Also, he didn't care about the politics of this standoff between the United States and the Soviet Union and

East Germany. To say that Sergeant Earl Crawford hated the U.S. Army, and by association, the United States government itself, was an understatement. They screwed him after Korea — so to hell with them.

"I'm listening," Earl said. "What kind of money are we talking about?"

Zimmermann's face lit up. Wachter smiled and bobbed his head up and down a few times.

"Oh, we're talking tens of thousands of dollars."

"Damn, Markus — now you're talking my language."

Nick's face showed no expression. He stared at Sergeant Crawford.

"Good. Now let's get down to brass tacks, as you Americans like to say. What my colleagues need most is information — but, from time to time, they also would like to get some actual equipment items as well."

Earl's mind went from point to point quickly. He went through a mental list of whom he knew in the battalion, and at Warner and Will Kasernes, and even Flak and Sheridan Kasernes in Augsburg. Surely, he could get almost anything he wanted. He would have to use his special carrot and stick techniques, of course, but they had not failed him yet.

"Okay — I think we can do business," Earl said.

Zimmermann offered his hand to Crawford, and they became partners. Their handshake told Earl that now he was going to be into some big money. He asked himself why he hadn't thought of this angle before.

Zimmermann handed him an envelope. Earl opened it and found ten one hundred dollar bills. If he had any doubts about what he was getting into before, now they disappeared. He put it in his jacket pocket.

"How will I know what you need?" Earl asked.

"Look inside the envelope, you will find a list."

On the jeep ride back to Henry Kaserne, Nick drove in silence. Earl didn't look at Nick.

Finally, Nick spoke.

"Sergeant Crawford, I can't believe what I just heard back there. Are you working for our counterintelligence? That's the only reason I can think of that would make this okay."

"It's just business, Nick."

"No, it isn't. It's treason. It's wrong. Just like those murders were wrong. These are capital crimes."

Crawford took his own pistol out and held it so that the barrel rested on Nick's neck, just below his ear lobe.

"So help me, Nick — if you cause trouble for me about this — so help me ... I thought you knew that you are as guilty as I am in this."

42

TRAITOR

Nick knew exactly why he couldn't sleep that night. The knowledge that Earl Crawford was about to betray the United States — how could he even think that was okay? Twice during the night, Nick had gotten up, paced the floor, and stared out of the window.

The question — the only question, of course, was what should Nick do with what he now knew?

This was not about petty thievery — this was about treason. How could any American soldier think it was okay to help East Germans, or their bosses in the Soviet Union, in any form or fashion? No — Sergeant Crawford had crossed the line — he had gone too far this time, as if murder wasn't enough. Nick had tried to report the murders — it didn't work. Now what? He had to do something to stop this madman.

Nick had been selected for main gate guard duty on this day. He pulled himself together in order to look his best for the guard inspection. The Army had an incentive device whereby the sharpest soldier at guard inspection was designated as a supernumerary. The supernumerary did not stand guard, but could hang around and be available on call, in case he was needed. He could sleep upstairs in the guardhouse just inside the main gate, or he could hang out in the snack bar, service club, or the library, all in a building across the street from the guardhouse. At any rate, it was worth the effort for any soldier to try his best to be the supernumerary. The alternative was four hours on and four off, standing guard at the little guard shack in the middle of the front gate.

Nick was not selected to be the chosen one. Instead, he drew the first shift with Specialist 4th Class Darrel Hinton, an Alabaman with B Company of the 3rd Armored Rifle Battalion of the 46th Infantry. Their first duty was from 0800 to noon.

Hinton was not talkative, and that suited Nick just fine. Nick wanted to think through the whole situation with Sergeant Crawford. Was there any way Nick could stop Crawford before he got any deeper in his involvement with Zimmermann? Maybe not — it's possible that nothing can stop him. Various plans came and went in Nick's mind. When that chain of thoughts ended, Nick wondered if he should tell someone else about what Crawford was about to do. Should he tell anyone? Should he tell Vince — they had shared some of their secrets so far. But this was different — it was so big — so dangerous — that Vince might do something dumb, like getting involved with Crawford himself. Nick thought he could take Crawford in a fight. Maybe that's what he should do? But then what? Unforeseen consequences. After all, Crawford had threatened Nick if he caused any trouble about this business. Nick certainly didn't want to put himself, Vince, or anyone else, in danger.

Nick and Hinton were busy for the first hour, checking vehicles and documents of individuals and groups leaving Henry Kaserne for various purposes.

When a jeep or a truck stopped at the guardhouse, Nick would examine the documents authorizing the vehicle and men to leave, and he would write on a form attached to a clipboard. He recorded the vehicle number, the names of the occupants, the destination, and the time of departure. Then he would salute the officers, if there were any, and let the vehicle pass through. When the vehicle or pedestrians returned, they would be checked off the list.

Nick thought about Carol. He ached inside to see her again. He knew he would feel better if he told Carol more — especially if he could just use the words about how he felt.

Nick's second shift, from 1600 to 2000, was also busy. This was when many of the Henry vehicles returned to the kaserne.

Nick thought a lot about Carol — about how natural he felt when he was with her. About her humor, and her practical common sense, and the grit she showed when things were tough in her life. Nick was sure he loved Carol, even though he hadn't been able to define what that meant. He was sure he would gladly put his life in danger in order to save hers. The Army talked about that as the measure of love of one soldier for another, but Nick had only felt that way about a few men — Vince, for sure — and Sergeant Cervenka, and Sergeant Stark, and even Danny Maguire. The rest of them could all go to their maker — or the other place — it made no difference to Nick.

Nick liked it when it was busy at the front gate. He didn't have to think about Crawford. For that reason, Nick dreaded his last shift — midnight to 0400, usually a period of inactivity.

The lack of sleep the night before, and being alert and on his feet for eight hours already, meant that Nick was not in the best physical or mental condition during those cold and quiet hours. He had lain down on a cot upstairs in the guardhouse after his previous shift, but he hadn't slept.

He sat on a stool in the small guard shack with Hinton. They were both in their own thought worlds. Nick never once wondered or asked what Hinton was thinking about, Nick sipped on a cup of hot coffee.

Nick had a half hour left on guard duty.

The thoughts in Nick's mind turned into visions. Black vultures circling lazily in a night sky with a quarter moon.

Earl Crawford pulled the trigger as Nick stood against the cold stone wall behind the barn at Ebersdorf. The bullet took forever to reach Nick's brain. Nick jerked his head to the side as the bullet smacked into the barn wall.

By the time he was relieved at 0400, Nick had still not reached any decisions. He realized that to not make a decision was to make a decision — a decision to do nothing. So be it, he thought — he was too tired to think anymore. He said the Lord's Prayer, and asked God to do the worrying for a few hours.

43

ALTE PINAKOTHEK

Saturday, 3 December

Carol and Nick walked from her apartment to the Alte Pinakothet, the Old Picture Gallery. Carol had told Nick, several times, that she loved to spend time in this place that was filled with paintings by the masters. She looked forward to sharing her joy of art with Nick.

"I believe it was George Bernard Shaw who said 'you use a glass mirror to see your face, and you use works of art to see your soul'," Carol said.

The Alte Pinakothet's collections included many examples of European painting from the Middle Ages through the 18th century. The building, but not its art treasures, was destroyed by allied bombers during World War II. It was re-opened in 1957.

"Oh, Nick, look at this — isn't it beautiful?"

"Yeah, I guess so."

"Nick, you're a million miles away. What's wrong?"

"Nothing."

"Nothing? Are you so uninterested in great art that you can't even pretend to look interested?"

"Uh — I'm sorry, Carol. I was thinking of something else. Really — I really am sorry."

"Let's find a place to sit and talk. This isn't fun for me, either, if I can't do this with you."

They found a window alcove in a gallery with few visitors — a place with a padded bench — and sat down.

"Okay, Nick. I don't think I've ever seen you this way — this preoccupied. Please, tell me what's wrong."

Nick stared out the window. He didn't look at Carol.

"Nick?"

Nick looked at Carol.

"Carol, I don't know how to start, or even where to start. I've been arguing with myself for several days — no, I guess it's been several weeks already."

"Start wherever you want, Nick."

Nick looked away from Carol, and stared out the window again. Then he looked back at her.

"We've got time, Nick. And I want to hear what you have to say. If it's hard, then — take your time."

Nick hesitated.

"Okay. Three weeks ago, while we were in the field, I saw Sergeant Crawford murder four people."

Carol did a double-take.

"Oh, Nick, that's terrible."

"He said that I am his accomplice, and therefore, I am just as guilty as he is."

Carol remained silent. She took his hand and held it in hers.

"Of course, it was terrible. I can see it play out in my mind, over and over."

They sat in silence for several minutes more.

Carol looked confused. What did this mean? She wondered if what he had said was true? Was Nick as guilty as his sergeant? This young man who was her boyfriend — was he really guilty of murder? No, she couldn't believe that.

Nick had a good heart. He was a good man. Was she thinking that it could be true? Or else … what?

"Do you think you are as guilty as he is, Nick?"

"No. No, of course not. But I was there. I saw it happen. I told him I thought it was wrong. I told the captain, but he didn't believe me — he thinks it's all in my head — that I imagined it all.

"But, Nick, this was murder — it wasn't about seeing someone stealing cookies out of a cookie jar."

"Yes, yes, yes — I know that."

Nick swivel-nodded his head from side to side.

Carol watched Nick closely. She realized how difficult this must be for him to talk about this, and to confide in her.

"Go on, Nick. Talk to me."

"And then …"

Nick looked away again.

"And then — you were about to say …"

"Then, just a week ago, I was there when Crawford sold out his country. He made a deal to steal information and give it to the Communists. I saw it all, Carol. He took a thousand dollars from the commie, and promised to give him the information he asked for. He's a traitor to his country — to our country."

"A traitor, as well as a murderer," Carol said, as she shook her head back and forth.

"Yes."

Nick choked back a sob.

"He's a traitor, and a murderer, and a thief. I know that. I know how wrong he is. And yet — and yet, I don't know what to do about it."

"You've told me, that's a start."

"Yes, now I've told you. But I trust you, Carol."

Carol rubbed his hand softly.

Another minute of silence.

"What does your conscience say, Nick?"

"Ah — um — umphsph."

Nick laughed.

"My conscience?"

"Yes, Nick, your conscience — or think of it as your inner voice being your conscience, but, that the message is from your soul — what is your soul saying to you?"

Nick looked up, his expression serious.

"My soul?"

"Yes. Sometimes when I'm talking to my conscience, I realize that the voice responding to me is my soul."

"Wow," Nick said.

Again, Nick looked out the window in silence.

Finally, he looked back at Carol.

"My soul is screaming at me. *Do the right thing, Nick. Do the right thing — you know what that is — do it.*"

Carol let go of Nick's hand, rubbed his arm gently, and waited for him to continue.

"The right thing — what is the right thing, Carol? That's the problem for me. I've always taken pride in knowing the difference between right and wrong — but this, this is different, it seems."

"What are you afraid of, Nick?"

Nick chuckled and looked away again.

"Afraid of? I'm scared to death of what my dad would think if he knew what I've been involved in. I wouldn't be able to look him in the eyes if I ended up in an Army prison, or even if I were to get a dishonorable discharge. That's what I'm afraid of."

"But, what about yourself? As a man? As an honorable man — an honorable soldier? As yourself? What do you think? How would you feel if you were sent to prison, or were to get a dishonorable discharge? I mean, this is about murder, and treason. Wouldn't a dishonorable discharge be a fair price to pay in order to bring a murderer and a traitor to justice? You don't need a piece of paper — a discharge document — to have honor."

Nick didn't answer her.

"Nick, your dad isn't here. Those others who you value so much what they think of you — whose opinion of your reputation means so much? But they're not here. This is your life, and what you decide to do is your decision. This is your life — this is now."

"What do you think, Carol? What should I do? I don't know what to do."

"I think you do know what you should do. Listen to yourself, to your conscience, your soul. Do the right thing. They're telling you to do the right thing. That's what you want to do. That's what you did when you stood up for Danny."

Nick looked sat her with eyes that said, I know you're right, and I love you for listening to me and believing in me."

They walked back to Carol's apartment.

"I'm glad you told me what is bothering you, Nick."

Nick held her close, and kissed her tenderly.

44

What to Do?

Nick sat in the back pew of the Henry Kaserne chapel. After the service, he waited until only he and Captain Reynolds remained.

"Chaplain, may I talk with you?"

"Of course, Nick. Let's go into my office."

Nick held his cap and gloves.

"Now, what can I help you with, Nick?"

"Sir — we've talked before, but now I need to get more serious about this."

"Go on."

"I have information … I've seen some things …"

"Yes?"

"I've been very reluctant to talk about this with anybody."

Chaplain Reynolds did not say anything.

"I did talk with my girlfriend about this, as you suggested. I trust her."

The air smelled stuffy. Nick could see dust particles in the sun's rays shining through the window behind the chaplain.

"She said I should listen to my conscience — to my soul."

"And what do your conscience and your soul say to you, Nick?"

"They say that I should do the right thing."

"They are correct."

"This is hard for me, sir. Very hard."

"Of course, it is hard — sometimes, doing the right thing can cost you a great deal."

"How do I know what the right thing is? I mean, I know what I should do. I just don't know how to do it. That's what's so hard, sir."

The chaplain reached over and picked up a book on his desk — a Bible.

"Ah, here it is — do you remember this, Nick? Micah, chapter six, verse eight. *'He has showed you, O man, what is good; and what does the Lord require of you but to do justice, and to love kindness, and to walk humbly with your God?'* Does that help at all, Nick?"

"Well, yes. What I'm getting at has to do with justice. I didn't — maybe I still don't — don't think that handing out justice was my job. Isn't that up to God?"

"In the end, you're right. God has the last word in all matters. But in Micah, God is telling us to do justice. That could be the right thing you're looking for."

Nick stood up and paced back and forth in front of the chaplain's desk.

"What I know — the things I've seen — need to be reported to someone in authority, sir. And when I do that, if I do that, all hell is going to break loose — pardon the expression, sir."

"Are you talking about one person? Or more than one?"

"Oh, it's just one person."

"Has he hurt you personally, Nick?"

"Yeah — yes. But not as much as he's hurt others."

"He has hurt others, as well as you?"

"Oh, yeah — big time."

The chaplain waited for Nick to continue.

"Yes. But ... you see ..."

Chaplain Reynolds flipped through the pages of his Bible again.

"Here, in the book of Matthew, chapter eighteen, verses fifteen through twenty."

Nick sat down.

"*If your brother sins against you, go and tell him his fault, between you and him alone. If he listens ...*"

Nick stood up and began pacing again.

The chaplain read the entire passage out loud.

"I don't know, sir. I don't think that would work. The person I'm talking about isn't a normal man, someone who would think that way."

"Have you got a better idea?" the chaplain asked.

Nick looked out the window, and then back at the chaplain.

"No, sir, I don't. What I've already tried hasn't worked, and I can't think of anything else."

"Well, then — what have you got to lose?"

"Okay, I'll try it. I'll go and ask him to turn himself in. That's the answer. That's the right thing to do. Maybe, just maybe, it will work."

"Nick, I think you've made a wise decision. If things don't work out — they might very well go wrong — he might not agree to turn himself in — then come back to me and we'll talk about what should happen next."

"Thank you, sir — chaplain, sir."

45

CONFRONTATION

Monday, 5 December

Nick's first opportunity to confront Crawford was after the work formation — shortly after breakfast. The men of Tank Section moved to their tanks to start their daily maintenance tasks.

"Sergeant — can I talk to you?"

Nick walked away from the tanks, to behind the small maintenance shack, out of earshot of the other men.

Crawford followed him.

"What is it, hot shot? Need some advice from your war daddy? Your sweet honey giving you problems again?"

Nick chuckled. He looked away, and then back — straight into Crawford's eyes.

"No, sergeant, I don't need any advice from you, and if you give it to me, I won't take it anyway."

"You sassy bastard."

"No, what I have to say is some advice for you."

Crawford widened his stance, and put his hands on his hips.

"You see, as I've told you before — you've done some evil things — I've seen you do them. I know what you've done. Stealing from the Army; committing murder; and now you're a traitor to our country."

Crawford's face turned red. He lowered his arms.

"I think you know that what you've done is wrong. I think you know it's only a matter of time until you'll be held accountable for your crimes. I think the right thing for you to do is to turn yourself in. Go to Lieutenant Jensen. Go to Captain Elliott. Go to the CID. Take your pick. I have a hunch that you will have a sense of relief to get rid of the guilt you must feel."

Crawford was clenching his fists — then relaxing them — and then clenching them again.

"You're a good soldier, sergeant — a good tanker. You've been in combat. You've sacrificed for your country. Your record will stand for something — something good. Give the money back to Zimmermann and tell him to go to hell. And then, there were reasons for killing those men. Who knows, they might even call it justifiable homicide — that you're not really guilty of murder."

Crawford seemed to be relaxing his expression — then his face changed back.

"Guilty? Guilty, you say? The only guilt I feel is that I didn't kill you in that barn when I had the chance. You self-righteous asshole. You think your shit don't stink. You're so full of yourself, with all that phony goody-goody horseshit. Didn't I teach you anything? This is an evil world, son. It's kill or be killed. Do unto others before they can do it to you. It's get by, any which way you can. To hell with all your sanctimonious crap, Holloway. Now, get out of my sight, cocksucker, and don't you ever try to preach that fucking moral bullshit to me again."

Nick walked to his tank, with his head down. He knew all along that it wouldn't work.

46

M-14 Affair

Monday, 5 December

Later that morning, Nick was working alone inside the tank turret when Sergeant Crawford put his head in through the open hatch.

Nick looked at him. Was he going to point a pistol at Nick and pull the trigger? Nick had suspected before that there was something dangerously wrong with the man, now he was certain. Nick was looking at a psychopath. Funny, thought Nick, that Captain Elliott should think that Nick was the crazy one.

"Holloway — get out here — I've got a job for you. I need you to go sign out that new demo model of the M-14 rifle. Bring it to my room."

Crawford handed a piece of paper to Nick.

"Here's your authorization — give it to Tucker."

Nick had sat inside the turret since his confrontation with Crawford. He went through the motions of working, but mostly he had thought about his failure to convince the sergeant to turn himself in. Nick was upset with himself for being so naïve to think that Crawford would ever consider turning himself in. Now, Nick's plan was to skip noon chow and go back to see the chaplain again.

Nick wiped his greasy hands on a rag and took the note. He wondered why Crawford didn't get the rifle himself. But then — the man was a psycho. A fleeting question entered Nick's head. Nick shivered as he considered what Markus Zimmermann might have said — that he wanted Crawford to get him a new M-14 rifle.

As Nick walked from the tank park to the barracks, he thought about how he had been prepared to turn Sergeant Crawford in — maybe that's the next step. The notes Nick had written were lengthy and in detail. He had gone over them several times to make sure he was as accurate as he could be, and that he hadn't left anything important out. He hid the journal under his wall locker — by tipping the locker forward a little — and slipping the pages on the floor underneath the locker.

The arms room was located in the lower level of the company barracks, below the mess kitchen. Specialist Fifth Class Donald Tucker ran the arms room for the company. He owed his cushy job to Sergeant Al Richards, the supply sergeant. Richards, of course, was a close friend of Crawford.

Nick presented himself at the half-door that blocked entry to the arms room.

"Sergeant Crawford asked me to sign out that new M-14 for him," Nick said.

Nick handed Tucker the note from Crawford.

Tucker neither said anything, nor looked at Nick. He brought the rifle, held it in his arms, and laid a sign-out sheet and a ballpoint pen in front of Nick.

Nick signed and dated the slip, and then handed the sheet and the pen back to Tucker.

Tucker handed the weapon to Nick.

The M-14 was intended to replace the M-1 Garand rifle that had been the Army's standard infantry weapon since

1936. Over six million semi-automatic M-1s were produced — it was the American soldier's friend during World War II and the Korean War. With the creation of the North Atlantic Treaty Organization (NATO), there was a need for the U.S. to develop an infantry rifle that used the NATO standard 7.62 millimeter ammunition. It took until December 1960 for 3/34 Armor to receive a few demonstration M-14 rifles. One rifle for each company.

Nick took the rifle to Crawford's room.

Sergeant First Class Earl Crawford took the rifle. He didn't thank Nick.

Nick hesitated, wondering whether he should say anything more.

He decided to keep quiet, and returned to the tank park.

At noon, Nick was unable to find Chaplain Reynolds.

That evening, at chow, Nick was eating in the mess hall with Vince when the company clerk came up to him.

"Specialist Holloway — the old man wants to see you — pronto."

"What for?"

"Who do you take me for — Einstein? I don't know what for. I'm in the Army — I do what I'm told."

Nick and Vince took their trays, glasses, and silverware to the scullery window, and then walked down the hallway to the company commander's office.

Nick knocked on the captain's door, heard the word enter, and then went in and reported to his commander.

Vince stayed in the hallway.

In Captain Elliott's office were Lieutenant Jensen, Sergeant Crawford, and Specialist Tucker.

"Where's the rifle, Holloway?" Captain Elliott said.

"You mean the new M-14, sir?"

"That's exactly what I mean. Where is it?"

Nick looked at the blank face of Sergeant Crawford.

"I gave it to Sergeant Crawford as he directed, sir."

"Sergeant Crawford says he gave you no such order, and that you did not give him the rifle — but here on this sheet, it shows that you signed it out of the arms room at 0917 this morning," Elliott said.

Nick looked back at Crawford's steely glare.

"There must be some mistake, sir."

"The only mistake was the one you made, Holloway," Captain Elliott said.

"Sir, Vince Delvecchio saw Sergeant Crawford come to my tank, and I told him that Sergeant Crawford had asked me to go and get the rifle for him."

"Sure, you two are like two flies inside a bottle of syrup — you share everything, and he'd only lie for you. Did you tell anyone else what you were going to do?"

"Well — no — I didn't talk to anyone else before going to the arms room, sir. But Vince ..."

Nick did not want to get Vince into any trouble.

Captain Elliott's face showed only serious purpose. It showed no compassion or desire for objective truth.

Nick had that helpless feeling one got when he realized he had been trapped — when it was one person's word against another, and the other person wanted to harm you, or at least make you look bad. What made it worse — the other person had power over you.

"Sir, Sergeant Crawford gave me a chit to give to Specialist Tucker, authorizing me to sign out the rifle."

"Tell Specialist Holloway what you told me, sergeant."

In a clear and rock-steady voice, Crawford said that he asked Nick to make sure that all the radios on each of the four tanks were set to the prescribed frequencies. He said he never told Nick to go and get the M-14 rifle.

The captain held up the rifle sign-out sheet in his hand and waved it back and forth.

"Is this your signature?"

"Yes, sir, it is, but ..."

Nick looked at Tucker, who quickly shifted his eyes away — upwards toward the picture of President Eisenhower on the wall.

Tucker — you son-of-a-bitch — didn't you tell him about Crawford's note — the one that I gave to you?

"No buts about it — you're in trouble, soldier — deep trouble. Specialist Tucker — did you or did you not give the rifle to Specialist Holloway?"

"Yes, sir, after he signed for it, sir."

"Why did you give him the rifle? Didn't you question what he was going to do with it?"

"He said Sergeant Crawford told him to get it. That was good enough for me."

Nick's mind was searching for an answer. How could he convince the captain that these men were lying?

"Okay, Holloway — why did you take the rifle?"

"Sir, there's an explanation for this ..."

"All I want to know is why you did it — and where the weapon is now."

"Sir, I heard that Specialist Holloway has been in touch with a Soviet agent. Maybe he gave the rifle to the Reds," Crawford said.

"But, sir ..."

"I know you've been under a lot of stress, but this is carrying things too far."

The captain looked at his watch.

"That's it — save it for the MPs, Holloway."

Captain Elliott pushed a button on his desk phone.

The door opened and the first sergeant looked in.

"You called, sir?"

"Sergeant Dixon — call the military police. Tell them we have someone here who needs to cool off overnight — until he decides to come clean and tell us the truth."

"Yes, sir," Sergeant Dixon said as he closed the door.

* * * *

263

The MPs put handcuffs on Nick and took him to their jeep.

Vince stood in the hallway outside the captain's office. He saw the handcuffs on Nick.

"Nick — what's going on?"

"It's just a big misunderstanding, Vince."

"Should I call Carol?"

"No, no — don't call Carol. She'll just worry. This will all be cleared up in the morning. Just make sure you stay on the tank."

Nick was processed at the MP station at McGraw Kaserne. He was intrigued by the procedures the MPs followed. They were polite. They took his fingerprints. They took photos of him. They had him change from his Army fatigue uniform to a jail uniform. Then they took a written statement from him.

He told the truth.

In the morning, Nick was asked if he wanted to change his statement of the previous night. He replied no, saying his statement was the truth.

An hour later he was told that formal charges had been brought by Captain Elliott and the battalion commander. Nick was to face a general court-martial for the theft of a weapon, and possible charges of treason.

The MPs then took Nick to the division stockade at Dachau.

47

DACHAU

Carol Benjamin was called out of her German Literature class. The aide said it was important.

"Carol? This is Vince — Vince Delvecchio. I'm so glad I was able to get to you. Something's happened to Nick, and it's serious."

Carol's face paled. She felt the strength go out of her hand — she nearly dropped the telephone.

"Wha ... what's wrong? What's happened to Nick?"

No, Carol thought, it couldn't be — he couldn't be dead. She had been so sure of herself when she said he should listen to his conscience, and to his soul. Maybe his inner voices were not at all like hers. What had she done?

"He's in jail — well, the stockade, out at Eastman Barracks, in Dachau," Vince said.

"Jail? Did you say jail? Dachau? Why, Vince? Why? He's been fighting again, hasn't he? I knew it — I just knew it."

"No — he hasn't been fighting."

Vince told her about the missing M-14 rifle.

"Please, Carol, don't take this the wrong way. It's not

Nick's fault — he's innocent. I'm sure he's being framed, probably by Sergeant Crawford."

"Is he okay, Vince?"

"Yes. I saw him last night, when they took him away, and he said he was okay."

"You saw him? Last night? Why didn't you call me then, Vince?"

"I said I was going to call you, but Nick said no. He said you would worry, and that he was sure the situation would be cleared up soon."

"You should have called me last night. Maybe I … we … we could have done something then?"

"Carol, this is Nick we're talking about."

"Yes, I'm sorry."

Carol was in an office — a secretary was looking at her and listening.

Carol picked up the telephone and carried it to a nearby chair — about as far away from the secretary as the phone cord would allow.

"Vince, what can we do to help him?"

"I know, Carol. He needs us to go to bat for him. I talked with Captain Reynolds, the chaplain, just a little while ago."

"Nick talked highly of his chaplain."

"Yes, I think he's a straight shooter. Well, when I told him about Nick, he called a friend of his in the CIC, that's the counterintelligence corps, a Sergeant Barrett. I waited in the chaplain's office until this guy — this Sergeant Barrett — got there. He and Chaplain Reynolds are on Nick's side, Carol. That's important. Well, it turned out that Sergeant Barrett knows an Army lawyer who can help Nick — a Captain Evans. So, they called the lawyer guy and he is going to work for Nick."

"That's good, Vince."

"Yeah — let's hope it works."

"Vince — is there anything I can do? Should I call or send a telegram to his parents?"

"Oh, no, don't do that, Carol. Not yet, anyway. I think Nick would not want his parents to know. Not yet."

"Well — what, then?"

"I don't know, Carol. I asked the chaplain that same question. He said I should pray for Nick."

"Yes, at least that. Look, Vince, promise me that you will call me the minute you hear anything new."

"Sure — of course I will — definitely."

Neither spoke for a moment or two.

"You know, Carol. You must know by now that Nick is in love with you."

Carol's eyes filled with tears. She took out her handkerchief.

Finally, Carol composed herself.

"Thanks, Vince."

Carol hung up the telephone.

I know … I hope … he has to be innocent.

* * * *

Dachau
Tuesday, 6 December

The three inmates sitting with Nick at lunch called themselves Tom, Dick, and Harry.

"So — what's your name, then?"

"Nick — Nick Holloway."

"You hear that, guys? Says his name is Prick."

Tom, Dick, and Harry bent their heads backwards and roared with laughter.

"So, Prick — what you in here for?"

There was no way Nick could get up and leave the company of his new fellow prisoners. He looked around and saw nowhere in the mess hall where the company of other men might be more congenial.

"Oh — nothing really — nothing serious, that is. I heard my platoon sergeant say the lieutenant's brains were up his ass — so I took a flashlight and went to the lieutenant and asked if I could take a look-see."

Tom, Dick, and Harry laughed so hard that they almost fell off of their stools.

"Hell's bells — Prick — you is a okay trooper."

The word spread quickly among the prisoners. He decided he could even live with his new name — it was better that way. None of the prisoners were telling the truth. Nick knew no one's real name, or what unit they were from, or even why they were in the Dachau stockade.

The stockade was located in a complex of buildings — part of a U.S. Army installation named Eastman Barracks. A U.S. MP unit operated the jail — they called it the Dachau Confinement Facility. These buildings had housed the SS soldiers and administration staff that ran and guarded the Dachau concentration camp from 1933 to 1945.

Dachau had the distinction of being the first of the hundreds of concentration camps set up by the Nazis to hold, and eventually to kill, undesirable people. Jews, political and Christian dissidents, gypsies, homosexuals, communists, and others. When the camp was liberated by American troops in April 1945, the U.S. took over the SS barracks. The concentration camp itself was left as it was, with plans to make it into a museum in the future.

The 24th Infantry Division — Nick's division — used space at Eastman Barracks as a stockade.

The prisoners in the stockade worked in a laundry. Trucks came weekly from the 100 companies throughout the 24th ID with dirty laundry, and went back with clean clothing for the soldiers.

Nick's prison uniform was blue denim — it was too big

for him. He was told that the prison uniforms were standard U.S. Army fatigue uniforms left over from the 1930s. His cap was also blue denim — and floppy. The guards wouldn't let Nick keep his belt. Instead there was a rope to hold his trousers up. That made no sense to Nick. A prisoner could hang himself easier with a rope than with his web belt. Then again, Nick had learned that reason, logic, and common sense were not always part of the Army's ways of doing things.

Nick's job in the laundry was to sort the dirty clothing. The newest prisoners always got the worst jobs. He opened laundry bags and dumped the contents onto a table in front of him. Fatigue shirts went in one pile. Fatigue trousers on another. Handkerchiefs here, and underwear there. Part of his job was to soak the shorts that had shit on them. There were a lot of those.

The guy who carried the laundry bags from the truck into the laundry room was called the Bruiser. The two other inmates working in the laundry called him Sir Bruiser. Bruiser looked at Nick with mean and lustful eyes.

"You the guy they call the Prick?"

Nick didn't say anything. He nodded.

Bruiser smiled.

"I like that. What you in for?"

Nick was tired and preoccupied. He didn't answer the Bruiser.

Bruiser's face quickly went from grin to menacing.

"What da fuck — Prick — cat got your tongue?"

Nick didn't look at him. He tried to ignore Bruiser by focusing on what he was doing.

"Answer me — Prick. You hear me?"

Bruiser brought his fist down hard on the table in front of Nick.

Nick had always prided himself on not being afraid of any other man. He took pride in the commitment he made to himself in high school. He told himself then that he would fight anyone who threatened him, his friends, or the woman he was with. If the guy was bigger than he was — so be it. Nick's body might give out, but he would never of his own free will give in to another man.

Now, Crawford was another matter — he had the Army's authority behind him.

Nick stepped back from the table and waited for Bruiser to make the next move.

Bruiser wasted no time. He came at Nick with all of his bulk — with both fists flailing.

Nick sidestepped and the Bruiser's fists only stirred the air.

This went on for ten seconds or so, and then Nick found himself backed into a corner.

Bruiser lunged at Nick again. Nick dropped to his hands and knees and saw a way out through the space between the wall and Bruiser's legs. Nick started to dart forward.

But the Bruiser moved his leg and blocked Nick.

The blows came fast and frenzied.

Soon, all was dark for Nick.

* * * *

Nick woke up in the stockade's infirmary. It was night, but Nick had no idea what time it was.

A female nurse came to Nick when she saw that he was awake. She was older, maybe thirty. Nick thought she was beautiful — she was angelic.

"Hello, soldier — welcome back to the world. How do you feel?"

"What is your name?" Nick responded.

"My name is Lieutenant Thompson to you — Specialist Holloway."

"No — I mean your first name — what's your first name?"

The nurse looked at Nick.

"Angela."

Nick winced as he smiled. He knew both of his eyes were black, his ears and his eyebrows hurt something fierce, his lips were swollen, and his body ached with pain all over.

"I knew it," Nick said.

"Knew what?"

"That you were an angel. Tell me, were you there?"

"Was I where?"

"Were you there when Jesus was born?"

Nick did his best to wink at nurse Angela.

She made a move to turn, but Nick grabbed her hand.

"Please — don't leave yet. Tell me how bad it is — be honest — how bad am I?"

"You're very lucky, Nicholas Holloway. No broken bones — only two bruised ribs. No concussion, as far as we can tell — so far. No broken teeth. No, I'd say you need to thank your maker and our orderly, Corporal Weaver, for saving your life out there."

"And the Bruiser?"

"You never touched him. That man is an animal. He's in solitary confinement now. This incident will be added to the long list of charges already against him. His court martial is coming up next week, so the commandant doesn't want any more trouble from him until he leaves here."

"What's he in here for?"

"Murder. He smashed the head of his platoon sergeant against the side of an armored personnel carrier."

Nick wondered what it would feel like if he were to ram Crawford's skull into the hull of a tank.

48

FREEDOM

Nick was sitting at a table in a small conference room in the MP prison guard office. He had come directly from the prison infirmary.

Nick struggled to stand up as they entered. Captain Evans shook his head and motioned for Nick to sit down again.

Vince patted Nick on his good shoulder as Mike Barrett shut the door.

"Easy there, good buddy. No sling doesn't mean that shoulder is A-okay," Nick said.

"Sorry, Nick."

"Nick — my name is Michael Barrett. I'm a good friend of your chaplain, Captain Reynolds. And this, my good man, is the reason you're going to walk out of here today with us — Captain Gordon Evans, of the Staff Advocate General's office out of Heidelberg."

Nick had learned to mask his feelings so well that he showed no expression at the good news.

Captain Evans put his briefcase on a chair, and sat across the table from Nick.

Mike Barrett and Vince pulled chairs back away from the table and sat down.

"Specialist Holloway — I want you to tell me everything about this incident with the M-14 rifle — in as much detail as you can. We've got all day."

"There's not that much to tell — really," Nick said.

Nick gave the bare facts. How Sergeant Crawford told him to go to the arms room and sign out the demonstration M-14 and bring it to him. How Crawford gave him a note to give to the arms room custodian. How he signed for the rifle, and took it to Sergeant Crawford.

"That corresponds to the official statement you signed — to a T. Do you still stand by that statement?"

"That's the way it happened, sir. Why would I not stand by it?"

"And why would your company commander suggest that you were going to give the rifle to a Soviet agent?"

Nick wasn't ready to talk about Crawford and Markus Zimmermann. First things first — that was what Nick was thinking. He had to be sure he would get out of prison first — then he would tell all to this lawyer.

"I have no idea where that came from, sir."

"Good. That's good — very good. Okay, then — let's move along. You men wait here. I'm going to step out for a few minutes and make a couple of telephone calls. I'll be back in — say — a half hour or so."

"Nick — you don't look so good. Did you run into a door or did you slip on a bar of soap?" Mike asked.

Nick chuckled with pain. Vince laughed nervously.

"Neither."

Mike Barrett laughed.

The Bruiser has been taken care of, so why tell these guys about him.

They drank coffee and talked as they waited. Vince assured Nick that the tank was well taken care of.

Captain Evans came back in less than twenty minutes.

"You're free to go, Nick. Captain Elliott and Lieutenant Colonel Strickland are dropping the charges against you."

Vince cheered.

Nick smiled. Mike Barrett reached over and gently shook Nick's right hand.

"Congratulations, Nick," Mike said.

"So — aren't you going to tell us how you did it, counselor?" Mike asked.

"First of all, I called the arms room custodian — Specialist Tucker. He confessed to me that Nick had presented him with a note from Sergeant Crawford. Tucker still has that note."

"Then, I talked with the lawyer who was putting the case together for the court martial. He acknowledged that there was no evidence whatsoever that Nick committed an overt act of treason, as defined in Article 106a of the Uniform Code of Military Justice, or in Article three, section three of the U.S. Constitution. He then called Colonel Strickland and Captain Elliott, and they agreed to withdraw their complaint."

"And, what about the theft of the rifle?"

"They've also agreed to drop that charge — they're going to open a proper investigation about the missing rifle — it hasn't shown up yet. You'll no doubt be questioned about it again, Nick, but I don't think they will put all their eggs in a basket supported only by unsupported statements of Sergeant Crawford and Specialist Tucker."

"Wow — you are good," Vince said.

Captain Evans looked at Vince.

"Sir — I mean, sir — you are a good lawyer."

"What now?" Mike asked.

"I'm waiting now to hear that the MP commander here has received instructions to release Nick."

Captain Evans left the room again.

"Nick — I did some snooping around your company last night," Mike Barrett said. "I talked with a spec five

Stonehouse — the night baker for your mess hall. He said he'd been baking pies, among other things, the night after the rifle went missing. He said he stepped outside to take a smoke break, about 0230. That's when he saw Sergeant Crawford leave the barracks and go to his car. According to Stonehouse, Crawford was carrying a long object wrapped in a blanket. That could have been the rifle. Then he saw Crawford drive away in his car."

"Yeah?" Nick said.

"Well — I've been asking myself — why would Sergeant Crawford set you up like this? Why you, Nick? What's he up to?"

Nick told Sergeant Barrett what Crawford had done.

* * * *

Vince and Nick sat in the back of the jeep on the way back to Henry Kaserne.

"Nick — I called Carol — she knows about this."

"Good. Vince, you did the right thing."

When they arrived at Henry Kaserne, Nick asked Captain Evans if he could talk to him about something very important.

The captain agreed, and invited Nick and Sergeant Barrett to have lunch with him at the Warner Kaserne Officers Club.

They stopped at Headquarters Company's barracks first. Vince went to the room and got Nick's journal.

When the MPs arrived to arrest Crawford, he was gone.

49

Tarantel

Still celebrating Nick's release from Dachau, they went to the Tarantel night club in the Schwabing area near the University of Munich.

The Tarantel (tarantula) was a classy place — not at all like the GI bars on Goethe Strasse. The Tarantel billed itself as a jazz night club, and on that night the featured musicians were called the Terrence Williams Trio. The group was originally from Chicago, but at that time, they called Paris their home.

Carol was impressed — she had never been to the Tarantel. Nick felt good about that — he had chosen well, and Carol was in a good mood. Anything Nick could do to please Carol, made him feel good also.

But where was Sergeant Crawford?

Carol ordered wine. Nick — a glass of beer. He was practicing his limit of two beers, and it was working for him. Carol was enjoying her wine, and ordered another, and still another.

The leader of the trio invited people in the club to dance. It was a slow dance, and Carol loved the feeling of being close to Nick. Cheek to cheek. Nick held her close and they moved together to the music.

The song ended, Terrence Williams announced the band was taking a break. Nick and Carol sat down.

"That was wonderful," Nick said.

Carol was feeling a little tipsy from the wine.

"Yes — you're a good dancer. Is there anything you don't do well?"

"Well, I can't wiggle my ears," Nick laughed.

"Oh, come on, Nick — you're a good fighter, aren't you?" Nick looked at her.

"You're drunk," Nick said.

"Maybe I am — so what? Answer my question."

"What do you mean?"

"You didn't tell me the whole story about that fight you had with that Ben — Ben what's his name."

"Yeah, so — what do you want to know?"

"How did the fight end?" Carol asked.

Nick's head jerked a little. He looked directly into Carol's eyes.

"You said before that you lost the fight with Ben. How did that happen?"

Nick continued to stare at Carol.

"What have you heard? Did Vince tell Barb something?"

"Well — yes, he did. Vince told Barb about your fight, and Barb told me. She said you almost died."

"That … Vince … he should not have done that. He shouldn't have said that. He should have known better than to do that."

"I don't know, Nick. That's between you and Vince, whether he should have revealed that. The important thing is what happened. You could have died. That would have been terrible. Why didn't you tell me?"

"Some things are worth dying for, Carol. Soldiers know that."

"Yeah, sure. But don't you get yourself killed trying to save my honor, or whatever you were thinking. My so-called honor isn't worth your life."

"You sheltered schoolgirls apparently don't know anything about that — you just don't understand."

"Now, just a minute there, Nick. That's not true, and it isn't fair."

"That's another thing. You don't seem to realize that the world isn't fair. Sometimes we have to do what we have to do, period. That's reality, Carol — that's just the way things are."

Nick's voice had risen.

Carol felt her face flush. She couldn't believe how Nick was talking to her. Didn't he realize what he was saying? Or who he was talking to? And now he was yelling at her. Now she saw Nick as he really was, someone filled with immense condescension.

"As for biting Ben's ear off, that's all I could do to break his hold on me."

"You bit his ear off?"

Nick looked quizzically at her.

"Didn't Vince tell that part, too."

"No, he didn't. Obviously, he's got more sense than you do. You bit someone's ear off?"

Now, it was Nick's turn to stare at Carol with wide open eyes.

"I assumed ..."

"You bit his whole ear off? That's terrible. I don't care what you say, Nick, that was uncalled for."

"Carol — it wasn't his whole ear. Just that part at the bottom."

Nick pointed at his ear lobe.

"So what? It's not okay. The whole ear or just a little bite off the lobe — it doesn't matter. It was an awful thing to do — a despicable thing to do."

Nick stood up and leaned toward Carol with his hands on the table.

"So, now you're calling me despicable — like I'm a despicable human being?"

Carol stood up to face Nick.

"If the shoe fits, Buster Brown, wear it."

Nick looked around at the silent people staring at he and Carol.

"So, that's the way it is. Let's just be honest — one last time — let's put an end to this and say it's over. Because it is over, Carol. I can't be with someone who thinks I don't count for anything."

"Nick, you're not listening to me."

Carol started to cry, and sat down.

Nick took a ten dollar bill out of his wallet and threw it on the table in front of Carol.

"Here — this should be more than enough to pay the tab and get you a taxi home."

Nick walked away and out the front door.

Carol dried her eyes, held her head up straight without looking at anyone, and then picked up the money and left.

50

KIDNAPPED

Monday, 12 December

Earl Crawford raced through the main gate of the kaserne. He had no documents authorizing him to leave the camp. He knew that, but he had few options, and he didn't like any of them.

When he turned left off of Kollwitz Strasse onto Ingolstadter Strasse, he slowed down and checked his rearview mirrors. He drove a random route until he arrived at the apartment he kept in Munich — at Viktoria Luise Strasse 18. The only ones who knew about this place were Manfred and Aldo Neumann, and Sophie Gerhardt, but he hadn't heard from her for several months. Earl had been married three times, each lasted less time than the previous. It took Sophie about a month to see the real Earl Crawford. But, of course, the MPs must be scouring the city to find him.

A plan took shape in Earl's mind.

He thought about Nick's girlfriend. *What was her name? Ah, yes — Carol — Carol something. And she was a student at the University of Munich.* Crawford was trying to remember what he'd heard Nick say about the girl.

* * * *

Friday, 16 December

As he drove down Leopold Strasse and approached the university buildings, Earl decided he was certain enough about this girl that his plan might work. And if it worked out it could be a ticket out of the trouble he was facing.

He had seen a photo of Carol in Nick's wall locker. He tried to remember what she looked like.

Earl parked his car and walked to the front of the largest building. He stood behind a statue and waited. He kept one eye alert for MP jeeps, and the other looking at each student coming out of the building. There was a low probability that he would find Carol that way — but what else could he do? This was the third day that he had waited for her. He didn't know where the girl lived. He didn't know any other students who could lead him to her. He thought about grabbing one of the students walking by and asking if they knew where an American girl named Carol was? That scheme had even less chance of succeeding, he thought.

So, he waited. He looked at every female that came down the steps in front of him.

His plan was to take Nick's girlfriend — then Nick would be forced to help him get safely out of West Germany.

He waited for almost two hours. He started walking back and forth occasionally to work out the soreness in his legs. And then he saw her, or at least he thought he recognized her.

Carol came down the steps with her books held against her chest.

Crawford decided to approach her.

"Carol? Miss Carol?"

Carol stopped, facing him.

"Yes?"

"My name is Peterson — Sergeant Bob Peterson. I'm in

Nick Holloway's unit. He asked me to find you and bring you to the hospital."

"The hospital? What happened? What happened to Nick?"

"Well — he's not out of the woods yet, but the doctors are hopeful."

"Oh, no — Nick's been hurt."

"Please, ma'am — Miss Carol — won't you please come with me?"

Carol followed Crawford to his car and got in.

"Tell me more about Nick — I've got to know."

"Well, Carol — you see, I wasn't there when it happened — but what I heard was that a full 55-gallon drum of gasoline fell on top of him — landing on his legs."

"Is it bad, sergeant?"

"Well, they hope they won't have to amputate."

"Amputate?" Oh, no — Nick — no. I'm so sorry, Nick."

Carol started to cry and then to sob. Earl took out his handkerchief and gave it to her.

He drove across the Isar River and headed towards his apartment in the Haidhausen-South section of Munich.

Carol wasn't watching where he was driving.

When they reached Viktoria Luise Strasse 18, Earl parked the car.

"We've got to pick up this German doctor here. He's a specialist of some kind. You need to come with me — he was told over the telephone that you would pick him up."

Carol thought for a moment before responding.

"What?"

"I know it sounds strange, but truly, this is what we have to do. I'm not lying to you."

"Okay."

They got out of the car and went into the building. Crawford led the way up the stairs.

At the door to his apartment — 4G, Crawford inserted his key into the lock.

Carol stepped back.

"What …?"

She started to turn, but Earl grabbed her, put his hand over her mouth, and pulled her into the apartment. He shut the door behind him and secured both the deadbolt and chain locks.

"What is this? What's going on?" Carol asked.

"Calm down, Carol. You're going to be staying here with me for a while. If you don't give me any trouble — I won't give you trouble."

Carol started to scream.

Crawford put his hand over her mouth again, and pushed her towards a desk by the front windows. With his free hand, he opened a drawer in the desk and took out a roll of gray duct tape. He put a piece of the tape over Carol's mouth. When finished, he let go of her.

Carol ran toward the apartment door and was removing the chain lock when Crawford came up behind her. He lifted her up and carried her to a chair up against the wall.

"Listen to me. If this is the way you're going to be — little miss muffin — I'm going to have to tie you down good. How would you like that?"

Carol struggled to get free of his grasp, and she made desperate sounds behind the tape.

"Okay, then. We'll do it your way. Now — let's get a few things straight. I'm not going to rape you — I have no interest in that. Well, not now anyway — who knows, it could be fun. I don't want to hurt you — but if you give me cause …. You're going to be staying in this place for some time. I don't know how long it will take. It all depends on your boyfriend. If super-soldier Nick Holloway is smart and plays ball with me, nothing will happen to you — nothing at all. You will walk out of here a free woman if Nick cooperates. If he doesn't …"

He taped her feet together and her hands behind her back. Then he ran tape around her body and the chair.

Crawford closed the curtains and walked around the apartment to make sure all of the windows were closed.

"I'm going to leave you now for about an hour. When I get back, we'll have something to eat. We'll talk about how we're going to work out things for you to go to the bathroom and how and where you're going to sleep. Now, while I'm gone — you think about how you want to behave. The calmer and more cooperative you are, the better it will be for the both of us."

Earl walked to a nearby café that had an enclosed telephone booth.

"Hello, Markus …."

* * * *

17 December

Markus Zimmermann had finally gotten back in touch with Earl. His superiors had agreed to provide safe asylum status for Earl in East Germany. But Earl had to find his own way to the city of Hof, on the border between Bavaria and the DDR.

Earl asked Markus why he couldn't go to Vienna by train, and then take a Hungarian train to Budapest? Someone could meet him there. But Markus was adamant that he come directly to East Germany. Earl would be a STASI responsibility, and that was the end of the matter.

Crawford left the apartment and walked to the cafe that had a pay telephone inside. He stood before the phone and tried to gather his thoughts. What would he say to Nick? What could he say that would have the most effect on him? The effect that Crawford wanted? Maybe it would be better to let Holloway stew for a while. Give him time to think about the way things stood. No, time was of the essence now. He'll soon know that his girlfriend went missing, and he'll wonder what happened to her. Nick Holloway was a smart guy, and he would connect the fact that Crawford had gone AWOL at about the same time that his girl disappeared. Nick would figure out that Crawford had Carol. That should be enough for Nick to cooperate and help him get to Hof.

"Hello, Nick. Guess who I've got?"

When he was finished talking to Nick, Earl turned away from the telephone and walked out of the cafe.

He bought some groceries and beer and went back to the apartment.

Carol looked at him when he came in.

Crawford put the groceries away in the kitchenette, opened a bottle of beer, and sat down in a stuffed chair facing Carol.

Crawford looked at Carol.

Carol stared at him with hateful fire in her eyes.

This man is seriously disturbed, she thought. Didn't Nick recognize that when he first met him? Nick should have told me more.

51

AIR CRASH

Saturday, 17 December

Nick had cleaned up and dressed to go out, when the AFN (Armed Forces Network) announcer on Nick's radio interrupted the music.

It was 1430 when the music stopped, and the announcer spoke.

"Sad news, listeners. We've learned that not long ago, within the hour, there was a terrible air crash in central Munich. German authorities have released information that the airplane was a United States Air Force plane, carrying American students to England for their Christmas holiday from schools in Munich. We will continue to pass along any new details as we receive them."

Nick got up and paced the room. He ran his fingers through his hair. Since they broke up, just three days earlier, Carol had been in his thoughts almost constantly. Why had things gone so wrong? Why had he said such mean things to her?

No — it wasn't possible. She couldn't be on that plane. Okay, it was possible, but it just wasn't very probable. Still ...

Nick grabbed his jacket and ran out.

He ran to the gymnasium, opened the door, and ran inside, to the basketball court.

"Vince — Vince. Get dressed. Hurry up Vince — come on."

Nick explained what he heard on the radio as Vince got dressed. The two of them ran from the gym to the service club, where Nick called the Meier's. He didn't want to alarm Frieda and Arndt, but he had to know.

Arndt answered the phone this time. No, she wasn't there. He said he was sure that Carol wasn't going to England. She hadn't slept in her room on Friday night, but he thought she had just stayed overnight with one of her girlfriends.

Then Nick called the Osterheid's apartment. Nancy Johnson was there.

"Oh, Nancy — I'm so glad to hear your voice. I'm trying to find Carol. Do you know where she is? Did she stay with you last night?"

"No — no, I don't know where she is, Nick — and no, she didn't stay here last night."

"Did she say anything — anything at all — about going to England for the Christmas break?"

"No — I never heard her say anything like that. She did say that she once had a friend who married a guy who was now in the Air Force, stationed in England."

"Oh, no," Nick said.

Nick held the phone away from his ear for a few seconds.

"Did she say anything about going to Starnberg for the weekend?"

"No — I don't recall anything like that either."

"Look — Nancy — if you see her, tell her I need to talk with her — right away. It's very important."

Nick hung up the phone, and stood there in the phone booth holding his head down.

"What did they say?" Vince asked.

"Arndt thinks she spent the night with one of her friends,

but he's not sure — and he doesn't know who she might be with. Nancy Johnson said Carol knew someone in England, and that she might have gone there, but she thinks that's unlikely. Vince, I don't know what to do. Carol could have been on that plane."

They went back to their barracks and listened to the radio reports.

The plane was a U.S. Air Force Convair C-131D military transport plane. It had a crew of seven, and was carrying thirteen American students to Northolt air base near London. All were killed. The plane took off from Munich-Riem airport, and a few minutes later crashed into a streetcar on Bayer Strasse, near St. Paul's church in downtown Munich. Thirty-two people were killed on the ground.

A runner came to the room — Nick had a phone call in the orderly room.

Nick wanted to cry, but he choked it back. He ran to the orderly room. Vince went with him.

Hoping that it was Carol, but fearing the worst, Nick picked up the phone.

"Hello? Carol?"

"Nick — my boy, Nicky — guess who I've got sitting here in front of me. I've got your sweetheart — Carol is her name. Her ID in her purse says her full name is Carol Anne Benjamin."

"Why, you son-of-a-bitch, Crawford. You better not ..."

"Better not what, Nick? Harm her in some way? Have my way with her? Oh, Nick — whatever happens to this sweet and pretty young thing depends entirely on you. You better keep quiet, and help me out, Nick — or else — or else I don't know what I might do to your pretty little lady. You find me a way to safely get to Hof, on the border. Markus said he'd take care of me in the East. I'll call you later to find out what you've arranged."

The phone clicked and all Nick heard was dial tone.

52

SEARCH

"She's alive, Vince. But Crawford's got her."

"What the ..."

Nick breathed deeply.

"That was Crawford. He's got Carol and threatened to hurt her if I don't help him. He wants a way to get out of the country — to East Germany. Markus Zimmermann has promised him safety there."

Vince was speechless. He shook his head back and forth.

"And all this time we thought she was in that plane crash," Vince said.

Nick's mind had settled — somewhat. The relief that knowing Carol was still alive passed in an instant. Now he was done searching for what his next indicated step should be.

"I've got to talk to that Mike Barrett. Do you know how to get ahold of him?"

"No — the chaplain called him."

"That's it, then — I'm going to see Chaplain Reynolds. Vince — you go and find Lieutenant Dolan and tell him what's happened."

Nick ran out of the barracks, and across Patton Field to the chapel.

Captain Reynolds was in his office, working on his Sunday sermon.

"Slow down, Nick — and calm down," Reynolds said.

Nick stopped talking, took several deep breaths, and then continued his story about Carol and Crawford.

Nick stopped to catch his breath.

"We need to talk with Mike Barrett, chaplain," Nick said.

"Yes, you do. Mike's the only one I would trust on a matter such as this. I think Mike, being in counterintelligence, will be able to help you find Carol."

The chaplain didn't hesitate. He picked up his telephone and dialed.

"Elise? Mrs. Barrett? This is Captain Reynolds — Bruce Reynolds. I need to talk with Mike right away. It's an emergency."

Reynolds held his hand over the mouthpiece.

"She's gone to get Mike. He's entertaining — it's a birthday party for one of his children."

Nick's face remained impassive — his mind was elsewhere.

The chaplain was brief in his explanation to Barrett. When he had put the phone down, he told Nick that Mike was on his way.

When Sergeant Barrett arrived, Nick told him what he had told the chaplain.

The chaplain called the duty officer at the headquarters company barracks and made sure that passes for Nick and Vince would be ready when they got there.

"My guess is that Crawford has taken Carol to that farm near Ebersdorf. I know the way — it's about an hour's drive from here," Nick said.

Then Barrett called the nearest MP detachment and had them send two men to Henry Kaserne.

They picked up Vince and Lieutenant Dolan at Headquarters Company.

It was already dark, but Barrett drove as fast as he dared. The MP jeep kept up with him.

Nick was at his best when in tense situations. He knew he had some kind of gift in staying calm when he was in dangerous situations. That was one reason he thought he was a good soldier, and why he had wanted to stay in the Army.

Nick started talking again as they went through Ebersdorf. It was like a movie and its soundtrack playing out of his memory. He pointed out to Barrett the cafe where they met Manfred Neumann on their first visit to the farm.

When they approached the woods and the hill above the farm, Nick said they should park there and approach the farmstead on foot.

Nick told Barrett about the barn, where Crawford murdered the Germans.

Mike Barrett conferred with the MPs, and they agreed that Mike, Nick, Vince, and Dolan would approach the farm buildings directly down the road, while the MPs would go through the woods to the left, and approach the buildings from the rear.

All was silent at the farm. No lights were on in the house. No vehicles stood around.

Mike Barrett was holding a Walther PPK pistol as they neared the house.

The house was the logical place for Crawford to be holding Carol.

Nick noted that there was no smoke coming out of the house's chimney, and no lights were showing. He thought how miserable Carol must be in there.

They searched the house room by room. They went up into the attic, and down into the cellar. There were no signs that anyone had been in the house since the murders.

Carol was not in the house.

While the MPs secured the area as a crime scene, Mike, Dolan, Nick, and Vince searched the house. They were looking for anything that would lead them to where Crawford was holding Carol.

There was a desk in the corner of the living parlor. Mike Barrett sat at the desk and went through the contents in the drawers.

There was a log book of various stolen goods received by the Neumann brothers, and who they had been sold to and for what amounts.

Then there was a small packet of letters — from Earl Crawford to Aldo and Manfred Neumann. The return address was apartment 4G, Viktoria Luise Strasse 18, in Munich.

53

RESCUE

Sunday, 18 December

It was almost dawn when they got back to Munich.

Lieutenant Dolan went directly to Henry Kaserne to alert Captain Elliott.

Mike Barrett parked about a block away from Viktoria Luise Strasse 18, the building of Sergeant Crawford's apartment.

"Nick, I think this is best, that the three of us do this. To contact the MPs and the CID, and to involve the Munich police, would take time. They'll all be here soon enough. But with them here, it could also end up in a total circus — a SNAFU that could be a tragic screw-up. We have the advantage of surprise. You know Sergeant Crawford, and you know your girlfriend. But, we've got to do this right. If I understand what you said, Nick, Crawford thinks you don't know about this apartment. He thinks he's safe in there. Vince, you come with us to the apartment. It's more important that we have your muscle when we break into the apartment, than it is for you to watch the back entrance to the building. Okay?"

Vince nodded.

"I'm with you, sergeant."

"What do we do when we get into the apartment?" Nick asked.

"I'll try to get him to open the door — then we'll rush in — and get him down on the floor before he can do anything. But be careful, he might have a gun."

"Just so he doesn't shoot Carol," Nick said.

"Don't say that, Nick," Vince said sadly.

Barrett removed his pistol, and worked the slide to load it.

"Okay — let's go. Be quiet with the car doors."

The three entered the building and went up the carpeted stairs to the fourth floor. They walked down the hallway to apartment 4G.

A radio was playing inside. The smell of coffee was strong.

Mike Barrett knocked on the door three times.

The radio went silent.

No response came from inside the apartment.

Barrett knocked again.

"This is the Munich Police. Open this door. We need to ask you some questions," Barrett said, in German.

He knocked again — five times — harder this time.

"Open the door, please. We want to ask if you saw or heard anything three hours ago. Two muggers beat an old woman and took her purse. It happened on the sidewalk below your apartment."

Another minute went by.

"I don't speak German. Can you tell me what you want in English?" Crawford said.

Mike Barrett told again what he wanted — this time in English, with a fake German accent.

"No — we didn't hear or see anything. We've been here all night."

Carol's muffled squeals were audible.

Nick poked Barrett in the shoulder and signaled as if to say *let's go — let's break the door down and get in there.*

"Is someone in there in there with you? We must speak to them also."

"Only my woman and I."

Nick clenched his fists, and glared at Mike Barrett.

"Open the door — now — that is an order," Barrett said.

"No."

"Open now or I will have to call a squad of men here to open it by force. Do you want that, American? Of course, you don't. Be nice, American. Open the door, and we can get this business over with quickly, without any fuss."

The deadbolt lock was turned open with a soft clunk.

The door opened about two inches until the chain tightened.

Mike, Nick, and Vince, all put their bodies against the door. The chain broke and the door opened all the way.

Crawford's body was off balance as he staggered backwards. He pointed his pistol and pulled the trigger. A .45 caliber slug went into Vince's shoulder.

Vince went down to his knees. Barrett's two hands held Crawford's gun hand. Crawford's left hand was hitting Barrett in the face.

Mike pressed his fingernails into the underside of Crawford's wrist.

Nick had gone directly to the chair where Carol was tied up. She had duct tape over her mouth.

"Nick — Nick, come here — help me with this gorilla," Mike said.

Vince had stood up and was holding his bad arm while kicking Crawford in the shins.

Nick came over and wrested the pistol out of Crawford's hand. Then Nick put a hammer lock on Crawford. Nick and Mike together got Crawford on the floor — on his belly.

"Nick — untie Carol and bring that tape here. Then — take your belt off and help me — tie his ankles together."

Crawford was struggling and cursing.

Finally, Mike put his handkerchief in Crawford's mouth.

Nick went to Carol and put his arms around her. She stood close to him. She was shaking.

Finally, Carol started to cry. Nick held her, with her head on his shoulder as she sobbed. Nick patted her gently on the back.

Neither spoke.

About a dozen people had gathered in the hallway, some were peering into the room.

Mike Barrett looked at them.

"It's all okay, now. You have nothing to be afraid of now."

"I called the *Polizei*," an old man said.

"Good — that's good — thank you," Mike replied in German.

Mike gave his pistol to Nick.

"Keep an eye on him, Nick. I'm going to call the MPs," Mike said. "Carol — can you look at Vince's arm? We don't want him to go into shock."

Carol went to look at Vince's wound.

"I was so scared, Nick," Carol said. "I was sure he was going to kill me."

"I know. But it's over now. You're safe now, my darling."

Nick felt waves of relief and contentment.

"I'm sorry, Carol. I'm so sorry about everything. Everything I said. I didn't mean any of it," Nick said.

"And send an Army ambulance also," Barrett said into the phone. "We've got one man shot. And send a nurse too. A young woman was kidnapped and held here for several days."

Vince was glaring at Crawford.

"You son-of-a-bitch, Crawford. You shot me. What do

you think, Nick — will I get a purple heart for this?" Vince said.

"I'm sure you will, you deserve it," Nick said.

Vince grinned through his pain as Carol looked at his wound.

Mike Barrett hung up the phone.

"How's our kidnapper doing?" Mike asked.

"He's not going anywhere until the MPs get here," Nick replied, keeping the pistol pointed at Crawford.

Crawford was squirming and twisting and emitting pig-like squeals through his nose. His red eyes were wide open.

Nick and Carol were now sitting on a davenport. Nick held her close as Carol dabbed at her eyes with her handkerchief.

The Munich criminal police arrived first. The man in charge introduced himself to Mike as Günther Dengler. Mike explained what had happened, and that American MPs were on the way. Dengler released the other policemen, but said he would stay until the American military police took control of the scene.

Nick rode with Carol and Vince in the Army ambulance that took them to the U.S. Army's 2nd Field Hospital in Munich. The doctors wanted Carol to stay overnight for observation. Vince would need surgery.

Mike Barrett went home.

Nick slept in the hospital waiting room.

54

THE FUTURE IS YOURS, SOLDIER

Monday, 19 December

Carol was released from the hospital that afternoon. She had suffered no physical injuries, but she was still scared. Nick told her that Crawford was now being held by the MPs, and that he would never, ever, get out of prison.

Nick and Carol together visited Vince in his room, but he was asleep. A doctor told them that Vince's surgery that morning was successful, and that he would be okay. The big bullet went through his shoulder, but missed bones and blood vessels. He would be in the hospital for a week or more. He would spend Christmas in the hospital.

Carol went to a telephone and called Barb. She told her that Vince was okay, and that she could come to see him that evening.

Then Nick saw Carol to the Meiers' apartment. Frieda and Arndt were happy to see her safe. Nick could tell that Frieda would take good care of Carol. Nick told Arndt an abbreviated outline of what happened. He assured Arndt that Crawford was now in custody and that Carol was in no further danger.

Back at Henry Kaserne, Nick told the story to Captain

Elliott, Lieutenants Dolan and Jensen, and First Sergeant Dixon. Chaplain Reynolds and Mike Barrett were there also.

Captain Elliott told Nick that Sergeants Richards, Hairston, and Guzman had been arrested that morning. Mike Barrett explained what happened to Crawford after Nick went to the hospital with Vince and Carol.

Captain Elliott said that Nick had an appointment to meet with Lieutenant Colonel Strickland, the battalion commander, at 0900 the next morning.

* * * *

Wednesday, 21 December

The next morning, as Nick was getting ready to meet the colonel, the other soldiers of Tank Section gathered in his room. Nick enjoyed the new atmosphere of congenial camaraderie — but he didn't want it to go too far. For one thing, he hadn't forgotten how narrow-minded and mean some of the men had been before; secondly, Nick wasn't comfortable with what he saw as unwarranted hero worship; and finally, Nick had made his decision. He would not make the Army his career.

"Nick — you are the best. I mean it. For sure, you are the best," Ben Bartlett said.

"And congratulations to you, Ben. I wish you all the best at NCO Academy, and in the future."

Ben beamed when he heard Nick's praise.

"Hey, Nick, is it true that your nickname in Dachau was Prick?" Joe Flores asked.

"Yup — that's right. Kinda has that ring of truth to it — huh, Joe?" Nick said.

They all laughed at that.

Nick felt easier with the men. He thought that maybe — just maybe — the guys had grown a little for the better, as he hoped he had. Or maybe, just maybe, he had never really known them — never wanted to know them because he was always so sure that he was the one in the right, and they were wrong, simply wrong.

"Say, Bartlett — who's the new section sergeant? Or haven't they named one yet?" Nick asked.

"Jensen came out yesterday and said Reuben Ortiz is the new guy. He's being promoted to staff sergeant and will replace Crawford. Fred Carson's sort of pissed — but Ortiz has a couple years of time in grade on him," Bartlett said.

"Good — that's good. Ortiz will be a good one," Nick said.

Nick had Billy Dryden trim his hair, and then he showered and shaved. It wasn't every day that a soldier was summoned to meet the top officer in the battalion.

Nick put on his dress greens, buffed his black low-quarter shoes, polished his brass insignia and belt buckle, and checked his tie. He was ready. The other men all wished him luck.

Captain Elliott and Lieutenant Jensen walked with Nick across Patton Field to battalion headquarters.

"Remember, Nick — he's the battalion commander — so don't get informal with him. Whatever you do, don't call him Art. He goes batty if anyone calls him Art instead of Arthur," Lieutenant Jensen said. "But, you shouldn't even call him Arthur."

Nick looked at the lieutenant. He didn't roll his eyes, or nod his head, or say anything. What Nick did was talk to himself. *You fucking idiot. You really don't know much about anything, do you, lieutenant?*

Nick went into Colonel Strickland's office alone. He was greeted by this affable commander, Lt. Col. Arthur Strickland, who offered his hand to Nick before Nick could snap a salute.

The colonel had a reputation he earned as a tank platoon leader who had served with Patton, as Sergeant Stark had, at the Battle of the Bulge in World War II. West Point graduate and battle-hardened — Strickland was well respected in the 3/34 Armor. Nick couldn't remember ever hearing any criticism of the man.

"Specialist Holloway — may I congratulate you on a job well done. Your work and your bravery working undercover has opened the lid on that black-market operation that has given the CID such fits the past couple of months. On top of that, you helped the CIC stop an enemy agent in our midst. To think that he was a part of this battalion ..."

Strickland shuddered.

"Thank you, sir."

"Also, I want to apologize to you for acting so rashly and putting you through your ordeal at Dachau. I'm sorry for my part in that."

Nick nodded.

"And now for some good news. I am putting you — and Specialist Delvecchio as well — I'm putting you both in for the Soldier's Medal. You've earned it. You performed a heroic act that involved personal hazard and danger, while not in actual conflict with an armed enemy. Of course, one could argue that Sergeant Crawford was an enemy — a domestic enemy. We're putting the paperwork together now. I have no doubt that it will be approved. I will be so proud to pin that medal on your chest."

"Thank you, sir."

Nick knew the moment was coming. He'd been rehearsing his response in his head.

"Also, Specialist Holloway — I understand that we've been holding your nomination to go to the NCO Academy. I can tell you with pleasure that I am lifting that hold. Your nomination will go forward immediately. It will depend only on your re-enlistment — of course, I understand you are serious about staying in the Army. The future is yours, Holloway. Who knows — you could have a shot at becoming an officer — to go to OCS, or even to West Point."

"Do I have permission to speak, sir?"

"By all means — go ahead."

"Sir — I've given a lot of thought to this. I know I wanted to re-enlist. I wanted to be a professional soldier in the worst way. I have wanted to become the best soldier, and the best tanker, that I could become. I wanted to be a sergeant like Steve Cervenka, my former Tank Section sergeant."

"Yes — I know Sergeant Cervenka. A very good man."

"Well, sir — the bottom line is this: I no longer want to make the Army my career."

Nick waited — he feared the colonel's reaction.

Strickland looked Nick in the eyes, but didn't say anything.

"You see, sir — I want to go to college. I think I'll be better doing something on the outside — as a civilian — sir."

Strickland looked out his window.

"I'm disappointed, Nick — of course. You're the kind of man we need in this Army."

Then his smile returned.

"Holloway, you've got what it takes to be successful at whatever you do. I wish you the best of luck."

Nick relaxed.

"Thank you, sir — I'll do my best. And I'll always be proud that I was a soldier — and a tanker."

"If I may, specialist — whenever I get a chance to talk like this with one of our bright young soldiers, I like to ask for their ideas on how we can make this battalion better — how we can more effectively be combat-ready. Do you have any suggestions? What would you do differently if you were sitting in my chair?"

Nick thought for a few seconds. He had a lot of ideas, but he hesitated, fearing he might be considered insubordinate. He had never imagined that he would have a chance to voice his thoughts to the battalion commander — a man in a position to make changes.

"Go ahead — I'm ready — and don't worry, I already see

many things I wish I could change, but there are barriers that you don't see."

"Okay, sir. The first thing that is needed is to get the right people on the tank crews. Get the incompetents, the physically unfit, and the unmotivated men off the tanks — find other jobs for them. And then, reassign the physically fit and competent men out of their cushy jobs in offices, and onto the tanks. Also, make sure that each tank has a full crew at all times. In the almost two and a half years that I've been with Tank Section, we've never had a full complement of sixteen tankers."

Strickland was writing on a note pad.

"Second — we need to intensify our training for combat. We are supposed to be a combat-ready battalion, but we aren't."

Strickland stopped writing and looked into Nick's eyes.

"I would put more emphasis on gunnery training. I would put more emphasis on basic soldiering skills. I would find and use the best instructors across the battalion to make training more effective, and not just having NCOs as instructors.

"Third — I would insist on officers and NCOs getting to know their men better. They can't lead if they don't know their men, and they can't know their men if they don't talk to the men and earn their trust. This is especially true of our black soldiers. And, I would do away with shakedown inspections. The men resent them, and they do nothing to build trust."

"Fourth — I would intensify tank and equipment maintenance efforts. I would put more emphasis on maintenance inspections — make them more frequent and more thorough. I would make more timely delivery of maintenance supplies and spare parts a high priority in order to reduce the time that tanks are dead-lined and out of operation. This might need higher authority, but still — it's important, in my opinion, sir. Find a way to install ventilation for the turret's gasoline heater. Like boring a hole in the hull and installing exhaust conduits. You might remember Private Maguire, sir. He was on my tank crew. Danny died of carbon monoxide poisoning from heater fumes."

"Yes — I remember Private Maguire — a tragic loss. Is that it? Do have any more ideas for changes?"

"I do, sir. I would also change certain practices that affect morale, sir."

Nick wasn't sure how Strickland would react to his suggestions to change certain Army traditions that might be as old as the Army itself.

"Go ahead."

Strickland was ready, with his pen poised over his notepad.

"Sir — I would stop applying unit-wide punishments for the offenses of one soldier. There is no such thing as collective guilt, and therefore collective punishment is wrong. I understand the reasoning behind it — the idea that the other men in the unit will straighten out the offender. But even when it works out that way — the men resent it. The practice causes more damage to morale than you can imagine."

"Oh — I can imagine it alright. Is that all?"

"One more thing. I would try to train the noncommissioned officers about assessing appropriate punishments to fit the seriousness of the offenses. Too often I've seen excessive punishments for trivial offenses."

"Examples?"

"Sure — at an inspection just last week, one of our soldiers in Tank Section was found to have a thread — a thread only a half-inch long — sticking out of one of his buttonholes. He was given a 14 and 2 company punishment for that. That's not right."

"I agree with you on that one, Specialist Holloway. Anything else?"

"No sir. I've probably said more than I should have already. I'm sorry sir. I didn't mean any disrespect. I know there might be good reasons like the battalion not being given enough ammunition for gunnery training. I don't know ...."

"No need to be sorry, soldier, you weren't being disrespectful. I appreciate your thoughts and your honesty."

Colonel Strickland fanned the several pages he had written on his notepad. He stood up.

Nick followed and also stood up.

"How is your friend Specialist Delvecchio doing?"

"He was lucky, sir. The doctor says he's going be okay — as good as new — the doctor said."

"That's wonderful. Please — will you let me know if I can do anything for him."

"Sir — I'm not sure if you know this — Vince has re-enlisted and plans to stay in the Army. He's a good tanker — he'll be going to the NCO Academy. Well — Vince — Specialist Delvecchio, would like to get a Purple Heart medal. Is that possible, sir?"

Colonel Strickland broke into a wide grin, and then turned serious.

"I can see how he feels that way, but I'm sorry to say that's not going to be possible. I hope your friend will understand."

They walked together to the door.

"And how is your girlfriend, Nick? That must have been terrifying for her — tied up for several days — in the company of Sergeant Crawford."

"She wasn't hurt, sir — but she's still not over the fright of it all."

Strickland opened the door.

"Oh, Specialist Holloway, I just had an idea. Would you and your girlfriend — what is her name?"

"Carol, sir. Carol Benjamin."

They stood in the open doorway. Captain Elliott and Lieutenant Jensen stood nearby.

"Yes — Carol — would you and Carol like to join Mae

and I, and a few others, for dinner at our house on Christmas Day? We'd love to have you join us."

"Yes, sir. That sounds great. I'm sure Carol will like that."

"Good. Shall we say 1600 on Sunday then?"

"We'll be there."

Nick thought he would never forget the expressions on the faces of Elliott and Jensen.

55

CHRISTMAS EVE

Saturday, 24 December

Nick and Carol arrived at the Headquarters Company mess hall at 1430 — a half hour before the children were to be there.

Each year the company put on a Christmas program for the children of the Holy Angels Kinderheim — an orphanage in northeast Munich. Nick had volunteered to help at the previous year's party, and had such a good time that he again volunteered. Carol eagerly accepted his invitation to be part of the event.

A decorated tree stood along one wall, and Christmas-themed centerpieces were on the tables. Instead of the usual white tablecloths were red and green ones. Several tables had been put end to end along the other wall.

Nick noticed the disparity of a room that spoke of peace and love in its Christmas adornments, flanked by images of Patton and Rommel and war.

"Oh, Nick, it's beautiful — what part of this was your doing?" Carol said.

"I put tinsel on the tree last night."

"Oh, come on now, Nick — you? Doing something so not

soldierly? Oh, that's right — you've got only two weeks more to be a soldier. Are you practicing for the peace world? The real world? The land of round doorknobs, as you like to say?"

Nick laughed.

"Something like that," he said.

"Oh, here they come, aren't they so cute?" Carol said.

Four nuns led and shepherded twenty young children, from age three to about seven, into the mess hall.

Once all the guests had found themselves on chairs, First Lieutenant Patrick Dolan stood up and picked up a microphone.

"Welcome, welcome, welcome — and Merry Christmas to all — especially you little ones."

Dolan knelt down and took the hand of a little girl sitting next to Carol.

"You have found a friend. Isn't that wonderful, because Christmas is about friendship, and love, and peace, and the birth of our shepherd."

Carol picked up the young child and put her on her lap.

Dolan stood up and continued.

"As many of you know, Headquarters Company has a special relationship with Holy Angels Kinderheim that goes back several years. By way of introduction, I am Lieutenant Pat Dolan — now, I'll ask the members of our orphanage Christmas committee to stand."

Nick, Hal, and several other soldiers stood. Lieutenant Dolan pointed to each man and gave his name. Then he handed the microphone to one of the nuns, who introduced herself and the other nuns. She said the children were a little shy, but if you asked their names, in German of course, they would tell it.

"And what is your little friend's name, Carol?" Nick said.

"Ask her."

"Hello, little girl — what is your name?"

"Nick — she's German — she doesn't speak English."

"Oh, yeah — *wie heisst du?*"

The girl responded. Her name was Teresa, and she was four years old. Teresa clung to Carol like she was glued to her.

"What are you going to do with your life, Nick — now that you won't be a soldier?" Carol asked.

Carol knew that Nick had arranged to stay in Munich until her JYM term ended in May. Nick was going to stay with John Cooper and Larry Connors in their apartment. The Army would provide him transportation to the United States for up to one year. She knew that both Sergeant Barrett and Captain Evans had offered to let Nick help them.

"I'm not sure. Well, I'm sure I want to go to college."

Nick chuckled.

"And then?"

"There are a lot of possibilities. It would be better to stay in the Army. Here the choices are all made for me."

Nick winked at Carol.

She laughed.

Oddly, at that moment, Nick thought about the irony that Sergeant Crawford was sitting in the division stockade at Dachau, awaiting his own court martial.

"No — really — Nick?"

Nick shook his head back and forth.

"I don't know. I was impressed with that lawyer fellow — Captain Evans. You know — the guy that got me out of Dachau. I had a good talk with him. What he does really helps people. I don't know if I have what it takes, but I'd like to find out — if I could be a lawyer, I mean."

"I think you've got what it takes, Nick."

Nick looked at Carol's eyes — yes, she was sincere.

"Ho, ho, ho. Merry Christmas, everybody."

A soldier in a Santa Claus suit came into the room. Over his shoulder was a large cloth bag, bulging with what was inside.

Nick recognized him — it was the First Sergeant — Sergeant Dixon.

Lieutenant Dolan did a masterful job of bantering with Santa Claus.

Each child was called up to the front by one of the nuns. Santa gave the child a package with a toy inside. Teresa ran back to Carol with her package. It was a doll.

Then packages of caps, mittens, and scarves, one set per child, were given to the nuns.

When all of the presents had been distributed, and Santa Claus had made his jolly departure, Nick and Hal Washington got up and left the room. They soon returned carrying a piece of furniture.

Donations had been collected from the company's soldiers each payday. Then Nick and Hal had picked out and bought a Grundig radio and high fidelity record player, in a beautiful teakwood cabinet in the modern Danish style.

The nuns gasped and put their hands to their mouths when Lieutenant Dolan presented the gift to the orphanage. They cried as each one expressed their thanks to the soldiers.

Then it was time for refreshments. There was gingerbread, butter and marmalade, and four kinds of cookies, all baked fresh during the early morning hours by Specialist Stonehouse.

Teresa ran back to give Carol a hug, and then to the table to get another cookie.

Nick and Carol talked about going to the Christmas service at the chapel the next morning — and then having dinner at the colonel's house.

Nick felt at peace. Yes, he should have said something long before he did. Yes, he should have pushed harder after the murders, and sought justice sooner. No, he should never have said those hurtful words to Carol. The important thing, though, was that they were together again. Had he learned anything from it all? Nick hoped that he had.

Lieutenant Dolan called for quiet.

Candles were lit and the lights turned off.
The children began to sing.

"Stille Nacht! Heil'ge Nacht!
Alles schläft; einsam wacht
Nur das traute hoch heilige Paar.
Holder Knab' im lockigen Haar,
Schlafe in himmlischer Ruh!
Schlafe in himmlischer Ruh!

Nick recognized the tune and hummed along.

ABOUT THE AUTHOR

Ted Hovey served with the U.S. Army in Germany from 1960 to 1962. Ted and his wife, Mary, were married in 1971 and have lived in Roseville, Minnesota since 1999; they have two children and six grandchildren. After a career as an accountant and auditor, Hovey studied creative writing at Metropolitan State University and Hamline University. He is the author of *Ten Days in May* and *An Imperfect Man*.

CPSIA information can be obtained
at www.ICGtesting.com
Printed in the USA
FFOW04n0425151017
41049FF